MW01116347

WANT TO KNOW A SECRET?

A NOVEL BY

FREIDA MCFADDEN

Want to Know a Secret?
© 2021 by Freida McFadden. All rights reserved.

ISBN: 9798596462579

To Libby and Melanie (as always)

CHAPTER 1

APRIL

To: April Masterson
From: Unknown number

Want to know a secret?
Your son isn't where you think he is.

"As you can see, I've now got a tray of delicious, ooey-gooey fudge brownies, fresh from the oven!"

I use my oven mitts to hold up my tray of brownies to the expensive digital camera mounted on the tripod in my kitchen. I tilt the tray slightly, so viewers will be able to see the brownies. They look delicious, if I do say so myself.

"Now for a taste." I pick up the carving knife on the kitchen table. I cut myself a nice big square of chocolatey goodness and take a careful bite. When I first started doing this, I recorded myself eating treats multiple times, trying to figure out the right formula for not looking like a slob while I stuffed confections in my mouth. "*Mmm*. So good!"

Truth be told, I over-baked them by about five minutes. They taste a bit dry. But nobody watching will know it. That's the great thing about video.

I lay down the rest of the brownie. I only ever take one bite and that's it. Nobody wants to watch me gorge myself on their computer screen. "And there you have it, folks! My secret recipe for the most delicious brownies you'll ever eat." As long as you don't overbake them. "If you enjoyed watching *April's Sweet Secrets*, please subscribe to my YouTube channel."

And now I wave at the camera, my eyes connecting with the lens. "Good night, Mom!"

That's how I end every episode.

My show is called *April's Sweet Secrets*. My secrets are my hook. In every episode, I tell viewers a few "secret tips" to get their sweet treats to taste better than anyone else's. Want to know the secret to delicious brownies? The secret is melting good quality dark chocolate in with the cocoa powder.

I shut down the camera and detach the microphone. It's only after the recording has stopped that my shoulders relax. Even though I'm not recording live, I feel tense when I'm on the screen in front of my thousands of subscribers. Even after five years of doing this.

And now there's the question of what to do with all the brownies. A huge tray of them, sitting there, taunting me.

They may be slightly over-baked, but they're still delicious and I would love to stuff myself with two or three of them (or five). Unfortunately, I can't afford to eat even one. That's the ironic part—my career is teaching people to put together the most delicious treats, but I'm not allowed to touch them aside from that one bite on screen. I have to look good for the camera.

I'll put aside a few for my seven-year-old son Bobby—he's playing out in the backyard and he'll come back inside soon, hungry for snacks. He deserves a treat for not having interrupted me even once during the filming. It's something of a world's record!

And I'll bring the rest of the tray to Carrie Schaeffer later today. She's going through that horrible divorce, and I know she'll appreciate them.

I head out to the living room where I stashed my cell phone during the recording. My phone is a distraction that I can't have anywhere near me when I'm making these videos. Nobody wants to watch a video of somebody sneaking looks at text messages on their phone—it's *so* unprofessional. And sure enough, I've got several waiting for me.

The first text is from Julie, who lives two houses down from us and is my absolute best friend. She's a little intense, but that's only because she used to be an attorney in her previous life. You know, Before Kids. (BK.)

Are you coming to the PTA meeting on Tuesday?

She has asked me that question no less than five-thousand times. And the answer is always the same. Yes. *Yes*, I'm coming. I have come to every single PTA meeting in the entire time we have known each other. But I know if I don't answer this one time, she'll get snippy. So I quickly reply:

Yes, I'll be there!

Can you come twenty minutes early to help me set up the tables and chairs?

I groan. I knew I was going to get roped into that. But it's very hard to say no to Julie. And she means well. She's amazing as president of the PTA.

Sure! No problem!

I notice another unread text message, this one from an unknown number. Undoubtedly, it's a spam text message. Or maybe it's from a fan who somehow got my cell phone number. Every once in a while, my number seems to get out there, despite my best efforts to keep it secret. I've had to change it twice. I click on the message to view it:

Want to know a secret? Your son isn't where you

think he is.

I stare at the message on the screen. *What?*

A cold, sick feeling comes over me. Bobby is in the backyard. We have a fenced-in backyard, and he and I have an agreement that when I'm filming one of my videos, he's got to either stay out there or in his room. But about half the time, he finds a reason to interrupt me. I had been feeling proud of him that he didn't interrupt me this time.

This has got to be a prank. But even so, I'll go check on him.

My legs feel a little wobbly as I step onto the back porch and scan the grass, which is in dire need of trimming. I look around the yard, my eyes darting between the two trees and the little swing set that Bobby has nearly outgrown. I don't see him. Maybe he's hiding behind a tree or something. That kid loves to hide.

"Bobby!" I call out.

My only answer is a slight rustling of leaves.

"April?"

I whirl around, my heart pounding. My husband Elliot is standing behind me, dressed in an Armani suit. It's Sunday, but of course, he's on his way to work. I wouldn't expect anything different from my workaholic husband. It used to drive me crazy, but I've learned to accept it.

"I'm on my way out," he says. "Just wanted to let you know."

"Wait." There's a slightly hysterical edge to my voice.

"I don't see Bobby in the backyard."

Elliot straightens out his tie. It's his red power tie. He must have something important going on today. I remember the first time I saw him in that tie nine years ago, I swooned. I actually *swooned*. I had never met anyone like Elliot Masterson before. He was one of the most handsome and charismatic men I'd ever met. There was something in the back of my head, even then, telling me this man would be my husband and the father of my child someday.

But right now, I can't appreciate how good he looks in his suit and tie. All I can think about is who sent me this text message and where my son is.

"Are you sure he's not out there?" he asks.

"Yes!" I fish around in my pocket for my phone. "And look at this text message someone sent me!"

Elliot takes my phone and reads the text as he rubs at his scalp. It's very smooth—he must have shaved this morning. That's right—my husband shaves his head. He started doing it about four years ago, and I screamed and pulled out my can of mace when he came into the living room with his newly shorn head for the first time. I thought he was going to burgle me—he looked like a completely different person, and I hated it. But after a few weeks, I came around. The shaved head is sexy and virile, and admittedly better than his badly receding hairline.

"It's probably just a prank," he says, although there's a slight tremor in his voice.

"Why would somebody play a prank like that on me?"

"I don't know! You're a public figure. People know you. Maybe somebody's cookies didn't come out right and they're angry at you."

He's right that I have become a public figure lately. Everybody in our Long Island town seems to know who I am, thanks to my YouTube show. And truth be told, I have received a few creepy text messages over the years from viewers who tracked down my number. But nothing ever came of it.

"Maybe he's upstairs?" Elliot suggests.

It's possible. But I've been in the kitchen for the last hour, and he would have had to go past me to get back in the house. I would have seen that. So he must still be outside.

"He could be hiding..." I say. Bobby is at an age where he thinks it's hilarious to hide somewhere, and jump out and startle me at an inopportune moment. *Haha, I scareded you!* If he wasn't so darn cute, I would be furious.

Right now, it would not be cute.

"I'll go check upstairs," Elliot says.

"I'll check the side of the house."

I go out into the backyard, tugging at the bright red blouse that suddenly feels too hot. On camera, I always wear bright, solid colors. Usually, I change shortly after I finish making my video, but there's no time for that now. I feel my ballet flats squishing against the damp grass. "Bobby!" I call again.

No answer. But that doesn't mean anything. If he's hiding, of course he's not going to give away his location.

I stop for a moment and listen. Even though he's good at hiding, he is still only seven. At this point, he's probably giggling to himself. So I listen for giggling. Or crunching of leaves. But I don't hear any.

I get another sting of panic in my chest.

I venture further out into the backyard. I look along the side of the house, where we keep our garbage cans. It's a perfect hiding place for a little boy—I'm hoping to find him crouched behind one of the bins. At this point, he's giving me enough of a scare that I will definitely have to scold him: *Mommy was really scared! Next time, don't hide like that!*

I look behind the bins. Nothing.

Then my eyes fall on the gate to the backyard. It's the only way to get in or out of the backyard without going through the house.

The gate door is wide open.

With a shaking hand, I pull my phone out of my pocket. I bring up the text message one more time:

Your son isn't where you think he is.

My hands are shaking so much, it's an effort to respond: **Who are you? Where is he?**

I stand there, watching the screen. Waiting.

But there's no reply.

CHAPTER 2

I rush back into the house, just in time to run into Elliot, who is coming down the stairs. "Was he up there?" I ask.

For a moment, I have a sliver of hope, but then he shakes his head.

"Did you check all the rooms?" I press him.

He nods. "Yes. I didn't see him."

That stab of panic is starting to escalate. My legs have turned to jello. "He's not in the backyard. And the gate is open..."

My heart is doing jumping jacks in my chest, but Elliot still doesn't seem overly concerned. How does he do that? Is he really not worried or is he just so much better at faking it? He *is* a lawyer, after all. He's good at faking it.

"Don't freak out, April," he says. "You know Bobby. He probably went over to play with Leo."

Leo is Bobby's best friend, and conveniently Julie's son.

"Without asking me?" My voice sounds high and squeaky. "He wouldn't do that."

"Hmm. It sounds *exactly* like something he would do."

That's not true.

At least, I don't think it's true. Admittedly, Bobby has been testing some of the boundaries of what we will allow him to do lately. Maybe Elliot is right. Maybe he's playing at Leo's house right now. Although if he were with Julie, wouldn't she have mentioned it when she texted me about the PTA meeting?

"But what about that text message I got?" I say. I was willing to shrug it off as a prank before, but now that I can't locate Bobby, I realize it may be much more than that.

He just shakes his head. "I… I don't know…"

"I'm calling Julie," I announce. Before he can say anything, I reach for my phone and call Julie's number on speed dial. It rings five times, then goes to voicemail. "She's not picking up."

"She never picks up."

My heart is racing as I push past my husband. "I'm going over there."

Elliot is watching me, his eyebrows bunched together. "I'm sure he's fine. I bet anything he's at Leo's house."

"Yeah," I mumble.

"I mean," he goes on, "kids don't just get taken from the backyard. That's the kind of thing that happens in fiction. In real life, that never happens. It's really rare."

I stop in my tracks to glare at him. "I just got a text

message asking me where he is, and now I can't find him. You really think I'm overreacting?"

Elliot opens his mouth, but no words come out.

Bobby has taped one of his drawings to our front door. It looks like a turtle, which is his favorite kind of animal (this month). He's written his name in the lower right-hand corner, and in the upper right-hand corner, he's scribbled, "For Mom." Whenever he draws anything, he always writes that in the corner. Every drawing is for me.

A few hours ago, if I saw this I would have yelled at him for using tape on the wall. I've told him a hundred times that it takes the paint off the walls. Now when I see him, I'm going to hand him a roll of scotch tape and tell him to go crazy. He could cover every inch of the wall if he wants.

I yank open the front door, and Elliot follows me. "Do you want me to check Oliver's house?"

Oliver is Bobby's other friend on the block. He's all the way down at the corner. It seems unlikely Bobby would have gone over there. But you never know. "Fine."

I can't decide whether I should be happy that Elliot is taking this seriously and helping me to find our son, or if I should be terrified that he doesn't seem quite so certain anymore that we're going to find him any second now. But we decide to check both houses and meet back if we don't find him.

I don't want to think about what will happen if we

don't find him.

I practically sprint over to Julie's house. She lives on the other side of the light blue house with our new neighbors. It's a sixty-second walk. Of course, now the journey seems endless as I walk/jog in my flimsy ballet flats that I usually just wear around the house. Every pebble and crack in the pavement jabs my feet, but I barely notice it.

I keep telling myself Bobby is at Leo's house. And then I'm going to kill him for going there without telling me. But before that, I'm going to hug him and kiss him all over his sweet little freckled face.

Want to know a secret? Your son isn't where you think he is.

Who would send me a text like that? Did somebody snatch my son out of my backyard? What if I never see Bobby again? What if when I shoved him into the backyard to keep him out of the way, that was the last time I'd ever see him.

Oh God.

I am out of breath by the time I get to Julie's house, which is the biggest one on the block. And the newest. Elliot is a corporate lawyer, but Julie's husband Keith does personal injury law, and he really cleans up. Elliot does well at his job and I make good money through *April's Sweet Secrets*, but the Bresslers are the kind of rich where they throw hundred dollar bills into the fireplace for kindling.

But right now, I couldn't care less. I sprint up the steps to her front door and ring the doorbell. Twice.

No answer.

I pound on the door a few times. But nobody is home. All the lights are out and I can see through the open shutters that the living room is empty. Bobby isn't playing with Leo. The Bresslers aren't even home.

I take my phone out. The text message is still on the screen, taunting me. They haven't responded to me. I shoot off another text message:

Where is he??? Tell me now!!!!!!

No reply.

In the past, I've done a reverse lookup for phone numbers. You can get the information for free from the online White Pages. Maybe I can find out who sent me the text message.

My hands are shaking as I bring up the White Pages on my phone. It takes me three tries to successfully copy the phone number of the person who texted me into the search engine. I stand there, my legs trembling, as my phone hourglasses. Finally, the screen flashes with the result:

Unknown registrant. No name is associated with this number.

Whoever sent me that message did it from a blocked number.

I feel like I'm going to pass out. I know I need to call the police. But the idea of it fills me with sick dread, because a call to the police would be admitting he's really gone. The police will have to start searching for him. I can only imagine their questions.

When did you last see your son, Mrs. Masterson?

I was cooking in the kitchen and he went out to play in the backyard. And then I got this text message...

So you weren't watching him?

I feel a stab of guilt. I should have been watching him. I never should have taken my eyes off of him. But he was in our own backyard, for God's sake! With the gate locked! And he's not a toddler—he's seven years old. That should be old enough to play in his own backyard. Right?

I told him about Stranger Danger, of course. Never talk to strangers. Never go off with strangers. But I know Bobby. If a stranger offered him candy, he'd skip off with them in a heartbeat despite all the warnings. He's helpless to resist candy.

The police will have to organize some sort of search party. They'll check all the houses in a certain mile radius, then they'll have to extend to the parks and that wooded area at the edge of town. And the lake. Oh God, the lake…

I choke back a sob.

I've got to get back to the house. If Elliot hasn't found him, we'll have to call the police. And in the meantime, we should probably check with the neighbors. See if they saw a strange van, or a bearded stranger lurking around my house. And maybe they can trace who sent me that horrible text message.

As I jog back to our house, I happen to see the lights on inside the house of our new neighbors. Their white SUV—practically identical to mine, except an older model—is parked in their driveway. Just a week ago, a new family moved into the house after poor old Mrs. Kirkland passed on. I haven't even had a chance to stop in and say hello yet.

I hesitate near their driveway, staring at the mailbox with the name Cooper etched on the side. These people are right next-door to us. Maybe they saw something. This is not the introduction I wanted to have to our new neighbors—telling them I've lost my son—but I'm desperate. Every moment counts at a time like this.

I race up the steps to the blue house and rap my fist against the door. My hand is shaking badly. My whole body feels like it's buzzing. Who would do this to me? Why is somebody targeting me? This can't possibly be about a tray of burned cookies.

After a minute or so, the door swings open. A woman in her early thirties with olive skin and dark brown hair loosely pulled back into a bun stands before me. She has a plain face, but when she smiles, dimples pucker on either cheek, which gives her a sweet, friendly appearance. There's something strangely familiar about her, but I can't seem to place her.

"Hello," she says. "May I help you?"

"Hello." My voice cracks. "Um, my name is April. I live next door…"

"Hi, April." Her brow furrows in concern. "I'm Maria. Is everything okay?"

"No. It's not." My voice is shaking again, threatening to break. "My son, Bobby…"

I hear some shouting behind her, and before I can get out the rest of the sentence, my jaw drops open.

It's *Bobby*. Sitting in this woman's living room, playing with Legos with another little boy.

"Hi, Mom," he says, like I haven't nearly dropped dead of a stroke while looking for him. The rush of relief I feel almost knocks me off my feet.

"Bobby!" I scream.

I run over to him and drop to my knees on the floor. I don't know whether to shake him or hug him. I do a little bit of both.

"I had no idea where you were!" I cry as I press his skinny body to my chest. "I was so scared! You scared me so much!"

And now Bobby is crying. We're both crying and hugging each other. It's a bit of an embarrassing display in front of the new neighbor, but I don't care. What the hell was he doing here anyway?

"Oh my God, I am so sorry!" the woman, Maria, is saying to me. "He showed up on our front lawn and said you told him he could come over to play with Owen. I had no idea you didn't realize he was here!"

I look up at my new neighbor, studying her expression. Her brown eyes are wide and she looks embarrassed, apologetic, and almost tearful. She certainly doesn't look like a psychopath who just sent me a threatening text message and stole my son out of my backyard for a playdate. I don't think there's any chance of that.

I *do* believe Bobby might get it into his head to wander out of our backyard. Anyway, he and I are going to have a *very* long talk tonight. After I spend the rest of the day covering him in hugs and kisses.

I shoot off a quick text to Elliot: **Found him. He was at the neighbor's house.**

Elliot's response comes a second later: **Told you. Going to work now.**

How could Elliot not even want to see Bobby after he thought he was missing? I don't understand men at all.

"You must have been worried sick," Maria says. *She* gets it, at least. "I can only imagine!"

I struggle back to my feet, wiping tears from my eyes. "At least he was safe the whole time."

"Absolutely!" Maria offers me a smile, which makes me want to hug her. This woman found my baby. God knows where he would have ended up if he didn't come here. "And he had such a good time with Owen. Poor Owen doesn't have any friends in the neighborhood yet. I would be happy to have Bobby over again, with your permission, of course."

I'm not sure about that. After this, I may have to duct tape Bobby to my right leg. It might be challenging to do my show, but viewers would understand. *April's Sweet Secrets—now with a screaming second-grader in every episode!*

"That would be nice," I finally say. And I mean it. "By the way, I'm so sorry we haven't managed to connect yet. I was meaning to stop by in the next day or two."

Maria waves a hand. "No worries! It's so busy with school starting soon..."

"Yes, us too! It's been crazy, hasn't it?"

"Well," Maria says, "now that you're here, would you like to have some coffee while the boys play? Get off your feet?"

I shift in my flats. My right foot is throbbing. "That would be nice. Thanks."

I feel a rush of relief that Bobby is safe and sound in this woman's living room. He was never in any danger after all. Except I can't ignore the fact that somebody did send me a text message about him.

Of course, maybe the text wasn't as ominous as it sounded. Maybe whoever sent it saw Bobby leaving the backyard and wanted to warn me he was gone. Maybe the person was a good Samaritan.

But if that was the case, why did the text come from a blocked number?

I'm making too much of this. Bobby was never

missing. He's fine. And lots of people in our town have blocked numbers. I'm not going to panic over a text message. It's not like I haven't gotten my share of disturbing comments on my YouTube videos over the last several years. I need to just put it out of my head.

So I follow Maria into the kitchen for coffee.

CHAPTER 3

Maria's kitchen is small but incredibly cozy. It's about half the size of our kitchen. Maybe even less. But that makes sense, since Maria's house is about half the size of ours or maybe even less. But the kitchen suits her. It's small, no-frills, and everything seems very well organized. I appreciate a well-organized kitchen. I even have a show on the secrets to a well-organized kitchen.

"How do you take your coffee?" Maria asks as she gets the coffee machine going. "I've got cream and sugar."

Maria's coffee machine looks like the one my mother had when I was a little kid. It's old-school. She pours coffee grounds into a little filter and flips a switch to turn it on. I have to admit, I'm very particular about my coffee. A year ago, I bought a machine that makes espressos and cappuccinos right in the comfort of my own kitchen. It was not cheap, but I justified it as a business expense by doing an episode of *Sweet Secrets* about the secret to making the perfect cappuccino.

The secret, in case you were wondering, is using ice-cold milk right out of the refrigerator to make the perfect foam. (And also, purchasing a five-hundred-dollar cappuccino machine.)

"Cream and sugar would be great, thanks," I say. I glance out the window at our own house, clearly visible across the way. I left the lights on in the kitchen. "Actually, I made some brownies for you guys. I'll bring them by later."

I'll give her the brownies from my show today. I'll make something else for Carrie tomorrow.

Maria's eyes light up. "Owen would love that. I am hopeless in the kitchen, especially when it comes to baking."

"I've always been pretty good at baking," I say. "I have a little YouTube show about it."

"Oh, I know!" When I look at her in surprise, Maria's cheeks flush. "Sorry, a few people mentioned to me that you've got the show and I watched it the other day. You're sort of a celebrity around here, you know!"

Now it's my turn to blush. "Am I?"

She nods eagerly. "The show is great. I tried to make your homemade chocolate chip cookies, but I'm so hopeless, they came out terrible."

She rifles around in the refrigerator, looking for the milk. I can't help but crane my neck to look over her shoulder. I know it sounds crazy, but I am very curious about other people's refrigerators. Maybe it's because I love to cook so much. I feel like the inside of a person's refrigerator tells you a lot about them.

For example, Maria's refrigerator is just like the rest of her house. It's small and neat, without much inside, but very well organized. I spy a few pieces of fruit in the crisper, a container of milk, orange juice, a loaf of bread, and some cold cuts. I suppose they're the sort of family that gets takeout a lot.

"So what brought you out here?" I ask, as Maria removes the container of milk from her fridge. I quickly peek at the expiration date—she's got two more days.

She glances at the coffee machine. It's still churning. "Our last apartment was in a terrible school district. There was a lot of bullying at the school and nobody seemed to care. We wanted something better for Owen."

I nod eagerly. "The schools are amazing here. Owen will love it. What grade is he in?"

"Second grade."

I do my best to hide my surprise—based on his size, I thought for sure Owen was in first grade or maybe even kindergarten. "Same as Bobby! Who is his teacher?"

"Mrs. Reynolds."

My heart leaps in my chest. "That's amazing! That's Bobby's teacher. They're in the same class!"

Maria clutches her chest. "That's wonderful. I've been so nervous about Owen making friends, but it seems like he and Bobby are getting along great."

This is incredible. I had been hoping to have a neighbor that I could be more friendly with than elderly Mrs. Kirkland, but I hadn't dreamed of getting a neighbor with a little boy Bobby's age in the same class as him. It will be so nice for Bobby to have a friend on the block whose mother isn't… well, Julie. Not that I don't love Julie, but she can be intense. And Leo is so overbooked with afterschool activities, he never has time to play.

"Are you planning to join the PTA?" I ask.

She hesitates. "I wasn't sure. I got a flyer about a meeting this week. Do a lot of people join?"

"Oh my God, yes." I'm embarrassed to tell her how much of my life is consumed by the PTA. But at least I'm doing work for a good cause—my kid's school. "And Julie— she lives on the other side of you—she's the president of the PTA this year and she's going to push you to join. For sure."

A funny smile plays on Maria's lips. "Yes, I've already gotten a few notes from Julie. She says she's the… block captain?"

I groan. "Yeah, she pretty much made that up to feel important. It's not like we voted for her or anything. At least, I didn't. She organizes all the stuff on our block, like yard sales and the book club… that's next Thursday, by the way, in case you want to come."

"Yes, I saw the book was almost six-hundred pages. That seems a bit… challenging."

I lift a shoulder. "Honestly, I have no idea. We never discuss the book for more than a minute or two. We spend most of the time gossiping. Julie picks the books, and they're always the longest, most boring books in the world."

She laughs. "So it's okay if I didn't read it?"

"Heck yes. I sure haven't."

The coffee machine lets out an obnoxious buzzing noise that sets off a jab of pain in my left temple. I'm already planning to buy Maria a new coffee machine for Christmas. You can never start planning for Christmas too early. During all of December, I usually do Christmas-themed episodes of *Sweet Secrets*.

Maria pours me a cup of coffee in a white mug with a little crack on the side. I pour in some milk and a few teaspoons of sugar, then take a sip. Just as I suspected—it's awful. Barely edible. I'm definitely buying her a coffee machine. Something amazing. It will change her life.

Her eyebrows bunch together. "Is the coffee okay?"

"It's fine!" I pour in a little more milk in an attempt to make it tolerable. "Delicious. But you know, the secret to a really good cup of coffee in any machine is grinding your own beans. It's never going to taste as good if you buy coffee grounds at the supermarket."

Maria nods politely. "Oh, okay."

"Sorry!" I say quickly. "This coffee is fine. It's just… This is what I do, and it's hard to turn off the tips, you know?"

"Of course. And thanks for the tip." Maria takes a sip

of her coffee and seems to be genuinely enjoying it. Huh. "Anyway, I would love to join the PTA. I'll just have to see if I can fit it in with my work schedule."

"You work?" I can't disguise the surprise in my voice. Most women in this neighborhood are stay-at-home moms. With my weekly YouTube show, I do more than most.

She flashes me a self-conscious smile. "I manage Helena's."

Oh my God! So *that's* why she looks familiar!

She raises her eyebrows. "Have you heard of it?"

"Heard of it?" I shake my head. "I love Helena's! Your clothes look so great on camera. I could buy the whole store, except it would wreck my profit margin."

That's not an exaggeration. The last time I went to Helena's, it was a hide-the-credit-card-bill situation. They have incredible stuff, and it's also expensive. Whenever I look at the price tags, I want to cry. It's like a tease to have such beautiful clothing that I can't afford.

"Well," Maria says, "I get a thirty percent employee discount that you're welcome to take advantage of."

"Are you serious?"

She nods.

Okay, this really is too good to be true. This lovely woman is my neighbor, and not only does she have a son the same age as mine, but she can get me thirty percent off at my favorite clothing store in the entire world.

"Thank you so much, Maria," I say. "Believe me, I will

pay you back in brownies. Or chocolate cake. Or scones. I make really good scones."

She laughs, but I'm not kidding. I adore this woman. And I do make great scones. The secret is that you have to bake them close to each other. Scones like to be kissing.

I clear my throat. "So where is your husband? Is he at work?"

"Oh, no," she says quickly, as if such a thing would be ridiculous. And it *is* ridiculous. I still can't believe Elliot went to work after the scare we had. "Sean just stepped out to grab some groceries. He'll be back soon."

"What sort of work does he do?" I wonder if he's a lawyer like Elliot and Julie's husband. There are a lot of lawyers on this block. And bankers. Most of them commute into the city—I'm lucky Elliot has an office out on the island.

"He has a contracting business." She lifts her chin. "He started it from scratch. And in the last couple of years, it's taken off."

As if on cue, the front door lock turns. I jerk my head around just in time to see a guy with light brown hair and a well-trimmed beard lumber into the living room holding a bag of groceries. That must be Sean.

"Daddy!" Owen screams.

He abandons his Lego creation and propels himself at his father. What follows is several minutes of pretty adorable roughhousing between father and son. Owen loves it. Bobby looks on with a crease between his eyebrows, which makes me realize that this is something Elliot never does with him.

When Sean finally disentangles himself from Owen, he looks up and his eyes widen at the sight of me sitting in his kitchen. He clears his throat.

"Sean," Maria says, "this is April and her son Bobby. They live next door."

He straightens up and retrieves the bag of groceries from the floor. I can't help but notice his worn T-shirt and frayed blue jeans are a far cry from what my husband was wearing today. "Next door, huh? Are you the one who keeps leaving us notes about our car being parked wrong? Or are you the one who makes cookies on YouTube?"

I laugh. "Cookies."

A smile spreads across his lips as he deposits the groceries on the kitchen counter. "Well, then it's nice to meet you, April."

Sean's dark blue eyes meet mine as he sticks out a hand for me to shake. I can't help but notice that his palm is rough and calloused compared with my husband's. Hmm, Elliot might not be the hottest husband on the block anymore.

"Sean was planning to take Owen to the park to practice soccer," Maria explains.

My ears perk up. "Bobby adores soccer. Does Owen play a lot?"

"God, yes," Maria says. "He loves every sport, but

especially soccer. Sean used to coach back at his old school."

"Oh yeah?" I shouldn't be surprised. Sean looks like a natural athlete. "That's great. What coach do you have here?

Sean pauses in the middle of sorting the groceries. "Unfortunately, we were too late to get Owen on the team. I put him on the waiting list, but we're not hopeful."

I feel my eyes light up. I love helping people out with problems. "I'm really good friends with Mark Tanner, Bobby's coach. I could talk to Mark about putting Owen on the team."

Sean beams at me. "You think you could do that?"

"Definitely." I grin at the Coopers. "I'll just make him up a batch of chocolate cupcakes. Nobody says no to chocolate cupcakes."

"Thanks so much, April." Sean puts the last of the groceries—a dozen eggs—in the refrigerator and then pours himself a cup of that terrible coffee. He takes a swig of it black. "Hey, would Bobby like to come to the park with us to practice now?"

That is a very tempting offer. Bobby loves playing soccer, but Elliot never has time to play with him during the weekend.

But at the same time, I'm still shaken about Bobby going missing. Even though I found him after less than fifteen minutes and he was perfectly safe the whole time, the thought of sending my little boy off with a man I literally met two minutes ago leaves a bad taste in my mouth.

"April is a little shaken up," Maria explains to her husband. "Bobby wandered over here without telling her, and gave her quite a scare."

"Oh?" Sean looks at me with interest.

I shrug and try to play it off. I didn't even tell them about the creepy text message. "It was a bit scary when I didn't see him in the backyard."

Sean places a hand on his chest. "I promise, I will guard him with my life, April."

He isn't being facetious. I can tell he would keep a close eye on the boys. And probably protect them better than I ever could. I have a feeling if *his* son went missing, he wouldn't shrug it off and say he "probably went to the neighbors."

But even so, I don't quite feel comfortable yet. And anyway, I need to have a talk with Bobby about running off without letting me know. I still can't believe he did that. He definitely needs to be punished.

"Next time," I promise.

Sean grins at me. "Sure. Owen and I are usually kicking the ball around in the backyard, so Bobby is always welcome to join us."

"Or you could come to our backyard," I add. "Ours is much bigger, so there's more room to run around."

As soon as the words leave my mouth, I regret them. These people don't want me to point out that our house is twice the size of theirs. It's obnoxious. I didn't mean it that way anyway… I just meant that we have more space. That's all.

Sean doesn't seem offended, thank goodness. But now that he's home, Owen is overeager to get to the park. I expect Bobby to beg to go with him, but he seems agreeable to heading back home. That's good, because I don't feel like fighting with him right now.

"I'll see you at school drop off tomorrow," I tell Maria as I herd Bobby out the front door.

She waves at me. "Looking forward to it!"

Bobby is skipping all the way home, and to be honest, I feel like skipping too. Maria is amazing. I finally have somebody I can be friends with on the block who isn't super judgmental and bossy. And Bobby has a new best friend too. Also, Sean seems really nice. Really *really* nice.

"Maybe me and Dad can play against Owen and his dad at the park," Bobby says.

My stomach drops. Bobby doesn't know his father already went to work. Then again, you'd think by now he would expect it. But he still keeps hoping his father will stick around and take him out to play.

"Actually," I say carefully, "your dad had to go to work today."

Bobby's lower lip juts out and his face turns pink. "But that's not fair! He always goes to work on the weekend!"

Secretly, I agree with my son. But Elliot and I have to maintain a unified front. "You know your dad has a super important job."

A tear escapes from Bobby's left eye. He's still young enough that his response to anything unfair in life is to start crying. I wonder when that will change. "But I want to go to the park!"

"Listen." My voice takes on a firm tone. "I told you Dad needs to work. And anyway, you're being punished now. I've told you a hundred times not to leave the backyard without my permission. I'm very angry with you."

Bobby's brown eyes widen. He looks so much like his father right now. It's so strange to catch these little glimpses of Elliot in my son. "But I didn't leave without your permission! You said I could!"

I snort. "I most certainly did not!"

"Yes! Owen's mom said you told her it was okay!"

I shake my head. I can't believe how good of a liar my seven-year-old son has become. It's getting to be a problem. I'm going to have to watch out for this one. "That's not true."

"It is! She came to the fence and told me you said it was okay for me to come over!"

I think back to the text message and get an uneasy feeling in my chest. Is it possible Maria would send me that text message and then lure my son out of the backyard just to scare me?

There are a lot of crazy people out there. After all, *someone* sent me that text message...

I shake my head. No. No way. Maria was genuinely

shocked when she found out Bobby was there without permission—she couldn't fake that. And why would she do something so evil? Not that there aren't people in this town that dislike me, but I only just met the woman. The more logical explanation is somebody simply saw him leave my yard and wanted to give me a warning.

"Even if that were true..." Which it isn't. "You still should have gotten permission from me directly. You are never supposed to leave the backyard without asking me if it's okay. Do you understand?"

Bobby lowers his eyes. "Yes," he mumbles.

"What? I didn't hear you."

"Ugh!" Bobby does not like rules. He also doesn't like apologizing. He'd rather rip off his right arm than say sorry. "I told you, yes!"

He's saying yes, but I don't entirely trust him. I'm going to have to dole out some sort of punishment, like no TV for the rest of the week. He'll kick up a fuss about that one, but it needs to be done. I still can't believe he would just leave the backyard without telling me. And then to lie about it... Does he think I'm stupid?

CHAPTER 4

Dear parents,

Welcome to the Hopkins School Parent-Teacher Association!

We managed to exceed our fundraising goals last year, and this year we are hoping to exceed our total from last year! But we need volunteers to achieve the standard of excellence that is expected of our PTA.

I hope all of you will consider attending our first meeting at the Hopkins School Library on Tuesday night. We will be discussing all of our goals for the year, and how you can help us to achieve those goals!

The meeting is expected to last approximately three hours. There will be NO FOOD. If you do attend, you will be expected to stay for the duration of the meeting. I would also expect that when the meeting concludes, you will help us rearrange the tables and chairs back in the configuration they were prior to the meeting.

Important: all electronic devices should be powered down during this meeting. The welfare of your children requires your complete attention. Simply putting your phone on silent is not acceptable.

Hope to see you Tuesday night!

Your PTA President,
Julie Bressler

Breakfast is the most important meal of the day.

I had an episode of *Sweet Secrets* about French toast. Technically, it's not a baked good, but I love it and the episode was really popular. My secret for the perfect French toast batter is a pinch of brown sugar. And of course, brioche bread. Bobby always gobbles it up and asks for more. And so does Elliot, for that matter.

I cook it in a mix of butter and oil until it's perfectly crisp on the outside and still moist in the center. I love the way my boys' eyes light up when I put the plates down in front of them.

"You make the best French toast in town, April," Elliot declares as he shovels a bite into his mouth. "You're going to give me a heart attack, but I don't even care."

"Aw, you really know how to flatter a girl."

There are some cut up strawberries on the plate too, so that's the healthier element. But Bobby is meticulously eating around them. Oh well.

My own plate consists of an egg-white omelet and three strawberries. If I'm going to be on camera every week, I have to maintain my figure. So I never eat any of my sweet treats, and I go running three times a week. And speaking of looking my best, tomorrow I've got an appointment at the hairdresser to touch up my roots. My dark roots are very visible on camera—if I let it go, I always end up getting comments from viewers.

Elliot finishes his French toast in two minutes flat, then downs the rest of his coffee in a single gulp. Part of me is hoping he might stick around for a bit, but it's clear he's rushing to get to the office. Again.

I miss my husband.

"Sorry I've got to run." Elliot leans in to kiss me, and I let him, although I'm tempted to turn my head so he'll get cheek rather than lips. "I'm not sure if I'll make it back in time for dinner."

My heart sinks. "Elliot…"

"I told you, it's crazy right now at work." He chews on his lower lip. "Listen, if you can, why don't you stop by the office and we'll grab lunch together?"

I sniff. "Are you sure you'll have time?"

"Hey." He pulls me close to him and presses his lips against mine. Even after all these years, I still melt when he kisses me. Yes, my husband isn't perfect, but I love being married to him. "I can always make time for you."

Well, that's not really true. But I'll let that one go. Why pick a fight first thing in the morning?

Bobby is still taking his sweet time finishing his French toast, so I walk Elliot to the front door. He kisses me one last time, then hops into his Tesla and takes off, nearly smashing into the postal truck pulling up in front of our house. Considering how much money he spent on that damn car, you'd think he would drive more carefully. I own a white SUV that was voted safest car in the year I purchased it.

As he drives away, I go to my phone and load up the latest episode of *April's Sweet Secrets*. The brownie episode is still in editing, but the episode I recorded last week is now live. I made a chocolate soufflé. The episode took me forever to film, because my first set of soufflés totally fell. I had to do the whole thing twice.

I'm very pleased with the number of views I've had so far. It looks like I may surpass the views on my last video. I start scanning through the comments:

April, this looks delicious!

You are a master in the kitchen! You make it look so easy!

I'm making this for my next dinner party. Thanks, April!

Love that shirt on you! Red is your color. The soufflé looks great!

I smile at the first several comments. For the most part, everyone is very supportive. I mean, it's a baking show. There isn't much controversial stuff on there. But then my fingers pause as the comments abruptly change in tone.

Disgusting! Why would April think anyone wants to eat this pile of crap?

Looks like something my dog did!

I think she poured that soufflé out of some newborn baby's diaper.

One after another negative comment, filling the screen. I've received plenty of negative comments before, but never quite such a barrage of them. I thought the soufflé episode was really good. It came out looking just like a professional chef would make it.

A lump forms in my throat as I scroll down, waiting for the hateful comments to end. I finally get to the last one:

April's secret is that she is a terrible cook and a worse person. Trust me—I know.

My phone almost falls out of my hand. You would think after all these years, I would be able to ignore comments like that. And I can, for the most part. I even had an episode where I made fun of some ridiculous mean comments I've gotten over the years. But this onslaught... It's so unexpected. And the last one is especially disturbing.

Trust me—I know.

"Shit," I breathe.

"Mommy, you said the S-word!"

Oh God, where did Bobby come from? Ninety percent of the time, he's so loud that people down the street can hear him, but every once in a while he's like a stealth ninja.

I quickly lock my phone and lower the screen. "No, I didn't."

"You did! I heard you say it!"

"No. I said sheet. Like a sheet of paper."

"No, you didn't!"

I put my hands on my hips. "Bobby, we have to be at your school in fifteen minutes and you don't have your shoes on or your backpack ready. Did you even put your lunch in your backpack?"

"Yes…"

"So if I look in the refrigerator, I'm not going to find the lunch I packed for you?"

Bobby wrinkles his freckled nose. I make lunch for him every day, but for some reason, he has glamorized the school lunch, to the point where he manages to "forget" the lunch I packed with alarming frequency. So apparently, it's one more thing I have to police.

"Fine," he grumbles. "But Leo says only losers bring lunch from home."

I wince. I'm really glad Bobby has made friends with Owen from next door, because Julie's son isn't the best influence.

Bobby trudges off to pack the lunch I made for him. It's only when he's back in the kitchen that I take one last look at the final comment on my YouTube video:

April's secret is that she is a terrible cook and a worse person. Trust me—I know.

I log into my account, and one by one, I delete all the mean comments. There. Now it's like it never happened.

CHAPTER 5

Bobby has never once been tardy for school, and today is no exception. Despite what felt like an insurmountable number of tasks to complete before getting out the door, I manage to park my car outside the school with a comfortable five minutes left until the early bell rings. It's only a two-minute drive from our house to Bobby's school, which is why school bus service is not provided. Potentially, it is walkable. But we never manage to walk it.

Before I've even locked the door to my white SUV, I hear Bobby scream, "Leo!" And then he propels himself in the direction of his best friend.

I have to appreciate Bobby's enthusiasm. He always seems so excited to see Leo, even though they see each other essentially *every single day*. I can barely manage a smile for my own best friend, Julie, who is chatting with some other women as they wait for the bell to ring.

Julie used to be a lawyer before she gave up her job and

moved to Long Island, and she still dresses the part. She's wearing a pristine white blouse and a gray pencil skirt. Her hair is swept back from her face in an elaborate twist—she has the sort of classic beauty where she will look beautiful even when she's eighty. I had her on my show a couple of times demonstrating an upscale recipe, and those episodes always get lots of views.

Julie took over the reins as president of the PTA this year, and by all accounts, she's taking it very seriously. I've already received at least a dozen emails from her about it and we've yet to have our first meeting. I'm sure she'll do an amazing job. She's a great leader. I'm so lucky she's my best friend.

As I get closer, I notice Julie is chatting with Kathy Tanner. I freeze in my tracks. Kathy doesn't like me, for some reason. I don't want to talk to her, but I also don't want to stand alone. And God forbid I snub Julie. So I've got to go over there.

"April." Julie smiles at me. "We were worried… it isn't like you to be so late."

"Yes, well… Bobby was so slow in the morning. You know what I mean."

I don't want to tell these two women about the slew of horrible comments on my latest video. They would just laugh it off. *You have to have thick skin if you're going to be on the Internet, April.* But it isn't just about having thick skin. There was something incredibly disturbing about that final comment. Like it could have come from someone close to me.

April's secret is that she is a terrible cook and a worse person. Trust me—I know.

Who would write something like that?

"Bella makes her own breakfast every morning and is ready to go when I get downstairs," Kathy volunteers. "She is *such* an angel."

"Mmm," I say. "Bobby isn't quite there, I guess."

"Good thing your show is about cooking secrets and not child behavior secrets!" Kathy laughs.

I shoot Kathy a look. She smiles at me, but her eyes are cold. If I ever call her on her nonstop jabs, she insists she's just teasing me and I'm too sensitive. It's exhausting.

Is it possible Kathy could have been the one who left those nasty comments? I wouldn't put it past her.

"By the way," Julie says, "we wanted to get your opinion on something, April. Don't you think there should be a dress code for drop off and pick up?"

Kathy nods eagerly. "Look at all these mothers standing around in pajamas! It's such a disgrace. Honestly, it's embarrassing."

I look around at the scattered mothers gathered around the school entrance for drop off. I do see one woman carrying an infant in her arms and a toddler is attached to her left hand, and she does appear to be wearing pajama pants and slippers.

I look down at my own outfit. Yoga pants. A tank top.

A hoodie sweatshirt. Ballet flats again. I wonder if they're trying to tell me something.

"I mean," Julie goes on, "it's a terrible example for the children. We wouldn't allow *them* to go to school in pajamas, would we?"

"No," I say. "Well, except on pajama day."

"I'm going to bring it up at the PTA meeting tomorrow," Julie says. "Would you add that to the agenda, April? You're coming, right?"

Before I can answer in the affirmative, the early bell sounds off. The kids all pile into the front entrance. I wave to Bobby, but I'm not sure he notices. When he's around his friends, I might as well not exist.

Out of the corner of my eye, I see Maria Cooper and her son Owen hurrying toward the entrance. After Maria shared her concerns about Owen not having any friends at the new school, I had a talk with Bobby about being kind to him. Hopefully, Bobby will listen. Sometimes he does things without thinking and he's slow as molasses in the morning, but my son has a good heart.

After Maria deposits her son at the school entrance, I wave her over. After all, Owen Cooper isn't the only one who is new to town and needs friends. What kind of neighbor would I be if I didn't introduce Maria to all the other mothers?

"Maria!" I call. "Hi!"

Julie furrows her brow. "Who is that?"

"Our new neighbor."

"Oh." She frowns. "Those people are never home. I've stopped by at least five times to welcome her. And I left her two copies of the guidelines for the block, but she still keeps parking wrong."

Maria looks nice today. Her dark brown hair is tucked behind her ears and she's wearing these adorable dangly earrings that I saw once at Helena's. (I must take her up on that thirty percent discount!) She offers me a big smile as she walks over which makes her dimples pop.

"I was so worried I was going to be late," Maria sighs. "Owen is just so slow in the morning!"

"Bobby too!" I say. Finally—one other person who doesn't have a perfect child.

Julie sticks out her right hand. "I'm Julie Bressler. I'm your new next-door neighbor. And this is Kathy Tanner."

Maria takes Julie's hand, and I can see her wince. Julie has one hell of a handshake—she never holds back. I guess it's a holdover from her lawyer days. "Nice to meet you both," Maria says. "I'm Maria Cooper."

"I hope you're coming to the PTA meeting tomorrow." Julie gives her a pointed look. "You got the flyer, right?"

"Um…" Maria chews on her lip. "Sure. I think I can make it."

"I've been trying to stop in," Julie says, "but I can never find you. I'm impressed April managed to catch you."

Maria laughs. "Well, April misplaced her son at my house. So that's how we met."

Julie arches a perfectly shaped eyebrow. Julie has the best eyebrows ever. She won't tell us where she gets them done—she has some secret eyebrow threader tucked away somewhere. "Misplaced her son?"

My face grows hot as Maria recounts the story of how Bobby left the backyard and I had a panic attack looking for him. I know Maria doesn't mean anything by it, but the story doesn't make me look good. I don't want everybody to think I'm an irresponsible mother.

Even worse, when Maria is done telling the story, Julie and Kathy snicker knowingly.

"That sounds just like Bobby," Kathy says.

"What are you talking about?" I snap at her. "I've never lost Bobby before."

"Of course you have." Julie shakes her head at me. "Remember when we were at Whole Foods and he took off while we were getting food from the salad bar? You had the whole store looking for him! And then they found him stuffing cupcakes in his mouth in the bakery—there was chocolate all over his face."

"And at that art store," Kathy reminds me. "Remember he broke all that pottery and you had to pay for it?"

That is *so* unfair. I could name plenty of incidents where Julie and Kathy would come off looking foolish, but it's not a *competition*.

"Anyway," Maria says quickly, "Bobby was a pleasure

to have over. He was playing so well with Owen." She flashes me a quick smile. "Like I said, he can come over anytime. And if your son would like to come over, Julie, we'd be happy to have him too.

Julie mumbles something non-committal. She's never fond of making new friends. She'll probably be cold to Maria for the next year if the past is any indication. Unless…

"Hey, guess what," I say. "Maria works over at Helena's. She's a manager there!"

That manages to spark Julie and Kathy's interest. Like I said, we all love that store. Although between the three of us, Julie is the only one who can really afford it. I smile to myself as the two women pepper Maria with questions and ask if they can get a friend discount. I feel a little self-satisfaction that Maria offered me her thirty percent discount but tells each of them that they only get ten percent.

"Actually, I've got to head to work right now." Maria looks down at her watch regretfully. Then her eyes widen. "Oh... damn! We forgot Raffey!"

Julie frowns. "Raffey?"

Maria's cheeks color. "Raffey is this stuffed giraffe that Owen is really attached to. It's been helping him get through this transition period. I saw it on his bed this morning and I promised to bring it down for him so he could put it in his backpack, but I forgot with all the rushing around." She looks down at her watch again. "He's going to be crushed when he realizes he doesn't have Raffey. I'll just have to be late for work."

"Don't be silly!" I say. "I can go to your house and grab Raffey, and I'll bring him to Owen."

Maria cocks her head to the side. "Are you sure? I don't want to trouble you."

"It's no problem!"

"But—"

"Let April do it," Julie interrupts her. "This is her thing. She loves to be helpful."

Well, that's true. I do enjoy helping other people. But does she have to say it like it's an insult?

Maria's shoulders relax. "Thank you so much, April. You're a lifesaver."

I'm happy to do it. After all, what are neighbors for?

CHAPTER 6

The key to Maria's house is exactly where she said it would be: under the potted plant next to the front door. It's a horrible place to hide a key. If I were a burglar, that's the first place I would look.

I step into her tiny living room, which has been tidied up since I was here yesterday. Her television is smaller than ours and she doesn't have any sort of stereo system set up. I wonder how much money Sean Cooper makes as a contractor.

Now that Maria isn't around, I open up her refrigerator to get a better look. I shouldn't snoop, but it's just her refrigerator, for God's sake. Anyway, there's nothing very surprising here. She only has supermarket brand food items. I notice she has quite a lot of raw meat—far more than anything else. A pack of two pounds of ground beef. Steaks one inch thick, dripping with blood.

Then I look in the pantry. The supplies in there are embarrassingly scarce. She doesn't even have flour! Who doesn't have flour in their pantry? There's white sugar, but no brown sugar. No vanilla extract either. How does she bake anything without having vanilla?

Vanilla is just about my favorite ingredient. The smell of vanilla is known to directly impact the brain and induce a feeling of calmness. Maybe that's why I feel so calm when I'm baking.

All right, better go upstairs.

Our stairs are carpeted, but these aren't. Every step creaks under the weight of my flats. I reach the top of the steps and immediately see a room with a twin bed and colorful bedspread. Owen's room. The place where I'll find Raffey on his bed.

But my eyes are drawn to the room next to it. The master bedroom.

Yes, I'm curious. Is that so terrible? Elliot hates my curiosity. *Why do you always have to know everything, April?* But it's not like I'm going to take anything. I just want to see what her bedroom looks like. I'd like to see what sort of bedspread and sheets they have. Maybe take a peek in the closet. Nobody will even know. No harm done.

Like everything else in the house, the door to the bedroom creaks loudly as I open it up. The bedroom is decorated as simply as the rest of the house. A queen-sized bed in the center, a dresser on the side, a night table with a photo of Sean, Maria, and Owen together at Disneyland. A happy family.

The covers are not made up on the bed. Apparently, Maria doesn't require all the beds to be made before she leaves the house. That is an absolute rule at the Masterson house. I try to get Bobby to do his, but ninety percent of the time, I end up doing it. I look down at the covers, itching to make the bed for her. I mean, how could she just *leave* it like this? It's like leaving the house without buttoning your shirt.

Before I can give the matter any other thought, a noise makes me nearly jump out of my skin. It's coming from outside the bedroom. It sounds like footsteps.

Oh no, there's somebody else in the house.

I've got to get out of here.

My heart is slamming in my chest as I make a run for the door to the bedroom. As it swings open, I nearly run straight into Sean. Who looks absolutely stunned to see me.

Also, he's wearing nothing but a towel.

His mouth is hanging open and he's gripping the towel with his right hand. "You… What are you…?"

"I'm April," I say quickly. "We met yesterday. I was here with my son Bobby."

He just shakes his head. His hair is damp, and I have to say, I underestimated him yesterday when he was wearing a T-shirt. Oh my *God*, this guy has a nice chest. So many muscles. It must be from all the manual labor. Or sports. Either way, it's making me a little weak in the knees. "But what are you *doing* here?"

"Maria sent me." I swallow so hard, I'm sure he must

hear it. "Owen forgot Raffey, so she sent me to get it for him." When his expression is still blank, I add, "You know, his toy giraffe."

Sean looks at the door to the master bedroom, then back at me. "That's *our* bedroom though."

"Right. I was confused."

I watch Sean's face, hoping he'll buy it. Although mostly, I'm hoping he manages to hang onto that towel.

"I'll just grab the toy and go." I bat my eyes innocently. "Is that Owen's room over there then? I wasn't sure."

I should have been an actress. Really.

Sean looks me up and down. "Don't worry about it. I'm heading out now anyway, so I'll bring Raffey to Owen."

"Are you sure? I don't mind."

"Yeah. I'll take care of it."

Sean doesn't seem that thrilled with me. I guess I can't blame him, since he caught me snooping in his bedroom. Still, I'm determined to make nice. Elliot always says that I have a desperate need for everybody to like me, and I can't say he's entirely wrong.

"Well, his school is only a couple of minutes away," I say. "It's the Hopkins school. On River Street."

He looks at me like I have two heads. "Yes, I know where my son goes to school."

"Oh."

Well, it's not completely crazy that he wouldn't know. I'm not entirely sure Elliot knows where Bobby goes to school. We were going to see Bobby in a play at the end of last year, and Elliot started driving us in the entirely wrong direction until I corrected him.

"By the way," Sean says, "where did you get the key?"

"Key?"

He raises his eyebrows. "The key. To the house. Where did you get it?"

"Maria left it under the potted plant by the door."

He swears under his breath. "I told her not to leave it there. Any burglar could find it in two minutes."

"It's a safe neighborhood."

"Still."

Sean holds out his hand to me, and for a moment, I stare at it, confused at what he wants me to do. Then I realize. He wants his key back.

I fish around in my pocket until I come up with it. I place it down in his calloused palm, and he closes his fingers around it.

"Thanks, April," he says.

It takes me another second to realize that what he's really saying is, *Get the hell out of my house, April.* So I get the hell out of there.

CHAPTER 7

Text messages between April and Elliot Masterson:

April: **Would you like me to pack a picnic basket for us or do you want to go out to lunch?**

April: **Actually, I think I'd rather go out.**

April: **What do you think about going to that new French place?**

April: **I keep passing it and it looks so good.**

April: **OK, on my way out the door!**

April: **See you soon!**

Elliot: **OK**

It's a twenty-minute drive from our house to Elliot's office in his Tesla, but when I take my SUV, it's closer to half an hour. I don't speed. Ever.

After I get back home, I change out of my unacceptable school drop off clothing into something a little prettier. I put on a summer dress—it's yellow, which Elliot says is my best color. Of course, that's because I have blond hair. With dark roots, but nobody needs to know about that if I keep my hairdresser appointment for tomorrow.

I release my hair from my mom ponytail (which I alternate with my mom bun), I brush it out, and I even get out my curling iron. It takes forever, but when I look in the mirror after it's all done, I decide it was worth it. I clean up good.

I did consider packing a picnic basket for him. I used to do that in the early days of our relationship—I'd bring the basket to his office and we would eat at his desk together. But then again, I'm supposed to be angry at him for skipping out on our family time. He owes me a romantic lunch out.

I park in the lot outside Elliot's office building and take one last look in my compact before I head upstairs. His office is on the third floor, and the elevator is painfully slow, but I don't want to break a sweat before our lunch together. So I endure the elevator.

Elliot's receptionist, Brianna, always stands guard outside his office. I keep in good shape, but Brianna is, without a shadow of a doubt, absolutely gorgeous. Her legs are long and shapely, and her blond hair is shinier and thicker than mine. And her skin is like porcelain. I may be a YouTube star but she could be a movie star. It's painfully clear which one of us is the wife and which is the hot secretary.

And this woman works with my husband all day every day. I try not to think about it.

When I approach Brianna's desk, she's on the phone. From what I can hear, it sounds like a personal call. And when I clear my throat, she holds up a finger.

This goes on for a full two minutes. Is it just me or is her behavior completely unprofessional? If it were up to me, she'd be gone.

"I'm just going to go inside," I say to Brianna.

She flashes me an irritated look. "I've got to go, Niki," she says. She puts down the phone and finally gives me her full attention. "I'm afraid you can't go in. Elliot said he's very busy and not to be disturbed."

I roll my eyes. "We've got lunch plans. He told me to come here at noon."

"Yes, well." She shrugs. "His plans have changed. He's got a meeting in fifteen minutes, and he was very clear about not wanting to be disturbed."

"For God's sake, I'm his wife!" I fold my arms across my chest. "He didn't mean *me*."

"I'm sorry," she says in that irritatingly bland voice of

hers. "There is no lunch on the calendar. I'm afraid I can't let you in."

That's not true. She obviously *could* let me in if she wanted. She simply doesn't want to.

Well, I'll show her.

"I'm calling him," I inform her.

I yank my phone from my purse and select Elliot's cell number from my favorites. The only other favorites listed are Julie, Shady Oaks Nursing Home, and Bobby's school. I wait while the phone rings in my ear.

And I wait.

And I wait.

My whole face feels very hot by the time the call goes to voicemail. He definitely has his phone in there. He texted me less than an hour ago. He could answer it if he chose. But he's choosing not to.

Brianna smiles with satisfaction. "I could book you for lunch later in the week if you'd like?" She taps on her keyboard a few times. "He has an opening on Friday. Should I put you down?"

"No, thanks," I manage.

She clucks her tongue. "In the future, you really should make an appointment. That way you don't have to drive all the way down here for nothing."

I hate this woman. I really do.

"Look," I say, "I just want to talk to him for a minute. That's all."

"As I said…" She smiles up at me. "Elliot is *very* busy

right now. I'm sure he'll contact you when he has a free moment."

I've had enough of this. I move to the side of the desk, planning to blow past her, right into Elliot's office. But before I can reach the door, she jumps out of her seat, quick as a flash, and steps in front of me, blocking the door.

"I'm afraid you can't go in there." Her eyes meet mine. "As I said, he's busy."

I hold her gaze. Brianna is about my height, although I've got at least ten pounds on her. I wonder if I could knock her out of the way. For a moment, I'm tempted to try.

Brianna folds her arms across her chest. "Should I have somebody escort you out of the building?"

Great, she's going to call security to boot me out of here. I take a step back and jab at my phone one more time to call my husband. Again, the phone goes to voicemail, only this time immediately. I take a shaky breath.

Then the message appears on my screen:

So sorry. Forgot about meeting during lunch. Will make it up to you.

I look up at Brianna, who still has that smile plastered on her face. I truly don't care for this woman.

Call me as soon as you can, I type into my phone.

"Would you like that Friday lunch appointment?" Brianna bats her heavily mascaraed eyelashes at me. "You should book it now, while it's still free."

I don't even answer her. I do an about-face and leave the office before I burst into tears.

I don't even bother with the elevator this time. I go straight for the stairs. At this point, who cares if I'm sweaty? It will be hours before I see Elliot. I'll probably be in bed by then. All I want is to go home and take a nice hot shower, then binge-watch some series on Netflix. Or maybe I'll bake something. That always helps me relax.

I wish I could talk to somebody about this. I can't tell Julie. She won't get it. She's married to a lawyer too, but she takes her husband's long hours as a given. She would never consider traipsing out to his office for lunch. Frankly, sometimes I think she likes the fact that he's not around much. I might feel that way too if I were married to Keith.

At times like these, I wish I could talk to my mother. It's like a deep ache inside my chest. Unfortunately, my mother developed early Alzheimer's several years ago. Right now she's a resident at Shady Oaks nursing home, and having a meaningful conversation would be out of the question.

She barely knows who I am anymore. But every night, the staff of her nursing home plays one of my videos for her. That's why I always end my episodes by saying, "Good night, Mom." I want to make sure my mother still remembers who I am.

Sometimes I feel really alone.

But it doesn't matter. I'll get through this on my own.

I just want to go home.

When I get downstairs, my phone buzzes in my purse. My heart leaps in my chest—maybe Elliot's meeting got canceled and he wants to have lunch after all. Take that, gorgeous young secretary.

But when I pull out my phone, I see another blocked number has left me a text message:

Too bad you don't know the secret to making your husband happy. Unlike Courtney Burns.

I stare at my phone, my mouth hanging open in disbelief. I look around the parking lot, trying to figure out if somebody is watching me. Did somebody see my husband reject me during my attempt to have lunch with him?

But the parking lot is empty except for me. There's nobody around. And as opposed to the message yesterday, it's obvious what the intent of this one was. I look up at the window to my husband's office, wondering if Brianna could have been the one to send the text. Is it possible she's the one torturing me?

But how would Brianna know about Courtney? That's the distant past. It's *over*. Nobody knows. Just me and Elliot. Well, and one other person.

Words can't hurt you, I try to tell myself. I wish I could believe it.

CHAPTER 8

Dear parents,

For those of you who will be supporting your child's school by attending the PTA meeting tonight, please arrive promptly at 6 PM. Stragglers are very disruptive to the meeting. For this reason, the doors to the library will be locked at 6:01.

Julie

Elliot lets out a low whistle when I come into the kitchen dressed in a long-sleeved chiffon dress that I paid far too much for last month. "Wow, April," he says. "Are you sure you're just going to a PTA meeting?"

I roll my eyes, but he does have a point. I dress better for PTA meetings than I do for pretty much anything else in my life, even my videos. After all, the image I'm trying to portray on *Sweet Secrets* is that of a wholesome housewife.

But the dress code for these PTA meetings just keeps getting stricter and stricter. We're all trying to live up to Julie's standard.

Bobby looks up from his bowl of macaroni and cheese that Elliot made for him. Elliot can only make Kraft macaroni and cheese and frozen chicken nuggets. That's it. But to be fair, those are Bobby's two favorite foods.

"You look pretty, Mom," Bobby comments.

I ruffle my hand through his red-tinged brown hair. "You don't have to sound so surprised."

Bobby studies me for a moment. "Mom, are you having a baby?"

Aaaaaand my confidence flies out the window. "What?"

"Dylan's mom is having a baby," Bobby explains. "And Lena's mom is having a baby. And I don't have any brothers or sisters."

I smooth out my dress over my belly, hoping it doesn't even remotely look like I have a baby bump there. I glance over at Elliot, whose hopeful expression mirrors Bobby's. The truth is, Elliot and I want another child. He would have liked three or even four, but the fact that I haven't managed to get pregnant with even a second is a source of tension.

There's part of me that wonders if he thinks of me as a failure for not managing to conceive again. He's been gently pushing me to see a fertility specialist, and a few months ago, he mentioned he went to a urologist and got his sperm checked. His sperm were perfect, of course. He had superstar, Olympic sperm. So the implication is that if we're not pregnant with his Olympic sperm, it must be because of me.

Ironically, we had no trouble at all getting pregnant with Bobby. Actually, we jumped the gun a little bit on that one. But nobody noticed my baby bump in my wedding dress.

"No," I reply patiently. "We're not having a baby."

"Yet," Elliot adds.

I shoot him a look. The last thing I want is for Bobby to go around telling his friends that his parents are trying to have a baby. How long will it take for that to get back to the other parents?

But Elliot just shrugs. He thinks I'm going to get pregnant any month now. He doesn't get it.

"Well, I'm going to head over to Maria's house," I say. "Are you two going to be all right? You know Julie makes us shut our phones off?"

"I think I can handle a few hours alone with Bobby."

That remains to be seen. Whenever I go out, Elliot always texts me the most inane questions. He's a high-powered attorney, but sometimes it feels like he can't find his right hand without me. The last time I went out and he watched Bobby, he sent me a text asking where the milk was. *The milk is in the refrigerator!* If it's not in the refrigerator, you shouldn't be drinking it!

"Dad, can we play Nintendo together?" Bobby asks.

Elliot frowns. "I have a ton of work to do, Bobby. Can't you play by yourself?"

"I guess." Bobby drops his head and looks down at his macaroni and cheese. He loves playing Nintendo with Elliot, but I'm not surprised he doesn't have time tonight. I've tried to play with him, but apparently, I "suck."

Maria offered to drive us both to the school tonight. Parking is sparse, so we agreed it would be a good idea to carpool. And it will be a chance for me to get to know my new neighbor better.

I limp over to Maria's house in my new Sergio Rossi pumps. It's colder than I thought it would be, and I hug my wrap around my chest as I shiver. I consider going back for a coat, but I'm almost at Maria's house. We'll be in her white SUV in a few moments.

I hit the doorbell, but I don't hear any chimes within the house. Maybe it's broken. I wait for a few seconds, then bang on the door. After another few seconds, I hear footsteps, and the door swings open.

Damn, it's Sean.

He's the last person I want to see after that awkward encounter yesterday. Also, the last time I saw him, he was shirtless. And now I'm having trouble picturing him *not* shirtless. It makes me a little breathless all of a sudden.

"Hi!" I say brightly. "I'm—"

"April." He flashes me a crooked smile. "I remember." He steps to the side so I can slip past him. He smells like wood chips. "Come on in."

He doesn't seem angry, at least. Maybe he bought my story about wandering into the wrong room. Then again, he doesn't seem stupid or naïve either.

"Maria will be down in a second," he explains. "She's still deciding on… shoes, I think."

"Oh, she shouldn't stress so much about what she's wearing," I say. Even though I spent two hours picking out my outfit for tonight.

"That's what I said." Sean shrugs. "So what is this thing tonight at the school?"

"Parent-Teacher Association," I explain. "It's where parents help fundraise for the school and plan fun and educational events for the kids."

"Oh." He scratches at his beard. "Should I be going to that then?"

I laugh.

He frowns. "Why is that funny?"

"Oh." I blink at him. "I thought you were joking. Fathers usually don't go to these meetings."

"Really?" He focuses his blue eyes on me. "Why not? I'm a parent. What if I have ideas about fun and educational events for my kid?"

"Well…"

He's not making an unreasonable point. But the fact of the matter is that fathers simply don't go to the PTA meetings. In the two years I've been going, I've only seen one father there, and he was a bit creepy. One of those men whose eyes were always focused just a little bit below your face, if you know what I mean. And he spent fifteen straight minutes gushing about how much he liked my cooking show, and especially this one sweater I wore.

But before I can stammer out an excuse that wouldn't be offensive, Maria appears at the bottom of the stairs and saves me. "Sean, you don't want to go to a PTA meeting. You'd be bored stiff. And anyway, Owen is expecting to take you down in ping-pong tonight."

Sean cracks a genuine smile. "No way. I'm still the ping-pong master. He's not going to be able to beat me until he's at *least* eight."

"Don't be silly. He's letting you win."

Sean grins wider and takes in Maria's appearance. She's wearing a dress like I am, which is a navy blue color that complements her dark blue eyes and is short enough to reveal some pretty shapely legs. He grabs her arm and pulls her in for a kiss that lasts for several seconds. She giggles, loving it. I drop my eyes.

"Don't stay out too late," I hear him murmur in her ear.

I look down at my nails, which I had done in a tasteful light pink a few days ago and still seem intact. I don't know why Sean and Maria's display of affection is making me so uncomfortable. Elliot kisses me all the time. But I can't help but think that he never kisses me quite like *that*. Not anymore, at least.

And I can't help but think that my husband isn't as sexy as Sean Cooper either. But that's a thought I'm going to push completely out of my head. Permanently.

————

The first thing Julie says to me and Maria when we walk into the Hopkins School library is, "You're late."

Even though we are, in fact, half an hour early.

Maria looks at me in confusion, but I quickly say, "I'm sorry. What do you need us to do?"

Julie makes a tutting sound. "I told you. We need the desks and chairs arranged in a circular formation. *Circular.* Do you know what I mean, April?"

"No problem."

She steps out of the library to make a phone call, leaving me and Maria to do the dirty work. Maria keeps casting looks in my direction, but after a few minutes, she finally speaks up. "Why do you let her talk to you that way?"

I'm busy myself getting one of the desks arranged just right. If they don't meet her standards, we'll have to redo it. "What way?"

Maria straightens up. "I'm sorry, I know she's your friend, but she's so bossy. I would never speak to somebody like that. You're not her slave."

I let out a sigh. "I know. But you have to understand that Julie is like royalty here. Everyone respects her so much. The only way I got started with *Sweet Secrets* is that Julie told everyone they should watch it."

"That's nice of her, but still."

"Listen," I say. "If you're nice to Julie, she'll do anything for you. But she expects you to do what she says in return."

Maria adjusts one of the chairs. "I'm sorry, April, but I'm *not* going to let Julie push me around the way she pushes you around."

She looks like she has something else to say, but mothers are starting to come into the library, and we can't risk anyone hearing us talk trash about Julie. That would get back to her in an instant.

The PTA meeting starts promptly at six o'clock, with Julie presiding at the front of the room. It's the first meeting of the year, which means she starts out with a PowerPoint presentation about all the amazing things we accomplished last year. She was the vice president then, but she did most of the work—Julie is a natural leader. Yes, she can be bossy, but she's *very* good at what she does. I can't even imagine what she was like as a lawyer. I bet she was terrifying.

"Thank you all for coming tonight." Julie folds her arms across her chest as she stares out at the impressive showing. She's also very good at getting people to participate. "As you know, our school does a great job, thanks to Mrs. Donnelly here." She gives a nod to our principal, who I know from experience will be largely silent during this meeting. "However, the PTA is essential in providing extra fun and educational events for our children like school trips and book fairs, and your participation is essential to that."

Without further ado, Julie launches into a PowerPoint summary of everything the PTA does and has done, and will continue to do in the future. It goes on for well over an hour, and it's very hard to keep from yawning. The only thing keeping me from doing it is knowing I would hear about it forever from Julie.

I'm also starving. I had a bite to eat before I left the house, but somehow I'm still hungry. (Maybe it's the baby growing inside me—*not*.) My stomach has a hollow feeling and I'm scared that any moment it will let out an embarrassing growl. I once suggested I bring a tray of brownies for the PTA meetings, but Julie was adamantly against it. I don't know how you can be adamantly against *brownies*, but she was.

I clench my abdominal muscles, trying not to think about food. It helps. A little.

"As you all know," Julie is saying, "one of our big fundraisers is the biannual silent auction. For those of you who don't know, this is when we solicit donations from other parents and you can bid online. We will announce the winners at the fall carnival. This year, the silent auction is again being run by April Masterson, who did a phenomenal job last year."

I raise a hand to acknowledge a smattering of applause. The silent auction is a lot of work, but as Julie said, it's a huge fundraiser. This town is super rich, and people donate extravagant items. Mink coats. Six tickets to a Taylor Swift concert. The year before last, somebody donated a boat. An actual *boat*! A nice one too, not just a rickety wooden rowboat.

"This is a big job," Julie says, "and April can't do it herself. Would anyone else like to volunteer to co-chair the silent auction?"

I hold my breath, hoping it won't be Melody Taylor, who "helped" me last year. The quotation marks are very appropriate in this situation. Melody did nothing. She had no idea what was donated or how much money we made.

A hand goes up to my right. "I'd like to help," Maria says.

I let out a breath of relief. Maria will be an amazing co-chair. Even though I've only known her a couple of days, I can already tell.

"Thanks," I say.

Julie nods, but her attention is distracted. She's looking at the corner of the room, where a new parent I don't recognize has her phone out and is talking to someone on the other line, one finger in her ear. I wince, knowing what's coming.

"Excuse me," Julie says sharply. "We're trying to have a meeting here."

The woman might have been able to save herself if she had shoved it back into her purse immediately, but instead, she keeps the phone in her hand and flashes an apologetic smile. "Sorry, this is an important call…"

There isn't a trace of sympathy on Julie's face. "If you insist on disrupting our meeting, I'm going to have to ask you to leave."

The woman smiles—she thinks it's a joke. The smile fades from her face when she realizes Julie is one hundred percent serious. "Oh, well, I'll just be another minute…"

"No." Julie's dark eyes are like ice. "You should leave. And you can come back after you've dealt with your personal issues."

"But I—" The woman looks wildly around the room, like she thinks somebody might stand up for her and point out how ridiculous this is. When she realizes that's not going to happen, her shoulders sag. "All right."

We all watch as the woman does the walk of shame out of the library. She mumbles something under her breath, but lucky for her, she doesn't say it out loud.

CHAPTER 9

Comment on *April's Sweet Secrets* YouTube video:

You can see April's dark roots showing. Her hair is a lie. Just like everything else about her.

I never thought I would be a soccer mom, but that's what I am.

It's not as big a deal as you think. At the second grade level, soccer is not that intense. We meet every Saturday morning at eight at the middle school athletic field (parking is extremely competitive). The kids practice for thirty minutes while the parents gossip, then they play for another thirty minutes against another team while the parents cheer them on.

Bobby is on the uncreatively named Team B, which is coached by Mark Tanner, who is fortunately much more pleasant than his wife, Kathy. Mark coached Bobby's team last year too and did an amazing job, so I was pretty excited to have him again. And I was so sure I could convince Mark to let Owen Cooper join the team that I told Maria to bring him this morning.

Julie's son, Leo, is also on Team B, which I don't think is any coincidence. Sometimes we trade off who brings the boys to soccer, especially when the weather gets nippy. Okay, it's not so much a trade-off as Julie asks me to bring both boys in. But I don't mind. I like to watch Bobby play.

Bobby is less than excited to be here. He was moaning when I dragged him out of bed and wasn't thrilled about putting on his shin guards and his knee-length soccer socks. Yes, I had to buy soccer socks. They're like regular socks, but more… soccer-y? I don't know—I just buy what they tell me. Anyway, he usually has a great time playing, even though it's hard to get him here.

"What's with the Tupperware?" Julie asks as she looks down at the plastic tub in my hand.

"Oh!" I shake the Tupperware container. "I made cookies for Mark. I'm hoping he'll let Owen Cooper join the team, even though it's after registration."

Julie mumbles something skeptical under her breath, but I make the most amazing chocolate chip cookies. Nobody can say no to my cookies. Ever. Here's my secret in case you missed the episode: I use two tablespoons of milk powder, which makes the cookies extra chewy. Oh, and a sprinkling of sea salt on top. But I think everything can benefit from a sprinkling of sea salt. I tell my viewers that they need to throw away their regular salt and only use sea salt. *Toss it in the trash right now!* I told them on one episode, then I stood there and waited patiently for them to throw away the salt.

I see Maria heading down on the field with Sean and Owen just behind her. I guess the whole family decided to come. Gosh, I hope Mark says yes. I would hate to disappoint them.

Maria waves to me and sprints the rest of the way over to join us. "Did you talk to the coach yet?"

"Not yet," I say. "I wanted to wait until you got here." I hold up the Tupperware. "But I brought cookies."

Maria looks just as skeptical as Julie did, but she's never tried my cookies.

Now that she's here, I stride across the field to where Mark is talking to another parent. Mark has been coaching soccer for years. He's in his mid-forties with mostly silver hair and light blue eyes that crinkle when he smiles. When he sees me, he gives me that eye-crinkle.

"April!" he says. "Are those for me? Dare I hope?"

I hold out the Tupperware for him. "I made them with just a touch of sea salt on top. Like you like them."

"Yum."

I glance over at the Cooper family, waiting anxiously at the sidelines. "I was wondering if I could ask for a favor, Mark."

His brows bunch together. "Yes…?"

"My friend Maria's son Owen is an *incredible* soccer player." Well, I assume so. "But they just moved here and were too late to register for soccer. I was just wondering if he could join Team B."

Mark hesitates. "I don't know if I'm allowed to…"

"I know," I say quickly. "But maybe he could be on the team… you know, unofficially. He could step in for kids who are out sick. You know as the weather gets colder, there are more and more no-shows."

"Right." Mark is nodding as he looks over at Owen Cooper. "Well, let's see how things go today. I think it should be okay, unless some of the other parents complain."

The only other parent who might complain is Julie— she's such a stickler for the rules. I wonder if a discounted dress from Helena's might be enough to win her over. Because cookies sure won't.

"Thanks, Mark!" I say. "You're the best. And don't worry about the Tupperware. We've got tons of it."

I go back to the sidelines, flashing an enthusiastic thumbs up. I can't tell who looks happier about it between the three of them. Probably Sean.

"So that's it?" Maria says. "Owen is on the team? Just like that?"

I bob my head up and down. "Just like that! I told you I make good cookies."

Julie rolls her eyes dramatically.

Owen races onto the field, excited to get to play. Practice will be starting in a couple of minutes, but some of the kids are already kicking the ball around. Right away, I can tell how good Owen is. Even though I only barely grasp all the rules of the game, I've noticed there are always a couple of kids on each team that stand out as being particularly good. Owen is one of those kids. Of course, that's what happens when your dad coaches the team.

I had worried Sean might be an awkward addition to our group, but he couldn't seem less interested in talking to us. He is watching the practice intently, giving Owen silent instructions with his hands. It's obvious he's barely restraining himself from leaping onto the field.

"Sean should volunteer to coach next year," I tell Maria.

"Oh, he definitely will," she says. "He loves it. Even after the sports season ends, he and Owen go to the park every day to practice. Football, soccer, whatever."

"How nice," Julie says vaguely.

What's that like? I wonder.

"Leo is very good too," Maria observes. She's not just being nice. Leo is probably the best kid on the team. Well, he was until Owen showed up. "Does your husband work with him a lot?"

Julie bursts out laughing. It is sort of funny if you know Keith. First of all, he spends most of his waking hours at work in the city. And even if he didn't, he looks like ten minutes of soccer practice would give him a heart attack.

"No," she says dryly. "We hired a professional soccer teacher to work with Leo."

"Oh." Maria blinks. "Well, that's great."

She seems shocked, but she shouldn't be. That's how things are in this town. I might have tried to hire a coach for Bobby, but I was hoping Elliot would pick up the slack. I'm starting to realize that's not going to be the case though.

With only ten minutes left of practice, Carrie Schaeffer shows up with her son James. That's the Carrie whose husband left her for the babysitter, which is all anyone can think of when we see her these days. It's courageous of her to still show up for sports practice. Especially at eight in the morning on a Saturday.

Carrie trudges up to us, looking like she's about to collapse. She's got big purple circles under her eyes, which probably doesn't help her measure up better against the young babysitter. I lean over and give her a hug. She hugs me back so tightly, it hurts my ribs.

"How are you doing?" I ask her.

"You know, the same." She lets out a long breath. "And thank you again for the casseroles and cookies. I would starve to death if not for you, April."

"It's the least I can do."

She's looking at Maria curiously, so I quickly do the introductions. "Maria, this is Carrie. Carrie, this is Maria—she's my new neighbor."

Carrie raises a hand in greeting. "I'm the one who got

dumped for the babysitter. Just so you know."

Maria's mouth falls open and Julie snorts. "For God's sake, Carrie," Julie says.

"What?" Carrie shrugs. "Everybody's talking about it. You would probably tell her right after I left. I might as well own it, right?"

I respect that. I don't think I would be nearly as upbeat in her situation. That's why I make sure that all the babysitters I hire are very plain. Our current sitter is postmenopausal. Not that I don't trust Elliot, but he's already got Brianna at work. Why tempt fate? Especially after...

No, I promised myself I wouldn't think about that anymore. It's the distant past.

Carrie spends the next several minutes sharing her tales of woe. Her husband has been sending the husband-stealing babysitter over to pick up the kids on his days with them. It's been driving Carrie crazy, and when she complained to him, he said, *What's the big deal? She was their babysitter.*

"I'm *this* close to running him down with my car." Carrie holds her index finger and thumb a millimeter apart. "Nobody would blame me. I'm sure of it. I'd probably just get community service."

I wouldn't blame her. Honestly, when I hear some of her stories about his shenanigans, sometimes *I* want to run him down with my car myself. And I would make sure

Carrie had a good alibi if I did it.

Carries attention gets distracted by something in the field. After a second, I realize she's looking at Sean, who is in a huddle with Owen, giving him some instructions. "Who is *that*? Single dad, I hope?"

Maria laughs. "No, that's my husband."

"Oh, sorry." Carrie hesitates. "Actually, not sorry. He's *hot*. Even hotter than Coach Mark. Lucky you."

Maria laughs again, but this time her cheeks turn pink.

The game is about to start up with the other team, but before it does, Bobby separates from the other kids and runs over to me. His lower lip is jutting out.

"I don't want to play," he says.

Oh great. I can't even imagine what it is this time. At the last practice, we spent the entire game searching for an open restroom or porta-potty. You would think they would have something available when there are so many young kids around.

"What's wrong, sweetie?" I ask.

"I don't want to play," he repeats, more insistently.

"Can you tell me why?"

His eyebrows scrunch together. "The other boys are better than me."

Oh no. I didn't think he had noticed how much better Owen was at soccer than him. But he would have to be blind not to. "No, they're not."

"Yes, they are! Leo is better and Owen is better…"

I bite my lip. I can't help but think to myself that if only

Elliot practiced with him all summer like he promised he would, we wouldn't have this problem.

"Listen, Bobby." I put a hand on his skinny shoulder. "The point of this game is to have fun. It's okay if a couple of kids are better than you. And if they're on your team, you're more likely to win the game, right? And that's fun, isn't it?"

Bobby thinks it over for a minute. "I guess so."

"The important thing is to try your very best. Just hit the ball as hard as you can."

Bobby cracks a smile. "You mean *kick* the ball."

I return his smile. "You kick the ball in soccer? I didn't know that."

The great thing about Bobby being seven is it's usually easy to tease him out of a bad mood. After my little pep talk, he goes right back onto the field with enthusiasm. But maybe we do need to think about hiring somebody to give him extra lessons.

"Is Bobby okay?"

I turn my head and see Sean is standing next to Maria now, backing off to let the kids play their game.

"Yes, he's fine," I say quickly.

He clears his throat. "Listen, Owen and I practice soccer every Sunday. Bobby is welcome to join us anytime."

I feel my cheeks grow warm. "Oh, I wouldn't want to bother you."

"I don't mind. It's better with more kids." He smiles.

"It'll be fun."

"Well… okay." I feel like a weight has been lifted. Elliot was never going to take Bobby to the park to practice. "Thanks so much! Really."

His blue eyes meet mine. "No problem."

I look over at Maria, but she's not smiling. I try to catch her eye, but her attention seems focused on the field.

I have to say, I don't entirely understand the soccer rules. I just find sports very uninteresting in general. Elliot will sometimes watch the game on TV, and I always go to the other room. But I get the general idea. One team is supposed to get the ball in one net, and the other team is supposed to get the ball in the other net. That's enough to follow the game. Everything else is just extraneous information.

Bobby is not playing particularly well today. He's had a few games where he's made a lot of goals and been happy on the way home. That's not the case today. But the team is doing well, largely thanks to Leo and Owen. Julie is cheering enthusiastically from the sidelines every time Leo scores a goal. She's her kids' biggest cheerleader.

I, on the other hand, am mostly shouting words of encouragement. "Come on, Bobby!" I call out. "Hit the ball!"

He looks up and makes a face at me.

Owen is kicking a ball down the field. Bobby is near the goal, but so is Leo. Owen looks between the two of them, and I'm certain he's going to pass the ball to Leo. But at the last moment, he kicks it in Bobby's direction. Bobby looks just as surprised as I feel, and he fumbles as he tries to kick that soccer ball as hard as he can, hoping to make his first goal of the game.

But the ball doesn't go into the goal. It sails into the air, right at Leo Bressler's face.

Which explodes in a fountain of blood.

CHAPTER 10

I don't think I've ever seen so much blood. It was just a soccer ball, for God's sake. It's not like somebody shot him in the face. But there's blood gushing out of Leo's nostrils, quickly staining his white jersey as the boy sobs hysterically.

It's making me a little queasy, to be honest.

Julie screams, of course. I can't blame her, but it is a touch overdramatic. I mean, it's just a bloody nose. Although as I said, it's a *lot* of blood. Even Mark looks a bit sick.

Thankfully, Sean has jogged over to the boy and seems to have the whole thing under control. Julie gives him some tissues from her purse, and he gets Leo putting pressure on it and tilting his head back. The first set of tissues gets soaked with crimson, but the second set fares better.

"My poor baby!" Julie cries as she tries to hug him. "We need to take you to the emergency room."

"I don't think that's necessary," Sean says. "The bleeding seems to be stopping. I think he's fine."

"But his nose could be broken!"

"I don't think so."

Julie puts her hands on her hips. "Well, how do you know? You're not a doctor."

"I've got some idea. I broke mine—twice." He taps the bridge of his nose, which is slightly crooked. "I think he's okay. But you can take him in if you want."

"Gee, thanks," Julie mutters.

"I'm okay, Mom," Leo says bravely. He's a tough kid. You kind of have to be if Julie is your mother.

Julie turns around to glare at me. "This is all Bobby's fault. What is wrong with that kid?"

My mouth falls open. "What are you talking about? It was an accident."

Julie snorts. "*Please.* I heard him telling you how jealous he was of Leo. And you were telling him to kick the ball as hard as he could. He was aiming right for Leo's face."

I look at Bobby, who is hanging his head in the corner. A tear slips down his cheek. He didn't hurt his best friend on purpose. If he could aim like that, he'd be the best kid on the team.

"It's nobody's fault," Mark speaks up. "Sometimes kids get hurt during the game. Bobby didn't mean to hit him. Now, Julie, if you want to take Leo to the emergency room—"

"Yes!" she snaps. "That's exactly what I'm going to do."

Julie grabs her son roughly by the arm and the two of them march off the field while Leo protests. God, I hope his nose isn't broken. She'll probably sue us.

No, she won't really sue us. She's just upset because her son is gushing blood from his nose. Julie can be very dramatic when she's upset, but I'm sure she'll calm down.

I start to go over to Bobby to see if he's okay, but Sean is already bent down next to him, talking to him quietly. Sean's shirt has Leo's blood all over it, but he doesn't seem bothered by it. I can't hear what they're saying, but I see a tiny smile spread across my son's face.

While I'm watching Sean and Bobby talking, my phone buzzes inside my purse. It's another text message. Probably Elliot, saying he's off to the office for work. Saturday wouldn't be complete without my husband rushing to work.

I pull out my phone and read the text message:

I know the secret of why Mark Tanner let you talk him into that other boy joining the team. And if you tell anyone about these messages, everyone in town will know it too.

I frown at the screen, an uneasy feeling in my chest. Then a second later, a photograph appears.

I gasp out loud.

"Are you okay?" Maria is squinting at me. "You're not squeamish, are you? That was a lot of blood."

"No, I'm fine," I say quickly.

"Do you need to sit down?"

I shake my head vigorously. "I'll be fine. Just… I need a minute."

I step away from the crowd of parents and kids. I look at the screen of my phone, and the whole world seems to disappear around me. My fingers are shaking as I type in the words:

Who are you and what do you want from me?

I wait for an answer. But like before, there's no response.

CHAPTER 11

Fine. Yes, I have a secret that isn't the sort I would advertise on my YouTube show.

I kissed Mark Tanner.

It's not like me at all. At *all*. I'm a good person—I swear. I brought Carrie Schaeffer no less than ten casseroles since her husband left her. When I'm driving, I always let people cut in front of me or make turns. They say that what you do when you drive shows what kind of person you really are deep down.

It was nothing. Just one kiss. Barely even a kiss. Mostly lip, hardly any tongue.

It all started when I was running the spring bake sale for the PTA, and Mark had volunteered to help me set up. Then he volunteered to give Bobby some soccer lessons. At first, it was just friendship. Nothing more. Mark would invite me out for breakfast after I dropped Bobby off at school. He would stop in during the day when Elliot was at work. But nothing happened.

Not that this is an excuse, but it wouldn't have happened if Elliot were around more often. I mean, he spends more hours at work than he does at home, and that includes sleeping hours. And even though I knew I shouldn't have, I started to complain to Mark about how little I saw Elliot anymore. How little attention he paid to me. How infrequently we had sex lately.

And then one day, while we were talking in my kitchen, he leaned forward and kissed me.

Of course, that's as far as it ever went. The one kiss. I enjoyed it for maybe a split second, then I came to my senses and pushed him away. Of course I did! I couldn't go through with something like that. I couldn't do it to my husband or Mark's wife. It was just *wrong*.

Yes, I felt neglected by Elliot, but I still loved him. And also, can you imagine what my *Sweet Secrets* viewers would think if it got out that I was cheating on my husband with another man?

I explained all this to Mark. And he totally got it. And now we're just friends again. That's it.

Yet somehow somebody has a photograph of Mark and me taken during that one kiss, snapped through my living room window.

One thing. I do *one thing* wrong in my entire life, and now I'm being threatened with it.

I have no idea what they plan to do with it. But a

photograph like that could destroy my marriage if Elliot ever saw it. If it got out on the Internet, it would destroy my cooking show—part of my image is being a wholesome home cook, and nobody will want to watch me if I'm a cheating bitch. Nobody would believe that it just happened one time, and I pushed him away. This photograph could mean the end of my life as I know it.

I need to figure out who's doing this. And what they want from me.

But one thing is certain. This person means business.

CHAPTER 12

Comment on *April's Sweet Secrets* YouTube video:

Here's a secret you don't know about April Masterson:

She dropped out of culinary school after four months. Is this the person you want to be taking cooking lessons from?

This afternoon, Sean took Bobby and Owen to the park to practice soccer. Bobby was so excited about it. There was a part of me that was scared he was never going to want to play soccer again after the incident with Leo (who did *not* have a broken nose, by the way), but fortunately, the pep talk from Sean worked. He told me excitedly that he was going to get really good at soccer like Leo and Owen.

My latest video on making brownies went up this

morning. Immediately, there was an onslaught of nasty comments. A lot of them just said my brownies looked gross, which they absolutely did not. But a few of them were more pointed.

Like the culinary school dropout one. I never told anybody about that. I used to have this idea in my head about being a chef, but as soon as I started culinary school, I realized it wasn't for me. So I dropped out.

It's not something I'm proud of. We always teach Bobby not to give up. And the commenter made a good point. Why should people take cooking lessons from a cooking school dropout?

Anyway, I deleted all the negative comments.

To take my mind off the whole thing, I went to visit Maria at Helena's. I figured it must get boring for her in the middle of the afternoon. Also, I had an ulterior motive: I wanted to use her discount. There's a silk scarf that I've been admiring at the store for ages, but I just can't justify how much it costs. I'll never hear the end of it from Elliot. But with her discount, maybe it will be okay.

I feel intimidated the second I walk into Helena's, like I always do. It's strange because Maria herself is not intimidating. But this store is. It's bright and shiny, with handbags and scarves and shoes and perfumes on little shelves along the walls. The clothing is in the back, and I'm scared to even look at the prices.

My YouTube channel is doing well. It's made me a minor local celebrity. But I'm not making the sort of money from it where I could drop a couple of grand on clothing. Maybe someday, but not yet.

The store is nearly empty, as I predicted, and Maria is sitting quietly at the desk in the back. The door jingles as it closes, and I notice that a man is standing next to the door wearing a uniform. He's also built like a linebacker. Security. I guess they need it in a place like this.

"April!" Maria looks thrilled to see me. "What are you doing here?"

"Shopping." I join her at the desk and rest my purse on top of it. "Also, I thought I'd keep you company. The boys are playing soccer."

Maria beams. "I know! It's so cute."

"Sean is so good with the boys." I try to keep the jealousy out of my voice. Her husband is not only really sexy, but he's also a great dad. I definitely wouldn't say that first part though. "I'm surprised you don't have half a dozen kids."

"Actually," she says quietly, "I can't have kids."

I look at her in surprise. "Did something happen with Owen's birth?"

She hesitates a moment, then shakes her head. "I'm not Owen's birth mother. His biological mother… died several years ago. He doesn't even remember her. I adopted him after Sean and I got married."

"Oh." The questions swirl around my brain. I had no idea Maria wasn't Owen's biological mother. I wonder how

Sean's first wife died, but I can't ask that. She must've been very young though—it was undoubtedly something tragic. "You and Owen look alike."

She beams. "Thanks. People say that a lot." She raises her eyebrows at me. "How about you? Are you one and done?"

I toy with the chain around my neck. "Um, not exactly." I haven't talked to anyone around here about our fertility problems, but something about Maria makes me feel like I can open up to her. "Elliot wants another baby, but no luck so far. So…"

"I'm sorry! That's so frustrating. Have you done IVF?"

"No, nothing like that." God, I can't even imagine being shot up with hormones. The thought of it makes me ill—I'm afraid of needles. "But we're off birth-control and… you know, crossing our fingers every month."

Maria reaches out and pats my hand. "For some people, it can take time. But I'm sure it will happen! You had Bobby, after all. So everything must be working all right."

"Yes. That's true." I sigh. "It's just that… I know how badly Elliot wants another child. I feel like… I'm letting him down."

"April, don't be silly!" She reaches out and squeezes my hand in hers. Her palm is warm and dry. "I'm sure Elliot loves you no matter what. And worst comes to worst, there are tons of fertility treatments out there."

"Yes, I know…" And now I'm tearing up. "Sorry…"

"Don't apologize!" She squeezes my hand again. "Do you need a tissue?"

"No, I've got one…"

As I rummage around in my purse, looking for a tissue, I hear the jingling of the bell at the door to the store. A customer.

"Do you need to go help her?" I ask.

She shakes her head. "Let her browse a bit first."

I turn to look at the girl who has entered the store. She's maybe in her early twenties with white-blonde hair and puffy, sexy lips. She looks very familiar. I keep getting this feeling about people—that they look familiar to me. It scares me a bit, considering my mother has early-onset Alzheimer's. Am I losing my mind? Is this why I can't remember anyone?

Oh God, that is not a thought I need to be having right now.

She's looking at one of the Prada purses. She seems awfully young to be able to afford such a nice purse. I wonder if she has a sugar daddy looking out for her. She can't possibly think she could shoplift with that big guy at the front.

And then it hits me who she is.

"Maria!" I hiss. "That girl…"

Maria frowns and leans in close to me. "You know her?"

"No, but…" I look back at the girl, just to be sure. Yes,

I'm sure. "Do you remember Carrie, from soccer practice?"

She nods.

"That's the babysitter! That's the one who stole her husband."

Maria's lips form an "oh." She cocks her head to the side. "Poor Carrie! I can't even imagine how I would feel if some twenty-one-year-old babysitter stole Sean away from me."

"I know…"

I wonder if Maria gets jealous about Sean. He does seem incredibly loyal to her. But she must realize how attractive he is. And, if I'm being completely honest, he's far more attractive than she is. I wonder if she could have landed a guy like him if he wasn't a single dad.

Then I feel guilty for those thoughts. Maria may not be beautiful, but she's a lovely person. I'm sure Sean likes her for her *inner* beauty.

Maria chews on her lower lip, watching the babysitter browse the purses. "Maybe I should throw her out."

"And miss out on the huge commission? Please. You don't want to have a *Pretty Woman* 'Big mistake' moment, do you?"

"I don't care about that. Look at her—she's probably not going to buy anything anyway." She narrows her eyes. "But it's not enough, you know?"

"Well, what else could we do?"

A slow smile spreads across her face. "Watch this."

I watch the whole thing. Maria picks up a necklace

from one of the displays, then she goes over to the babysitter, and sweetly asks if there's anything she needs. The babysitter shakes her head no. And as Maria walks away, she silently drops the necklace into the babysitter's purse.

Then she returns to the desk, smiling like nothing happened.

"Oh my God," I breathe. "I can't believe you just did that."

"And it's about to get better. Just watch."

She's right. A minute later, the babysitter attempts to leave the store. The overhead alarm goes off like there was a break-in at the prison. The bodybuilder pops into action, stepping in front of the door to the store and grabbing the babysitter roughly by the arm.

"Miss," he says. "Do you have any store merchandise in your purse?"

She wrenches her arm free, her expression indignant. "No. Of course I don't!"

"You set off our alarm. I can't let you leave without searching your purse."

The babysitter looks like she might refuse, but she's obviously in a bind. This big guy is not going to let her leave without checking her purse. So she thrusts it at his chest. "Here. Knock yourself out."

It's almost too horrible to watch, because I know what he's going to find. It takes him all of five seconds to yank out the necklace inside. The tags are still intact. The babysitter's eyes go wide.

"I didn't put that there! It… it must have fallen inside…"

The guard shakes his head. "I'm afraid we're going to have to call the police." He looks to the back of the store. "Maria? We have a shoplifter here and I'm calling the cops."

I only wish Carrie were here to see the look on the babysitter's face. She looks like she's about to pee her pants, especially when Maria strides over with a cold, almost chilling expression in her eyes. Maria can be pretty badass when she wants to be. I wouldn't have thought so.

"Please don't call the police." The babysitter is crying now. "*Please.* I swear I didn't take the necklace. I don't know how it got in my purse."

Maria's expression is impassive. "It doesn't help to lie."

"Please, you have to understand…" The babysitter swipes at her eyes. "I got arrested for shoplifting a year ago, and the judge said if I got caught again…"

"I'm sorry." Maria doesn't blink. "Our store policy is to prosecute all shoplifters."

The babysitter is still sobbing as they call the police. It's funny because I always thought of my friend Julie as the person you could never mess with. But as it turns out, Maria is not somebody to mess with either.

I would never want this woman to be mad at me.

CHAPTER 13

To: Book Club Group
From: Julie
Subject: Re: Food items

Please share with the group which item you will be bringing as a refreshment to our book club meeting this week, so that we don't replicate dishes. I will be bringing mini quiches from Giorgio's.

To: Book Club Group
From: April
Subject: Re: Food items

I was thinking about making apple pie turnovers. Does that sound good to everyone? Or if not, I could just make a tray of brownies. Whatever you guys want!

WANT TO KNOW A SECRET?

To: Book Club Group
From: Carrie
Subject: Re: Food items

I will be bringing the heart of the babysitter on a stick. Kidding! Unfortunately. I'll probably bring chips and dip.

April, my vote is for the turnovers. The last time I ate one of your brownies, I gained five pounds.

To: Book Club Group
From: Julie
Subject: Re: Food items

Please no store-bought salsa, Carrie.

To: Book Club Group
From: Maria
Subject: Re: Food items

April, apple turnovers sound amazing! Although ever since I tasted your brownies, I've been craving more.

Would mini pizzas be OK to bring? We've got a bunch in the freezer.

To: Book Club Group
From: Julie
Subject: Re: Food items

Maria, mini pizzas? I assume you are joking.

I've got a tray of apple turnovers balanced in one hand as I walk over to Julie's house for our book club. I've also got the book in my purse, which is weighing it down considerably since the book is about five billion pages long. It's called *Feathers of Life*, and it's about a guy raising a bird.

I tried to read it—I really did. I got about two pages in, and I was just *done*. I simply couldn't go on. I think it was the part where he was at the pet store, picking out varieties of birdseed. Life is too short to read boring books.

Julie gets uppity about us not reading the book, but for starters, she's the one who always picks the book and they're always terrible. Also, we never end up actually discussing the book. We talk about it for five minutes, then we end up discussing our husbands for another thirty minutes, then our kids for another thirty minutes, then clothing for another thirty minutes. Really, there's no time to discuss the book. If I came to the book club hoping to discuss the book, I'd be pretty disappointed.

As I walk past Maria's house, I see Sean on their front lawn, raking leaves. Nobody on our block rakes their own leaves. But the Coopers don't have the kind of money that everyone else does. And Sean doesn't seem upset to be raking leaves. He's whistling to himself as he does it. He's making it look fun. Half of me wants to say to hell with the book club and go rake my own lawn.

I raise my hand in greeting. "Hi!"

He stops for a moment and wipes sweat off his forehead. Even though it's a nippy fifty degrees right now, he's wearing only a T-shirt. "Hi, April. Maria is already at the book club."

"Oh, great!" I hesitate, not quite wanting to move on yet. "Listen, I want to thank you again for helping Bobby with soccer."

He grins at me. "Don't mention it. I told you, it's more fun with more kids."

I adjust the tray of apple turnovers. "Would you like an apple turnover? I just took them out of the oven fifteen minutes ago."

His eyes light up. "If they're anything like your brownies, hell yeah."

I peel back a tiny bit of the plastic wrap, enough that Sean can pick up one of the turnovers. He takes a bite and groans.

"Jesus Christ, April." He takes another bite. "These are

really, really good. Where did you learn to bake like this?"

"My secret is that I cook the apples in my own homemade caramel."

"Oh, right." He points a finger at me. "You have that YouTube show where you've got a different secret for every recipe, right?"

I feel my face flush. "You watched my show?"

He pops the rest of the turnover in his mouth. "Yeah. Maria put it on the computer. You're pretty good in front of the camera."

"Well, thanks." I smile. "Would you like another one?"

He laughs. "I would, but are you sure you'll have enough for the book club?"

"Oh, don't worry about it. I made way too many. Take two!"

He looks hesitant, so I remove the two extra turnovers myself and hold them out to him. (My hands are clean—I have excellent hygiene when it comes to handwashing. The secret to good food is good sanitary practices.) After a couple of beats, he takes the turnovers from me, and I feel his thumb graze my palm. At his touch, a tingle goes through my body.

All of a sudden, I'm feeling a little breathless. Sean's eyes are on me, and I expect him to start eating the turnovers, but he doesn't. He's just looking at me.

"I'll put these inside," he says. "Don't want to ruin dinner."

"Sure," I breathe.

His blue eyes are still on my face. "Thanks, April."

"You're welcome," I manage.

I tear my eyes away from him. I can't let him know what I'm thinking. Maria is becoming one of my best friends. I can't be having these thoughts about her husband. And after that whole mess with Mark, I don't want there to be even a hint of a scandal around me. It's stupid to even think about it a little bit.

That kiss with Mark was a one-time thing. I learned my lesson.

Sean heads back inside the house, and I hurry the rest of the way to Julie's place. She'll kill me if I'm late, and I'm already in dangerous territory. Julie cannot be charmed with delicious apple turnovers.

I'm the last one to arrive, but everyone is still standing around, so we haven't officially begun yet. I place the tray of apple turnovers on the dining table with the other food and go around to greet my neighbors.

"April!" It's Chelsea Buerger, who lives at the end of the block. I haven't seen her since the start of the school year because her nanny has been getting the kids, and she looks great. Her forehead is so smooth. I wonder if she got Botox. I can't ask though. Her husband works for the Yankees, and they're loaded.

"Hi, Chelsea." I give her a hug. We hug a lot in the club for some reason. Hug hello and hug goodbye. "What's up?"

"You're doing the silent auction again this year, right?"

she asks.

I nod. "That's right."

"Are you still taking donations?"

"Absolutely. What do you have to donate?"

Chelsea's face is shining. "How about four box seats for a Yankees game?"

Wow. We could get thousands for that. "Chelsea, that's amazing!"

A few of the other women are listening in, and this announcement has gotten everyone's attention. "I'll definitely bid on that," Leah Morgan says. "My husband would be over the moon."

"And I'll outbid you," Jean Rothenburg pipes up.

"I'll put it up on the website as soon as I get home," I promise.

Julie rolls her eyes, but she's got to be secretly pleased. Parents at the school can bid on items in the auction similar to eBay. They know what other people are bidding, and they all try to outbid each other to get what they want. Sports tickets are always a big item. That's why the silent auction earns so much money for the PTA.

"All right." Julie claps her hands together. "Let's take a seat and start our discussion."

We all take our seats around the dining table, and I make a point to sit down next to Maria. It will be fun to exchange meaningful expressions with her during the book club. She winks at me. "I see you went with the turnovers."

"Yes, they came out really delicious."

She licks her lips. "I can't wait to try them."

"I gave a couple to Sean on the way over, and he thought they were really good."

Maria frowns. "You gave a couple to *Sean*?"

Why did I say that? It seemed innocent enough, but now that I'm hearing the words on my lips, I wish I could take them back. "He was raking leaves in the yard, so…"

"Oh."

"I mean, just to thank him for helping Bobby with soccer. You know?"

Kathy Tanner is sitting across from us at the table, and she seems to have overheard our exchange. "April is just *so* generous," she says. "She's always got a treat for anyone who wants it."

I cringe at the edge in her voice. She suspects something happened between me and Mark. But she doesn't *know*. Not for sure.

Or maybe she does know. Maybe *she's* the one who texted me that photo. To torment me.

But no. If Kathy knew for sure, she would skip the barbs and go straight to scratching my eyes out. And anyway, nothing happened between me and Mark. It was just one kiss, for God's sake! And nobody needs to know about it. Not if that picture doesn't get out.

Maria gives me another strange look, but she doesn't say anything else. She can't possibly be jealous. All I did was pass her husband on the street and offer him some pastries.

And his hand brushed briefly against mine, but she doesn't even know that part. I mean, I'm married. So…

"Maria!" Carrie is sitting across from us and looks like she's already had a glass of the wine Julie put out. I also notice the chips and jar of salsa from the supermarket on the table. "I heard you did something amazing. The babysitter is now out on bail!"

Grateful for the change in subject, I say, "I wish you could've been there, Carrie. Maria is my new hero."

Maria glances at me, then smiles at Carrie, making her dimples pop. "I didn't do anything. We were just upholding the law."

Carrie giggles. "Well, then I have to thank the *law*. Apparently, this isn't her first offense and she might actually go to *jail*. Or at least get probation. My lawyer says it will give me a great argument for getting full custody. So thank you." She winks at Maria. "The law."

For a moment, I feel uneasy. Of course, I loved the idea of getting revenge on this woman who stole Carrie's husband. But it seems wrong that she should be going to jail for something she didn't even do. I didn't even think about it that way. I figured she would just get a slap on the wrist and maybe some embarrassment.

"All right," Julie says. "It's time to discuss the book. That is what we're here for. You all read it, I assume?"

Everyone says yes, including me. Even though I didn't.

"So." Julie folds her arms across her chest. "What did

you think?"

"Well, it was interminably boring as usual, Julie." Carrie rolls her eyes. "There was literally nothing I liked about it or want to discuss."

"But you have to admit there was an interesting symbolism with the bird," Julie says.

"What symbolism?" Chelsea says. "I thought it was just a bird."

Julie clucks her tongue. "The bird was clearly a symbol for the child Tom always wanted to have."

"And what were the worms a symbol for then?" Jean asks. "His penis?"

The other women dissolve into giggles. Just as the laughter is dying down, Chelsea says, "Speaking of worms, you're not going to believe what I found in the pocket of David's coat yesterday when he got home from school. Beetles! Like, six of them!"

Oh, thank God. We're done discussing the book. Julie's lips are set in a straight line, but there isn't much she can do about it. We don't come here to discuss the book. We come here to drink wine and chat about our lives. The book in book club is arbitrary.

But just when I think I'm home free, Maria picks up her copy of the book and starts flipping through it. "Actually, I really liked the part of the book with Gisele. That was my favorite part."

Julie's eyes light up, excited that for once, somebody else wants to discuss the book. "I *agree*. I thought that was so moving."

Maria pivots in her chair and rests her brown eyes on my face. "What did you think of Gisele, April?"

I freeze. I can't believe Maria is doing this. She *knows* I didn't read the book.

"Well," I say. "I thought Tom's relationship with Gisele was really nuanced."

Julie is nodding. She loves it when people say things are nuanced. "Oh, I agree."

Thank God, I somehow bullshitted my way out of that. I'm off the hook.

"Which particular nuance did you find most interesting?" Maria asks me.

I stare at her, my mouth hanging open. Why is she doing this to me? She can't possibly think I read this horrible book. "I just thought it was very…" I'm grasping at straws here. "Romantic."

Obviously, that was the wrong thing to say. Julie is gaping at me, and I hear a couple of giggles.

"April," Julie says, "Gisele was Tom's *dog*."

Oh. Whoops.

"Did you even read the book?" she hisses at me.

"I read part of it. A large part of it."

She rolls her eyes. "Gisele was introduced in the second chapter!"

Everybody in the room is looking at me. So I didn't read the stupid book about the stupid bird guy. So what?

"The rule," Julie says tightly, "is that you have to read the book to come to book club. This is not a social group."

She's looking at me pointedly. Is she throwing me out? Does she expect me to leave?

"Oh, for Christ's sake, Julie," Carrie says. "Leave her alone." She winks at me. "If she leaves, she might take the turnovers with her, and I don't think I could handle that."

Julie gives me a sharp look, but doesn't say another word about it. Still, the whole experience leaves me feeling awful. I mean, who actually reads the book for book club? Julie was acting like I was worse than Hitler. Although the amazing part was all the other women had apparently read it.

But what made me most uneasy is that Maria was the one who instigated the whole thing. I'm certain I told her I never read the book club books.

Didn't I?

CHAPTER 14

Maria and I walk back together to our respective houses after book club is over. I've got the mostly empty tray of apple turnovers and she's clutching her copy of the bird book to her chest. I watch her profile in the moonlight. There are moments when Maria looks pretty, but in the nighttime shadows, she looks old. The light casts dark shadows under her eyes and around her mouth.

"That was fun," Maria says. "I'm so glad I went."

"Yes…" I look down at my ballet flats. I hadn't wanted to say anything about what she did, but I can't stop thinking about it. "By the way, I thought I told you I hadn't read the book."

"Hmm?"

I clear my throat. "We were talking the other day and I said I hadn't read it. But back there, you kept asking me about it. And it was… you know, awkward."

"Oh!" Maria's eyes widen. "I'm so sorry about that,

April. I didn't realize you hadn't read it. I liked it. I couldn't put it down!"

She couldn't put *that book* down? Is she kidding me? "Well, I just get busy, and sometimes I don't have time to read it."

"Of course. I know how busy your life is. It's not a big deal."

But there's an edge to her voice. Is she being sarcastic? Does she think I shouldn't be busy? Or that I am less busy than she is? "I mean, I have to run through recipes for my show every week. And the silent auction is taking up so much of my time. Also, I've been cooking dinner every night for Mrs. Wright. You know, that elderly woman on the next block who broke her hip last month?"

Maria nods. "I know. It's so busy, isn't it? Anyway, don't worry about it. Nobody but Julie cares if you read the book."

I let out a breath. Maybe I'm reading too much into this. Maria has a lot on her mind, and I can't expect her to remember every little thing I tell her.

But on the other hand, she had such a strange look on her face when I told her I had given those turnovers to Sean. Could it possibly have something to do with that? Was this some sort of revenge for talking to her husband?

But that would be crazy. Nobody is that jealous. She said she forgot, and I'm sure she's telling the truth.

After dropping Maria off at her house, I walk the rest of the way to mine. Bobby is surely asleep by now, but there's a light on in the living room, which means Elliot is still awake in there. I look down at my watch and see that it's nearly ten o'clock.

The drapes are partially open, and I can see Elliot through the window. Good—he's still awake. Maybe we can have a drink together.

Then I hear my phone buzz inside my purse.

Immediately, my heart jumps in my chest. Getting text messages has become terrifying. What if it's another picture of me and Mark? Or something worse? But at the same time, I have to look. I fish my phone out of my purse and stare at the screen:

Shh. Your husband is in the middle of a secret phone call.

That's when I realize that Elliot is sitting on the couch, but he's not watching television or on his computer. He's on the phone.

I can't hear anything he's saying, but there's a tiny smile on his lips as he speaks into the receiver. Who would he be talking to this late? It couldn't be someone from work, could it? He doesn't look like he's having a work conversation.

I look down at my phone again. The words are still on the screen, taunting me. I want to ask them who they are again, but I know they won't answer.

I press my ear against the window, which is freezing cold against my cheek. It doesn't help. I can't hear a word. I better get inside before somebody sees me.

I try to be as quiet as I can when I open the front door. It occurs to me too late that I could have gone in through the back. The second I step inside, I hear Elliot's voice. "Gotta go."

Well, he sure got off the phone fast when he heard his wife coming in.

"Hi, honey." He jumps to his feet and comes to greet me at the door. "How was your book club?"

"Great." I try to keep my voice even. "What have you been up to?"

"Oh, nothing too exciting."

"Doing work?"

"Yeah, mostly."

Who were you talking to just now? I want to ask him the question, but I also don't want to sound like a crazy jealous wife. I can't figure out a way to ask him the question without it sounding that way. And I can't tell him about the text messages I've been getting—not after that threat they made about circulating the photo of me and Mark.

I push past him and go to the kitchen with the tray containing five remaining turnovers. I had meant to store them in the refrigerator for later, but instead, I shove one of them into my mouth. Then another. God, these are good.

Before I know it, the turnovers are gone. The apple and sugar and flour feel heavy in my stomach—I never indulge myself like that. I can't believe I allowed myself that moment of weakness. Tomorrow I'll have to make up for it.

I start washing the tray, because I can't go to bed with dirty dishes in the sink. And God forbid Elliot would ever help me with that. Elliot wanders into the kitchen, yawning. He rubs a hand over his bald scalp. "I'm exhausted. Want to go up to bed when you're done?"

The hot water feels nice on my cold hands. I love washing dishes. I find it relaxing. "I guess."

He puts his arms around my waist from behind, and I feel myself stiffen. Who was he talking to on the phone? It's driving me crazy. I could ask him, but he'll just lie and blow it off. What's he going to say—*oh yeah, I was just chatting with the woman I'm having an affair with.*

"Hey." I clear my throat as I turn around. "Could I use your phone for a second?"

His expression freezes. "For what?"

"Mine is out of batteries and I want to look something up."

"What do you need to look up?"

Great question. "Bobby has a half-day one day next week and I can't remember what day."

Ooh, that sounded very legitimate.

Elliot frowns at me. "You need to know that *right now*? At ten o'clock at night?"

"I need to plan for the week." And also, I need to take a peek at his call list.

He glances over at the refrigerator. "Isn't that a list of all the holidays and half days posted on the fridge?"

Dammit, he's right. My organizational skills have backfired.

My brain is struggling to come up with an alternate reason to look at his phone, but before I can, he kisses me on the cheek. "I'm going upstairs. I hope you can come join me soon."

I watched him trudge up the stairs to our bedroom. Those text messages are getting me paranoid. Just because he was on the phone when I walked in and then quickly hung up, it doesn't mean he was doing anything suspicious. It doesn't mean he's cheating on me.

Although it wouldn't be the first time.

As soon as I finish the dishes, I take out my phone one last time. I look at the text message, still on the screen. After a moment of hesitation, I swipe to delete the message.

CHAPTER 15

Owen and Bobby are becoming best friends. And honestly, it's a relief.

There's nothing wrong with Leo Bressler, Bobby's former best friend. Except for the fact that his mother is Julie. Don't get me wrong—I love Julie. But sometimes I get the distinct feeling she doesn't care much for my son. Every time Bobby goes to Julie's house, there's some sort of a problem. The last time he went over, she went on and on about how he didn't take his shoes off and now there was dirt on her white carpet. I swear, she acted like he had committed *murder.*

Who gets a white carpet when they have young sons? Tell me, *who?*

Maria doesn't have carpeting at all, and she doesn't have a hysterical meltdown if you don't remove your shoes the second you step through the door. I swear to God, Julie makes the mailman take his shoes off to deliver her mail.

This afternoon, Bobby and Owen are having a

playdate at our house and are out in the backyard, while Maria and I sit in the kitchen and discuss the silent auction. We have gotten a record-breaking number of donations so far, and people are bidding enthusiastically on the app. The bid for Chelsea's Yankee tickets just surpassed $3000.

"Don't take this the wrong way," Maria says as she takes a sip of peppermint tea, "but people in this town are too rich for their own good."

"I agree." I pick up one of the raspberry tartlets I made earlier this afternoon and pop it in my mouth. I did a show on raspberry tartlets a few months ago—the secret is using vanilla bean rather than vanilla extract for the pastry cream. I'm allowing myself exactly two tartlets and that's it. "But I'm also wildly jealous."

"Well, of course." She giggles and picks up her purse, which she had hung on the back of her chair. "By the way, I brought something for you. A present."

"A present?" I clap my hands together. I will never be too old to be excited about getting a present. "What is it?"

She pulls a little white box out of her purse and slides it across the table. A white box. That can only mean jewelry—maybe something from Helena's.

I crack the top open and see a necklace-length chain inside. There's a charm on the chain, which is a tiny silver woman with a squiggly circle on her abdomen. Well, it's not really her abdomen so much as her giant pelvis.

I'm not entirely sure how to react.

"It's a fertility charm," Maria says. "My sister used that

to conceive my niece and my nephew. She says it really works."

"I see…"

"You're skeptical," Maria notes. "I don't blame you. I am not into all this weird charm voodoo stuff either—I mean, it sure didn't work for me, but I have other issues. But my sister was trying to have a baby for five years, and one month after she got this charm, she got pregnant."

I raise an eyebrow. "Interesting."

I look down at the charm again. It does seem rather hard to believe that a necklace could be enough to get me pregnant. If I told Elliot, he would laugh at me. He would tell me to go to that infertility specialist and finally get worked up.

I shudder. I really, really don't want to go down that path.

"Anyway, my sister is done having kids," she says. "So you can keep the necklace and wear it if you want. Hey, what have you got to lose?"

That's true. "Thank you. I appreciate it."

"But for the record," Maria adds, "I don't think there's any chance Elliot would leave you because you can't get pregnant again."

I close my fingers around the tiny silver charm. "You haven't seen his secretary. She's gorgeous. And *really* young. Probably very fertile. He could probably get her pregnant just by looking at her the wrong way."

"Oh, come on! Elliot wouldn't do that to you."

I swallow. "Yeah. I'm sure you're right."

Maria excuses herself to go to the bathroom. She's been over enough times lately that she doesn't have to ask where it is. Even though we haven't known each other that long, there are times when I feel like I've known her for ages. And I've completely forgotten about what she did to me during that book club. Well, I haven't forgotten it, but I know she didn't do it on purpose.

I glance out at the backyard, to where Owen and Bobby are playing together. They look like they're playing tag. I still feel uneasy about how Bobby disappeared from the backyard that time. And the text message. But then again, nobody stole him—he left on his own volition, according to Maria. Either way, I've been keeping a much closer eye on him lately, especially now that the text messages have continued. The only thing besides school I allow him to do is go to the park to play soccer with Sean Cooper. I trust Sean.

A buzzing sound draws my attention away from the backyard. It's coming from Maria's purse. Her phone must be ringing on silent.

I start to call out her name to tell her she's got a phone call, but then I realize something. Her iPhone is lying on our kitchen table.

I glance over at the hallway leading to the bathroom. No sign of Maria. I get up out of my seat and look down inside her purse to see what's making the noise. I try not to touch anything, because I don't want her to think I've been going through her purse, even though I sort of am.

There's a phone in there. A flip phone.

Why does Maria have a flip phone in her purse when she has a perfectly good iPhone? That is really strange. It looks like one of those burner phones that you can buy with a prepaid card if you don't want somebody to track you down. But why would Maria have one of those?

I glance at the hallway one more time, then quietly remove the phone from her purse. It stops ringing just as I get it in my hand. I open it up and see a number on the screen, but no name attached.

Why would Maria have a burner phone? Who has she been calling with it?

And then I think of all those text messages from blocked numbers. That couldn't be *Maria*, could it? Why would she do something like that? It doesn't make any sense.

And then a text message appears on her screen:

When can we meet?

My mouth falls open. Is Maria having an affair? Is she cheating on Sean? I can't imagine Maria doing something like that, but why would she have a burner phone in her purse and be arranging clandestine meetings with someone?

The area code on the number is local. It's somebody from around here.

I look for a scrap of paper to scribble down the number, but before I can find one, I hear running water from down the hallway. I quickly snap the phone closed and drop it back into her purse. I can't let her know I was digging around inside her purse.

"Mom!"

I nearly jump out of my skin at the voice coming from behind me. It's Bobby and Owen. Their hands are caked in fresh dirt, and my son also has some on his cheeks. That's a good indication they've been having fun.

"Mom, Owen pushed me!" Bobby whines. He scrunches up his freckled nose.

Owen folds his skinny arms across his chest. "No, Bobby pushed *me*."

I groan. "Can't you both say you're sorry?"

"No!" Bobby looks affronted. "Owen pushed me! He pushed me off the swing and I fell on the ground."

Admittedly, Bobby's pants legs are caked in dirt. But that's nothing unusual.

Owen blinks eyes that are rapidly filling with tears. He has Maria's dimples even though he's not biologically related to her, but he has his father's blue eyes with long eyelashes. He looks like the sort of kid who will be handsome someday. A real ladykiller, but he doesn't know it yet. "I *didn't* push you. I was on the swing and you said it was your turn, but it *wasn't*. And then you pushed me off."

Thankfully, Maria emerges from the bathroom at that moment. The boys reiterate their dilemma to her, both of them insisting that they were pushed. At this point, I really don't care who pushed who. I'm sure even if Owen pushed Bobby, he didn't mean anything by it.

"You both need to say you're sorry," Maria says firmly. "*Now.*"

After a bit more coaxing, both the boys mutter apologies. I don't know what's so hard about saying sorry. It's like apologizing is physically painful for them. I say sorry about a hundred times a day. Even if it's not my fault.

"I better take Owen home now." Maria flashes an apologetic smile. "I think the boys have had enough of each other today."

"Would you like some raspberry tartlets to go?"

She looks longingly at the plate. "I would, but I shouldn't. Honestly, April, I'm going to gain twenty pounds living next to you."

We hug goodbye and Maria drops her iPhone into her purse. I'm dying to ask her why she has a burner phone, but I suspect anything she tells me will be a lie. I still can't believe she's having an affair. Especially when she's married to Sean, who is crazy sexy.

But the other explanation is too disturbing to consider.

After Maria and Owen leave, I decide I better get Bobby in the bathtub. I turn to look at my son, and that's when I noticed the darkening red patch on the right knee of his jeans.

"Bobby!" I cry. "What happened to your knee?"

"I told you, Owen pushed me off the swing!"

I roll up the pants leg while Bobby squirms. When I get it up over his knee, I gasp. He skinned his knee really badly. His entire kneecap is covered in blood and it's streaming down his leg. Bobby takes one look at it and bursts into tears.

"I told you!" He howls. "It huuuuuuurts!"

That's how little kids are. They don't even realize they have any pain until they see that they're injured. But I have to admit, this is an impressive wound. It's going to call for the first aid kit I've got in the hall closet. And Bobby is going to complain the whole time I'm cleaning it up.

But more significantly, it means Bobby was the one telling the truth. Owen pushed Bobby off the swing and then lied about it.

For a moment, I consider giving Maria a call. If Owen pushed another kid and then lied about it, she would want to know, right? But then again, boys love to roughhouse. And it's not like Bobby got a broken arm. It's just a scrape.

So I don't call Maria. But next time I see her, maybe I'll mention it.

CHAPTER 16

It's eight-thirty at night, which is Bobby's bedtime, and Elliot still isn't back from work.

This has been happening more and more lately. It used to be just an occasional thing, but now it's more like twice a week. But this is the first time Elliot hasn't responded to my text messages asking when he'll be home. It's like I'm just supposed to accept that he'll be home at some unknown time in the future, and not worry about it.

I'd be a lot less worried about it if Brianna wasn't with him. It's not that I don't trust him, but…

I still don't know who he was talking to on the phone the other night. But I haven't gotten any other text messages. Maybe whoever was harassing me decided to leave me alone.

I read Bobby his usual bedtime story. He loves the *Goosebumps* books, even though I'm worried they give him nightmares. I sit on the edge of his bed, recounting the story of the ventriloquist dummy that came to life.

"Are you sure this isn't scaring you?" I ask him.

Bobby rolls his eyes. "No! It's not scary. It's *funny*."

Whatever. "Okay, well, it's time for sleep."

"But Dad isn't home yet!"

I pull my phone out of my pocket and see if there are any text messages from Elliot. Nothing.

"Can you call him?" Bobby asks.

I had been trying not to be an annoying wife, but now that Bobby is asking me to call him, I feel like it gives me a license to do it. I select Elliot's number from the list of favorites and it rings on the other line.

And rings.

He's not picking up.

"Sorry, Bobby." I disconnect the call before it goes to voicemail. "He's really busy at work."

Bobby's lower lip trembles. "But he *always* says good night."

I let out a sigh. My only other option is to call the number for his office. At least then I'll know if he's on the road or not. Ordinarily, I wouldn't do it because it means speaking to Brianna. But it's late enough that I'm willing to make an exception.

I dial the number and it rings three times before Brianna's peppy voice comes on the line. "Elliot Masterson's office. This is Brianna."

Great. Not only is he still at work at eight-thirty at night, but he's with his gorgeous secretary. All alone.

"Um, hi." I clear my throat. "This is April."

"Who?"

"April *Masterson*. Elliot's *wife*." I grit my teeth. "Is Elliot still at the office?"

"Yes, he's still here," Brianna reports.

There's an interminable pause. "Well, can I talk to him?"

"Oh. I'm sorry, that would be impossible. He's very busy."

Bobby reaches out to tug on my shirt sleeve. "Is he coming home soon?"

I clear my throat. "His son is about to go to sleep and would like to talk to him. You really can't put him on the line?"

"I'm so sorry." But she doesn't sound sorry at all. "I'll let him know to give you a call when he has a chance."

"You really can't put him on the line for two seconds?"

"I'm afraid not."

I want to slam down the phone, but that won't do me any good. Brianna is the boss over there. She is the gatekeeper if I want to talk to my husband, and she is not letting me through the gate.

Of course, this is Elliot's fault for not texting me. Or answering his damn phone.

On the plus side, at least I know he hasn't crashed his Tesla on the way home and is lying in a ditch somewhere. I just have to wait and he'll be home eventually.

I give Bobby a few extra hugs to make up for the fact that Elliot isn't around. It takes some time, but I coax him into going to sleep. Elliot still hasn't texted me, so I leave my phone downstairs so I won't keep checking it, and I take a long, hot shower. A shower is my only chance of relaxing. If I sit and watch TV, I'm just going to be thinking about Elliot.

Maybe I should do a test bake tonight. I've been wanting to do a pound cake using ricotta cheese on my show. I haven't figured out the secret yet though. By the time I'm ready to film, I'll probably have turned out at least four ricotta pound cakes.

After about thirty minutes under scalding hot water, I feel a lot better. The hot water is so soothing. It's like getting a full body massage. I still feel angry at Elliot, but I can think about things differently. I know he's under tremendous pressure at work lately. He has a chance to make partner this year, and it's a big deal. I should be grateful to him for working so hard to support his family. I need to be more accepting of his long hours.

And then I hear glass shattering downstairs.

CHAPTER 17

Oh my God. Somebody's breaking into our house.

Worse, I left my stupid phone downstairs. So I can't even call 911 and tell the police about the break-in.

I told Elliot we needed a landline. He said it was a waste of money, but if we had a landline, I'd be able to call the police right now. Of course, if my husband got home from work at a *reasonable hour*, we wouldn't have this problem. He'd be home, protecting me. Like he's supposed to do.

I don't know what to do. My first instinct is to go into Bobby's room and make sure he's okay. But there's no lock on Bobby's door, so if I go in there, we're both sitting ducks. And there's no way I am waking Bobby up so he can freak out.

No, my best bet is to get to my phone. I've got to call the police.

I quickly throw on a pair of jeans, a sweater, and my slippers. I open the door to the bedroom quietly and listen for sounds downstairs to give me a sense of where the intruder is. I hold my breath, straining my ears.

I hear nothing.

Maybe whoever it was just grabbed my purse and left. Or maybe they heard sounds outside, got scared, and decided not to burgle me after all. Or maybe they're lying in wait.

Fortunately, all the lights are on downstairs. So it's unlikely somebody will be lurking around. Anyway, why would you break into a house where all the lights are on?

Hoping I'm not making a seriously stupid mistake, I make my way cautiously down the stairs to the living room. I still don't hear any noises to indicate an intruder. But I do see broken glass by one of the windows. It's cracked with a small hole in it, like somebody threw a ball at the window and it broke.

Maybe that's all it was. Maybe some kids were playing ball on the street and one flew through my window. Of course, the time of day makes that very unlikely.

And then I see the rock on the floor.

Somebody threw a rock through my window.

Thankfully, I'm wearing my slippers. I creep across the floor, doing my best to avoid the glass. I bend down next to the rock that penetrated my window. It's smaller than my fist but it did the job.

"April?"

I whirl around. Elliot is standing behind me, looking rumpled in his white dress shirt with his tie loose around his neck. He has a five o'clock shadow on his scalp.

"What happened?" His brows are scrunched together. "Is that a rock?"

"Somebody threw it through our window." I swallow a large lump in my throat. "I was upstairs and I heard it."

"Jesus Christ." He shakes his head. "What the hell? Who would do something like that?"

I shrug helplessly, not trusting myself to speak.

"Jesus," he says again. "Should we call the police?"

"What's the point? They're not going to do anything." I struggle to my feet, trying not to touch the ground because I don't want to get glass in my hand. "Why are you home so late? You didn't even text me."

"What are you talking about? I texted you like twenty minutes ago to tell you I was leaving!"

Oh. Well, that could be true. I haven't looked at my phone since I went upstairs.

I blink a few times, afraid my emotions are going to get the better of me. "I was worried about you. And Bobby kept asking for you."

Elliot's shoulders sag. "I'm sorry, April. Work is killing me lately. But I promise I'll try to be home earlier from now on."

I nod and pick up my phone from the coffee table, where I left it. Sure enough, there is a text message on the screen from Elliot, telling me he's on his way home. And then there's a second text message, from a blocked number:

Did you enjoy my little present, April?

I clasp my hand over my mouth to keep from crying out. Up until now, it was just words. Now there's a rock in my living room and a bunch of broken glass on the floor. Somebody's out to get me.

I only wish I knew why.

CHAPTER 18

I spend most of the next day cooking, just to get my mind off what happened the night before. By the time I'm ready to pick up Bobby from school, every inch of our kitchen table is covered with baked goods. I grab some lemon bars and cookies and hurry out the door to the school. I'm sure I can get somebody to eat them.

Carrie, Kathy, and Julie are waiting together near the entrance. Carrie groans when she sees my Tupperware. "Why do I feel like I'm going to gain five pounds in the next five minutes?"

I pull the lid off the container of lemon bars. "Come on, please take one. I'm overloaded!"

Carrie hesitates. "I shouldn't."

"Go ahead, Carrie," Kathy says. "Mark always says that April makes the best lemon bars in existence."

She shoots me a look as she says that. I shift uneasily. Could she be the one who threw a rock through my window? I wouldn't put it past her.

Just as all three women reach over to take lemon bars, I see Sean Cooper jogging over to me. He waves his hand to get my attention and calls out my name. It's hard not to notice him.

Carrie nudges my elbow. "I wonder what Maria's hot husband wants to talk to you about."

And then Kathy shoots me another look. "Yes. I wonder."

Oh God.

"April!" Sean slows to a stop in front of us. "I'm glad I caught you."

I smile at him. "Hi, Sean. Would you like a lemon bar?"

He looks down at the Tupperware container filled with my lemon bars. I make amazing lemon bars. My secret is that I put lemon zest both in the curd and also in the crust.

"That's okay," he finally says.

"Are you sure? Because—"

"Listen," Sean interrupts me. "Have you seen Raffey?"

Have I what? "Who?"

"Raffey." He smiles apologetically. "That's Owen's favorite toy. You know, the giraffe. We can't seem to find it anywhere, and Owen was freaking out last night."

"That's terrible!" I say.

I consider suggesting this is an opportunity for Owen not to be so dependent on a stuffed animal. He *is* seven years old, after all. But somehow, I don't think Sean will appreciate it.

"So anyway…" Sean scratches the back of his neck. "I was wondering if maybe Owen left it at Bobby's house?"

I shake my head. "Sorry, I haven't seen it."

"Well, maybe you could check his room."

I clutch the Tupperware to my chest. "Why would Bobby have it in his room?"

Sean's ears turn slightly pink. "I'm not saying he took Raffey from Owen, but—"

"April, remember when Bobby took Leo's Ninja Turtle?" Julie speaks up.

"That was three years ago. They were *four*." My cheeks burn. I can't believe they're accusing my son of stealing Owen's toy. Why would he steal a stupid stuffed giraffe when he's got a *Nintendo*, for God's sake? "I'll ask Bobby about it. But I don't think he would steal Owen's favorite toy."

"I'm just thinking Owen might have left the toy there," Sean says. "Will you check for me, April?"

"Of course." I force a smile, trying to make light of the whole thing. "But only if you try one of my lemon bars."

Sean takes a step back, like he thinks my lemon bars might be made of poison. "Um…"

"I promise. They're delicious."

Julie rolls her eyes. "For goodness sakes, April, you don't need to bulldoze the poor guy into eating your food!"

Everyone is suddenly looking at me as I feel my cheeks turning pink. Thankfully, the bell rings at that moment and the kids start filtering out. I still don't know what I'm going to do with all these lemon bars and cookies. But if Sean doesn't want any, far be it from me to force him.

Sometimes the kids play together after school, but not today. I hear Sean telling Owen they're going to the park, but he doesn't invite Bobby like he sometimes does. Julie and Kathy are talking together quietly with their boys running just ahead of them. I wonder if they're going to have a playdate. Usually, Julie invites me over after school, but she's hardly done it at all since the year started.

"Mom," Bobby says. "Can I go over to Leo's house?"

"I don't think so," I mumble.

"Why not?"

"Because he's busy."

"No, he's not. He told me he wasn't busy."

"Well, his mom is busy. Anyway, we're not invited."

"Can't you ask his mom?

Bobby has an amazing ability to never ever let anything go, but I manage to nudge him in the direction of my SUV. "Bobby," I say, "have you seen Owen's toy, Raffey?"

Bobby groans. "No! Owen kept talking about it all day. He's obsessed with that stupid toy."

I wonder where Bobby learned the word "obsessed." Probably from me. "So you haven't seen it?"

"Nope."

I still feel irritated that Sean basically accused Bobby of stealing that silly giraffe. Why would he even *want* it? He has much better toys than that at home. Like I said, he has a *Nintendo*!

Bobby complains incessantly about wanting a playdate, but I manage to coax him into the car. He pouts the entire way. By the time I pull into our driveway, I'm pretty much ready to snap. And then I see the woman standing at our front door.

The woman looks familiar, but I can't quite place her. But she doesn't look dangerous. She's in her fifties, with graying hair and a thick layer of padding on her abdomen. When she sees my car, she waves.

I have no idea who she is, but obviously, she knows who I am.

"Hello," I say as I get out of the car. I try to push away an uneasy feeling in the pit of my stomach. "Can I help you?"

The woman nods eagerly. "April, right?"

"Yes…"

"I'm Nancy." She smiles disarmingly. "Doris Kirkland was my aunt. You and I met while I was selling the house."

"Oh!" I return her smile. "I thought you looked familiar." I look back at Bobby, who is still in the backseat and messing around with his backpack. He always takes forever to get out of the car. "How are you doing?"

"Can't complain." Nancy shifts her oversized purse to her other arm. "Listen, I got a call from the new owners of the house, and they said they found one of Aunt Doris's boxes up in their attic. They told me I could pick it up. But…" She casts a glance at the darkened windows of the Cooper residence. "Do you know when they'll be back?"

I assume Maria is working this afternoon because Sean was the one who picked up Owen. They're probably still at the park.

"I'm not sure, sorry." I open the car door for Bobby, who still isn't budging. "Maybe an hour or two?"

She nods thoughtfully. "Are they nice people?"

"Yes. They are."

She smiles crookedly. "Nicer than Aunt Doris, I'm sure."

I laugh. "Oh, she was interesting."

"Now *you're* being nice." Nancy shakes her head. "Aunt Doris was a mean old lady. And she was proud of it!"

I tug at my jacket. Mrs. Kirkland was a bit grumpy at times, but I always chalked it up to her being lonely. Also, it didn't help that practically all of Bobby's balls ended up in her yard. You would think just by chance, some of them would *not* end up in her yard.

"My sister and I were sure she was going to live forever," Nancy continues. "We had a bet going that she would make it till a hundred. People like her always do. She probably would have if she had been wearing her life alert necklace." She clucks her tongue. "I can't imagine why she took it off."

I frown. "Life alert necklace?"

"Oh, you know." Nancy lifts a shoulder. "That button

you press if you've fallen and you can't get up. She was so pleased with herself for having gotten one, but then she wasn't even wearing it when she fell down the stairs. It was stuffed in a drawer in her bedroom."

A shiver goes down my spine. "Was that unusual for her?"

"It was. She was so anal about always wearing it." Nancy tilts her head to the side. "She was scared about breaking a hip, you know? I couldn't believe she didn't have it on. If this were a movie, I'd say for sure somebody pushed her."

I have a horrible sinking feeling in my stomach. I think I might be sick.

"I'm just kidding," Nancy says quickly when she sees my face. "I'm sure she just forgot. She was ninety-six, after all!" She takes her phone out of her bag, looks at the screen, then stuffs it back in. "Anyway, I can't wait any longer. If you see the Coopers, tell them I'll try to come back later tonight."

My head is spinning as I watch Nancy get back into her car. That was an incredibly disturbing conversation. Everyone on the block assumed poor Mrs. Kirkland had just taken an innocent spill down the stairs. She was ninety-six, after all, as Nancy said.

Elderly people fall. It doesn't have to be something sinister.

CHAPTER 19

Comment on *April's Sweet Secrets* YouTube video:

In every episode of the show, April says goodnight to her mother. Want to know a secret about April?

She hates her mother.

A few times a year, my mother guest stars on my show.

It's a bit of a challenge, to say the least. She is pretty out of it these days. But at the same time, she gets a huge kick out of helping me with cooking. I tell her exactly what to do—mix this, pour that—and she does it for me. The viewers love these shows. I get so many positive comments and usually a big uptick in hits.

That's why I want to do a show with my mother now. I've been getting so many negative comments lately. I desperately need some positivity right now.

Shady Oaks Nursing Home is about a forty-minute drive from our house. There were closer nursing homes, but I liked the feel of this one. When I walked in, I just got the vibe that it was a place my mother would like. It was expensive, but I was willing to pay anything. It's for my mother, after all. She deserves the best.

Unfortunately, my life has been so crazy lately, I only manage to visit once a month. Sometimes less. I feel guilty about it, but most of the time my mom is so out of it that she hardly even notices when I come. And I make sure the nurses play my show for her every night. I even bought her an iPad so she could watch it.

Shady Oaks has over a hundred beds, and it's a large, new-looking building of two stories with trees dotting the entrance. Not that the residents seem to spend much time outdoors. I had imagined my mother sitting outside on the lawn, but in all the times I've visited, I've yet to see one resident enjoying a sunny day.

To get inside the facility, you have to press a red button, which unlocks the front door. In order to leave, you have to punch in a four-digit code. Shady Oaks has a dedicated memory care unit, and it's not uncommon for those patients to try to escape. Fortunately, none of them can remember the code.

I head over to Shady Oaks with Bobby after school the next day. In one hand, I've got my camera and tripod, and in the other, I've got a grocery bag filled to the brim with ingredients.

Delilah at the front desk waves at me when I come in. She always has a great smile. "Welcome, April. Hi, Bobby! Are you two here to film again?"

I nod eagerly. "We're making no-bake cheesecake today."

"Sounds delicious! Leave some for me!"

"Actually…" I reach into my reusable bag of groceries—I always shop with reusable bags. "I brought some cheesecake bites for anyone who gets hungry in the meantime."

Delilah's face lights up as she takes one of my cheesecake bites. They're so easy to make. I probably break out my mini muffin tin about three or four times a week.

"Mmm…" She moans as she samples one of my cheesecake bites. "April, these are incredible!"

"Take another!" I smile as she eagerly obliges. "Also, I was wondering if you would be all right if Bobby hung out with you while I'm filming?"

She seems thrilled. "Of course!"

Delilah gets Bobby set up with some paper and magic markers, and I leave a few more cheesecake bites, then I go into the nursing home by myself. The memory unit is at the other end of the building on the first floor. I walk down the familiar, well-lit hallways, my wrist straining with the weight of the grocery bag. I always buy too much.

Peggy Lewis is waiting for me at the nursing station.

She has close-cropped gray hair and has worked here for over thirty years. I always offer her some pastries when I come, but I get the distinct feeling she doesn't like me. I think she judges me for not coming to visit more often. And another nurse confided in me that Peggy doesn't like the way I film episodes here, even though the rest of the staff get a huge kick out of it and I got the approval of the nursing home director.

I rest the bag of groceries on the counter in the nursing station and breathe a sigh of relief. "Hi, Peggy," I say in my most chipper voice. "How are you today?"

Peggy doesn't crack a smile. "It's been a rough day. We've had a few residents with behavior issues."

"But my mother is okay?"

She arches an eyebrow. "Are you asking if she's camera ready?" Without waiting for an answer, she adds, "She's fine. She's waiting for you in the kitchen."

Peggy doesn't offer to help me with my camera or my bag, but thankfully, two other nurses come over and practically fall over themselves to help me get set up. And they also help themselves to some of my cheesecake bites.

As promised, my mother is waiting in the kitchen. It's not so much the kitchen as it is a part of the dining area with a refrigerator and sink. You can't do any cooking per se in the kitchen, which is why we're going for the no-bake cheesecake.

There's a small circular table in the kitchen, and that's

where my mother is sitting. She's only in her sixties, but she looks much older. She could easily pass for eighty. Her hair is all white, even though she used to dye it when I was growing up. There are bags under her eyes and her cheeks are so sunken, they have shadows. Every couple of seconds, she smacks her lips, which I was told is a side effect of the medication. She's staring ahead, her eyes blank.

It's strange to see her like this, even after all these years. If there's one word I would have used to describe my mother before she got sick, it would have been "feisty." Or maybe "strong." She raised me all by herself after my father died, and she did a really good job. It's so hard to see her like this.

"Mom?" I say.

For a moment, she simply stares straight ahead. She's on several medications to control her agitation, and for a moment, I'm scared she's too out of it to participate in the show. But then, after a long hesitation, she looks up at me.

"Hello, April," she says.

I beam at her. "You remember me."

She doesn't respond to that.

"We're going to make cheesecake together, Mom," I say. "Won't that be fun? And I'm going to film it."

Her eyes fall on my camera, sitting atop the tripod. "Film it?"

"Yes! You're going to be on YouTube! Like a movie star."

My mother just sits there, contemplating this

revelation. I'm still not entirely sure whether she's up to helping me. But she doesn't have to do much. She doesn't even have to talk or stand up. Her dementia is so advanced, there's not much she can do anymore. But I can give her a bowl and let her do some mixing.

"April!"

I turn around and see Dr. Joseph Williams is standing behind me. Dr. Williams manages most of the patients on the memory care unit, and he's been my mother's doctor since even before she was admitted here. He was the one who helped me get her in here, and for that, I am eternally grateful. He's an amazing doctor—smart and compassionate.

"Dr. Williams!" I cry. "I'm so glad you're here! We were just going to start filming soon."

Dr. Williams flashes me a smile. He's in his early fifties and he always seems so in control of every situation. Whenever I see him standing there in his white coat, I feel comforted. "I knew that. Why do you think I came over here? I wouldn't miss it."

My cheeks flush with pride. Dr. Williams is so busy and so important, but he still gets a kick out of my internet show.

It takes me another half hour to get everything set up to start filming. I already have a no-bake cheesecake finished that I toss in a refrigerator. I'm not about to sit around here and wait for the cheesecake to be done. One of my secrets for filming is that I've always got a finished product already done before I start the show.

"All right, Mom," I say to her. "The show is about to start. Are you ready?"

My mother looks up at me. For a moment, her eyes lose that glazed look and she's her own old self again. She puts her hands on the table and struggles to her feet. "I'm ready."

Here we go...

"Hello there!" I say as I look directly at the camera. "This is April from *April's Sweet Secrets*. Today I'm at the nursing home with my wonderful mother, Janet Portland. She's going to be helping me out today, right, Mom?"

She stares at me for a moment. There's a little bit of drool in the corner of her mouth. She doesn't look like she's going to say anything. God, I hope she at least is willing to stir something in the mixing bowl.

"Anyway," I say, "I've got a recipe for you today that—"

"April." My mother's cracked voice interrupts my monologue. "April is my daughter."

I laugh and put my hand on her shoulder. "That's right. I am."

"April is my daughter," she says. "And she is pure evil."

CHAPTER 20

At my mother's words, the smile instantly drops off my face. "Mom…"

But it's like she doesn't hear me. Her eyes stare straight at the camera, which I desperately want to shut off. But I'm frozen in place.

"She locked me in here." The blinking red light ensures the camera is catching every moment of her little speech. Thank God we're not live. "She trapped me here. I'm a *prisoner*." Her gaze swivels so that her dark eyes are boring into me. Our small live audience seems frozen in shock as they watch this confrontation unfold. "You think I don't know what you're doing?"

The blood drains out of my face. "Mom, that's not true."

"You little ungrateful bitch!" she hisses at me.

And before I know what's going on, she has lunged at me. I don't know who is cutting my mother's fingernails, but they are not doing a good job because I can feel her nails ripping through the skin of my neck. It goes on for about two seconds before I feel her being pulled off of me by Dr. Williams and a nurse.

I collapse against the table, breathing hard. It takes three nurses to restrain my mother, who is screaming at the top of her lungs. "Let me go! Let! Me! Go! I want to get out of here! I shouldn't be here!"

I watch as they pull her away and bring her back to her room. Peggy and Dr. Williams follow down the hallway, but I stay put. I don't want to go anywhere near her right now.

My heart won't stop pounding. I gingerly touch my neck and when I pull my fingers away, there's blood on my hands. Well, at least she didn't bite me. But my hands won't stop shaking. How could she have said those things to me? Whatever medications she's getting, they're not doing the trick.

After about ten minutes, Peggy and Dr. Williams come out of the room to talk to me. I've just been sitting at the table, gorging myself on the no-bake cheesecake I brought. It's pretty clear we're not going to be able to film anything today.

"We have her restrained," Peggy says tightly. "But she's still very upset."

"Of course she's upset," Dr. Williams says in that calm, controlled voice. "She's incredibly confused and understandably wants to go home. It's very common to feel that way with her level of dementia." He furrows his brow.

"We had to give her some IM Haldol and Ativan."

I don't know much about psychiatric meds, but I know those are pretty serious ones.

"I feel so bad about this." I wring my hands together. "I *so* wish we could take her home. Maybe she'd be happier there.…"

"Right, but what would you do if she had an episode like this?" Dr. Williams folds his arms across his chest. "She could harm you or your family. This is the best thing for her, April. You know it is."

"I guess…"

"It is," he insists. "She's going to have occasional episodes like this, but in general, she's happy here. She can socialize with people like herself."

"Maybe…"

We all look at the doorway to my mother's room. The screaming seems to have stopped. At least for the moment.

"Can I go in?" I ask. "I want to talk to her."

Dr. Williams puts his hand on my shoulder. "You don't have to. And you should get your neck cleaned up. One of the nurses can get you a Band-Aid."

"I want to make sure she's okay," I say. "Please."

Finally, he nods. "Go ahead. But she's probably going to be pretty sedated."

My legs feel wobbly as I walk down the hallway to my mother's private room. They've shut off the lights in the room in an attempt to get her to quiet down. But even through the darkness, I can see both wrists are strapped to the bedrails.

Her eyes crack open. They're very bloodshot. "April," she croaks.

"I'm here, Mom," I say in a loud voice to make sure she can hear me. "I'm here for you. I'm always here for you."

"April, please." As opposed to the angry voice she used on camera, her voice is now a pleading whisper. "Please get me out of here. I don't want to be in this place anymore."

"I'm so sorry…"

"I don't have to live with you." Her words are coming out slurred. "I… I could get my own place. Somewhere far away. You'd never even have to see me. I wouldn't bother you. I promise."

Tears well up in my eyes. I remember how my mother used to walk me to the bus stop every single morning for school. My little hand would get swallowed up by her bigger hand, and I would feel so safe and secure. I just need her to be safe like that. But she doesn't understand.

"I'm sorry, Mom." I wipe the tears from my eyes with the back of my hand. "You have to stay here. It's the best thing."

But then her eyes flutter closed. And just like that, she's asleep.

My hands are still shaking as I leave the room. I wanted to include my mother in my show, but I can see now her dementia is too advanced. I can't attempt it again.

Dr. Williams sees how upset I am. He's perceptive

about things like that. He puts a hand on my shoulder again. "You can't let it get to you, April. You're doing the right thing."

I nod, not trusting myself to speak. Peggy is watching us and it makes me uncomfortable.

"It sounds like her paranoia is getting worse. I'm going to increase her scheduled antipsychotics." He takes a set of notes out of the pocket of his white coat and scribbles something down. "Hopefully she'll do better with that."

"Dr. Williams," I say, "isn't there anything we can do for her memory? Aren't there any treatments? A clinical trial she can be enrolled in? *Anything*?"

He shakes his head. "I'm afraid the treatments for dementia right now aren't great. We've already got her on Aricept and Namenda, and I haven't noticed any improvement. I think right now the best thing we can do for her is to manage her agitation. Before she hurts somebody… or herself."

"Okay… if you say so…"

He squeezes my shoulder. "Hang in there, April. I promise you this is the best thing for her. Don't beat yourself up."

I look in the room again, and my mother is now sound asleep. She looks peaceful. Dr. Williams is right. This is the best thing.

———

Before I leave Shady Oaks, I say goodbye to all the nurses and make sure they all try some of my cheesecake bites, and I let them know that the remainder of the no-bake cheesecake is in the fridge. The nurses at Shady Oaks are absolutely wonderful, and they take amazing care of my mother. I try to let them know how appreciated they are.

Elliot sometimes tells me I go overboard bringing treats for everyone, but I love doing it, and honestly, who doesn't like treats? Everyone appreciates it. And it's what I do.

When I get to the reception area, Delilah gives me a big smile. "So how did the filming go?"

"It got a little dicey," I admit. "My mom just wasn't... She was having a bad day." I swallow a lump in my throat. "Maybe she's getting too sick to do the shows."

"Oh, April..." Delilah reaches out to pat my hand. "You know how it is. There are good days and bad days. Dr. Williams will take care of her."

"I know. You're right."

Bobby is sitting quietly next to Delilah, drawing something that looks like a dinosaur fighting a ninja turtle. His tongue is sticking out of his mouth as he concentrates. He looks a lot like Elliot at this moment. Which makes me miss my husband. I feel like I've been seeing him even less than usual lately.

And then an idea occurs to me. Something that will cheer me up after this disastrous afternoon.

"Hey, Bobby," I say. "Do you want to go stop by Dad's

work? It's on the way home. And you haven't seen his office in years."

Bobby's eyes light up. "Yeah!"

I'm relieved. It was equally likely that he would think my idea was boring and lame.

It's a great plan. Brianna has been a total bitch to me, but she'll be nice to Bobby. She won't keep Bobby from seeing his father.

We hop back in the car and make the ten-minute drive to Elliot's office. I arrive at the parking lot of the building that houses Elliot's office just after four o'clock. It's good timing—he should be done with all his meetings for the day.

Just as I'm parking in the lot, I see a couple standing right outside the building. It takes me a second to recognize my husband and his beautiful blond secretary. I kill the engine and watch them for a moment through my windshield.

He's standing incredibly close to her. They're talking softly, and at one point, she reaches out and straightens his tie. It's such an intimate gesture.

Then Elliot makes a beeline for his car, gets inside, and drives off.

"Mom, aren't we getting out of the car?"

Bobby has gotten out of his booster seat and he's fumbling with the door lock. "Don't open the door!" I snap at him.

His eyes grow wide. "Why can't I open the door?"

Brianna is standing outside the building, just watching Elliot's car drive off. There's a distinctly proprietary expression on her pretty features.

"Why aren't we getting out of the car?" Bobby demands to know.

"I…" I swallow a lump in my throat. "It turns out Dad isn't here. We're going home."

Bobby cries in protest, but I don't care. I start up my engine and get the hell out of there.

CHAPTER 21

Dear residents of Pine Street,

Just a reminder for those of you with pets or who are considering purchasing pets:

There are no loud noises such as barking permitted on the block after 10 PM.

Please don't leave fecal matter from your dog on the street for the rest of us to clean up.

Pets should never be outside of the house without a leash. If they are in your backyard, I would expect them to be tied to a tree by their leash.

There is a limit to one dog per household.

Prior to purchasing a pet, you must submit a written application to the block captain (Julie Bressler). Your application must include the breed, weight, and size of the animal.

Sincerely,
Julie Bressler, Block Captain

This afternoon, Sean took the boys to the park to practice soccer.

I felt a bit uneasy about the whole thing, because Maria and Sean have been treating me somewhat coldly lately. I don't know why, because I'm perfectly nice to them both. It seems like Maria goes out of her way to avoid me lately.

Anyway, Maria is at work this afternoon, so it was just Sean and the boys. And Bobby was so excited about it, there was no way I could say no.

Also, the fall carnival is next weekend, and between helping organize that and squeezing in an extra episode of *Sweet Secrets* to make up for the one I didn't get to do at the nursing home, I've been overwhelmed. Two of our volunteers just backed out this week, so right now, I'm going to be selling tickets and also running the bake sale. And of course, I've got the silent auction to worry about. Helping with this carnival is a job in itself.

On the plus side, I haven't gotten any more mysterious text messages. Maybe whoever was harassing me decided I've had enough.

After spending the whole afternoon making calls to some of our sponsors and confirming the inflatable company got their payment, I decide to relax a bit with some baking. I pull out my recipe for a pineapple upside-down cake, which I haven't made in ages. I absolutely love pineapple upside-down cake. The buttery, brown sugary pineapple juice that seeps down into the cake from the slices on top make the cakes so moist, soft, and buttery. I did a show on pineapple upside-down cake last year. My secret is using tons of butter, and also substituting pineapple juice in the recipe for water.

And as luck would have it, it's cooling off just as it's time to pick up Bobby from the Cooper house.

I put the upside-down cake onto a plate and carry it over to the Cooper house. I remember how excited Sean was over my apple turnovers, so I figure he'll really enjoy this. Nothing makes me happier than somebody who loves my cooking.

I ring the doorbell with my right hand while balancing the cake on my left. After a few moments, the door swings open and Sean is standing there wearing jeans and a T-shirt, except the T-shirt does very little to conceal the muscles in his chest. His eyes widen when he sees the cake.

"I brought you an upside-down cake," I announce. "Fresh out of the oven."

"Wow…" He steps back to let me inside. "That looks great. But… well, I don't want to spoil dinner. So I better not."

"One piece isn't going to spoil your dinner!"

"Yeah…" He runs a hand through his thick brown hair. It makes me miss when Elliot used to have hair. "I better not."

Wow, great. Now what am I supposed to do with this huge cake? "Maybe I'll just leave it in the kitchen then. You can have some after dinner."

"Okay." Sean follows me to the kitchen, and while I gently lower my cake onto the counter, he hollers out to Bobby in the backyard that his mother is waiting. "He says he's coming."

"Okay, thanks."

He rifles through some papers on the kitchen counter. "Hey, can I ask you something?"

My stomach flutters. "Yes?"

He picks up a piece of paper and shakes it in his hand. "So I mentioned to Julie when I saw her the other day on the street that we were thinking about getting a dog. And today I found this taped to our door. Is she for real with this?"

I take the piece of paper. It's Julie's standard dog rules. "No, it's not a joke."

"Who does she think she is?" He shakes the paper again and it crumbles in his big hands. "I'm not submitting an *application* to her. It's my house and my property. If I want a dog, I'll get a goddamn dog."

"You should." It will drive Julie absolutely crazy. "You should get a pit bull."

He grins crookedly. He has a very cute smile. "You know, I think I will."

I really, really hope he gets a pit bull.

"Anyway." Sean looks down at the cake and then back at me. "So… are you going to grab Bobby or…? Because Owen has to get started on his homework…"

And that's when I realize he wants me out of here. He wants me to take my kid and get out. He doesn't want to sit around eating slices of pineapple upside-down cake. He doesn't want to chitchat about our kids. He wants me to go. *Now*.

"April?"

I startle at the sound of Maria's voice. Where did she come from? Why didn't I hear her key in the lock? Or her feet on the floor behind me? All of a sudden, she's just *there*.

"Hi, Maria!" I say in my most chipper voice. I whirl around to look at her, and she doesn't look happy. I'd say she looks downright pissed off. "You're home… early."

"Yes," she says. "That I am."

"Hey, hon." Sean goes right over to her and tries to put his arm around her waist, but she pulls away from him. He looks uncomfortable and scratches at his beard. "How was work?"

"Fine." Maria's brown eyes are still focused on me. "And how was your day?"

Before Sean can answer, I pipe up, "Sean brought the boys to the park. And I was picking up Bobby, so I brought over some pineapple upside-down cake."

"How nice," Maria murmurs.

And then we all just stand there in horrible,

uncomfortable silence.

Thankfully, the silence is broken by the boys finally storming back into the house. Both of their sneakers are caked in dirt, and my heart bleeds for Maria's floor, but she doesn't seem to care. She wants me out of here. They both do.

I don't get it. I wasn't doing anything wrong. I just came in to pick up my son and drop off some cake. Is that a crime? Yes, I was alone with her husband, but so what? It's not like we were *kissing*. He was barely even tolerating me.

"Bobby," I say in that same high-pitched chipper voice. I can't seem to make my voice normal again. I've lost the ability. "It's time to go home!"

"No!" Bobby stomps his sneakers on the floor, which isn't making the dirt situation better. "I want to stay. Can we stay for dinner, Mom? Please?"

Oh *God*, no. "I'm afraid not. Maybe another time."

"Why not?"

Would it be too much to hope for that just one time Bobby would accept my telling him no without asking why not? "Because we're busy tonight."

"We are? Busy doing what?"

"Busy having dinner as a family."

"But we can do that any night. Why can't we have dinner here tonight?"

Sean and Maria are both staring at me, waiting to hear what bullshit I'll come up with. "We'll do it another night."

"Why not tonight?"

"Because it's too last minute."

"So?"

Sometimes I want to throttle that kid. "I told you, Bobby, we'll do it another night!"

"When?"

Guh! Finally, miraculously, Maria takes pity on me. She bends down to talk to my son. "How about sometime next week, Bobby? We can order pizza."

If I said that, I'm sure he would've pressed me harder for a day, but he's better behaved around strangers than his own parents. He nods, and for the moment, that's the end of it.

Maria walks us to the front door so she can lock it behind us. I keep looking over at her, trying to read her expression. When I first met Maria, she seemed so sweet and uncomplicated. Now I don't know what to think anymore. I can't stop thinking about what she did to that babysitter in her store. And now she seems to have a problem with *me*.

And there's something about this house that makes me nervous too. Something I can't entirely put my finger on.

"Maria." I offer her my warmest smile when we get to the door—one I usually reserve for the camera. "Thank you so much for having Bobby over this afternoon."

She doesn't return the smile. "Well, Sean was the one watching them."

"Yes, but…" I take a deep breath. "I just wanted to tell you how nice it is having you next door. It's nice having a friend who lives so close."

"Yes." She still isn't smiling. "It *is* nice."

"Really." I know I should probably shut up, but I can't help babbling on. "This is exactly what I always wanted. I don't think I told you this, but for years, we had a neighbor living here who was just so unpleasant…"

"Doris Kirkland," she says.

I stop, my mouth hanging open. "Oh. I didn't know you knew her."

And then I think back to the other day, when Mrs. Kirkland's niece came by. How she had been talking about the life alert necklace. *She was scared about breaking a hip, you know? I couldn't believe she didn't have it on.*

If this were a movie, I'd say for sure somebody pushed her.

"Well, we bought the house from her niece." Maria shrugs. "Guess the name must've come up."

Coming over here with my pineapple upside-down cake was a mistake. I sort of want to go back to the kitchen and retrieve it, but I don't dare.

"Anyway," I say. "I just wanted to say thank you for being a good neighbor and… well, that's all."

Finally, Maria's lips curl into a smile. "It's nice having you as a neighbor too."

And then I get the hell off her front porch.

CHAPTER 22

Julie and Maria are coming over today to help do some last-minute planning for the fall carnival in a few days. I was nervous about having Maria over after that weird encounter when she found me and Sean alone in her kitchen, but she seemed perfectly normal at school drop off the next day. So it was hard to argue when Julie insisted we needed to talk about the carnival. It's always difficult to say no to Julie.

With everything going on, I have let cleaning fall to the wayside. We do have a cleaning woman who comes once a week, but in between, the house gets cluttered with Bobby's toys and the floors get muddy with his footprints. And everything gets so *sticky*. I swear, that child's hands are perpetually sticky.

It takes me about two hours to put away all of Bobby's toys, mop the floors, and vacuum, and I clean the kitchen and bathrooms top to bottom. At first, I tried to get Bobby to help, but that was a lost cause. And then I make a flourless chocolate cake. That is Julie's absolute favorite thing. It's the only thing she says is "worth the calories."

Maria and Julie are supposed to arrive at three o'clock, so by a quarter to three, I've got everything perfect. My house is sparkling clean, Bobby is occupied up in his room, and the cake is out of the oven. I'm about to sit down on the sofa to relax a bit before they arrive when my phone buzzes on the coffee table. I have a text message. From a blocked number.

Want to know a secret, April?

I stare down at the phone, frowning. I see the three dots, which means the person is still typing. I hold my breath, terrified to see what it's going to appear on the screen next. It's been such a long time since I got a text message from this person. I thought they had decided to leave me alone.

And then the words appear on the screen:

There's a surprise buried in your backyard.

I inhale sharply. What does that mean? A surprise in my *backyard*?

I look down at my watch. I still have at least ten minutes before Julie and Maria arrive. I'm not going to be able to concentrate if I don't check my backyard.

I hurry out the back door into our huge backyard. We hire a professional to mow our lawn because both Elliot and I are hopeless at gardening. So the grass is freshly trimmed, and it's a vivid shade of green. Well, all of it except for one little area.

I step out onto the lawn, feeling the soft grass crunch under my feet. There's a little patch, no more than a foot wide, where the grass has been uprooted. The dirt is loose, like somebody had been digging there.

Oh my God, what is in my backyard?

I run over to the corner of the yard, where we have a shovel that can be used for gardening and digging out the car in the winter. I don't have much time, but I have to see what's buried in my yard. I won't be able to think straight until I do.

I mean, it can't be a dead body. It's not big enough for that.

The dirt comes away easily. Somebody was digging here very recently. Maybe even today. I shovel out some of the dirt, wondering how deep I'll have to go. Then I shovel another mound of dirt. And another. And another.

And then my shovel hits something.

My hands are shaking as I reach down into the small hole I've created. I brush away some dirt, and then my hand touches fabric. I wrap my fingers around the object and I pull it loose.

"Raffey!"

In my determination to dig out the object, I hadn't realized Julie and Maria had come into my backyard. And now Maria is staring at the dirt-caked stuffed animal in my hand, her face pink.

"Maria," I sputter. "I…"

"I *knew* Bobby must've taken him," Julie says, almost triumphantly.

Maria marches over to me and yanks the dirty stuffed animal out of my hand. She looks down at the dirty giraffe, and her eyes fill with tears. "Look at it. How will I get this clean?"

"Actually," I say, "the secret to cleaning stuffed animals is to get a mesh laundry bag and—"

"Oh, shut *up*, April," Julie snaps at me.

I jerk my head back like she slapped me. I squeeze my fists together, not sure what to say or do. I wish I could tell them about the text messages, but I can't take that risk. Not with that picture of me and Mark floating around. "I don't know how this got in my backyard," I finally say. "But I'm sure Bobby didn't…"

"Oh, please!" Julie huffs. "The toy was buried in your backyard? How else could it have gotten there? Unless you have a dog we don't know about."

"I've got to get this clean," Maria mumbles. She doesn't lift her eyes to look at me. "I can't stay."

"We'll reschedule." Julie's voice is so kind and gentle, I almost don't recognize it. "Don't even worry about it."

I feel a lump in my throat. "I… I'm so sorry, Maria."

She nods, but she still doesn't look at me.

The two of them go out through the backyard without even passing through the house. I just spent two hours cleaning and they didn't even come into my house. All because of that stupid toy in the backyard. How did it get here anyway? Could Bobby really have buried it there?

But no. I got that text message about it. Whoever is torturing me put that stuffed animal in my backyard, just to humiliate me in front of my friends.

Which means whoever is sending me these messages was in my backyard.

I stand in the middle of my backyard, my hands coated in dirt, and I shiver. I run back into the house and find my phone on the coffee table where I left it. My hands are almost too shaky to type in my reply:

Please tell me what you want.

As usual, there is no reply.

CHAPTER 23

To: Fall Carnival Committee
From: Alice Knowles
Subject: Re: Carnival

I am supposed to help out tomorrow at the fall carnival at the beanbag toss. But I noticed tonight that I have a bit of a scratchy throat, so I don't think I'm going to be able to make it.

To: Fall Carnival Committee
From: Patty Westman
Subject: Re: Carnival

I was supposed to make brownies for the carnival, but I just realized that I don't have any eggs in the house! So unfortunately, I'm not going to be able to bring brownies as promised. That is, unless somebody wants to come to my house and bring me some eggs!

To: Fall Carnival Committee
From: Teresa Yu
Subject: Re: Carnival

I just realized that this weekend is my parents'
anniversary! I was supposed to volunteer at the bouncy
house for the 2-3 PM shift, but I can't do it because of
this prior obligation.

To: Fall Carnival Committee
From: Julie Bressler
Subject: Re: Carnival

The grocery store sells eggs, Patty.
Can anybody take Teresa's shift at the bouncy house?

To: Fall Carnival Committee
From: April Masterson
Subject: Re: Carnival

No worries, Patty! I'll make extra brownies!

To: Fall Carnival Committee
From: Sean Cooper
Subject: Re: Carnival

I am doing the 1-2 PM shift at the bouncy house, so I'll do Teresa's shift after. Unless it turns out to be my parents' anniversary too.

The fall carnival takes place on the first weekend of November.

It's a massive event. Because of the chilly weather, everything is set up in the large gymnasium of the elementary school. There are two bouncy houses (one for jumping and one with a slide), loads of games, and I am manning—what else?—the bake sale. People were supposed to bring in baked goods early this morning, but unfortunately, nobody ever does what they say they're going to do. But I have enough experience now that I anticipated it, so about three-quarters of the food on the table was made by me. I spent most of the morning baking.

The silent auction is still going as well and will be active until midnight. We're going to announce the winners tomorrow. I think we're going to break some records.

Strangely enough, the bake sale is not going very well. Usually, half the food is gone by an hour into the carnival. And I made all the baked goods everybody loves. I don't understand why nobody is buying anything. I've sold only one brownie and two cookies.

"Would you care for any baked goods?" I call to Carmen Landers, who is passing by the table with her five-year-old son. "We've got just about everything!"

"Mommy, I want a brownie!" the little boy cries. "The one with M&Ms!"

I did make two kinds of brownies. One with M&Ms and one without.

Carmen looks down at the table, then up at me, and she flashes me an uncomfortable smile. "I don't think it's a good idea."

"But Mommy—"

But Carmen is yanking her son away from the table, even as he's crying for a brownie. What's going on? Every other game or event seems to be doing great. Only the bake sale is crashing and burning. I don't get it.

And then Carrie comes over, looking much more tired and probably a lot older than the infamous babysitter. I feel desperate to make a sale, so I shove a tray of blondies in her direction. "I made your favorite," I say.

"Um." Carrie frowns. "I... uh, I'll pass."

What is going on here? "Are you sure? You love my blondies!"

She furrows her brow. "April, are you sure you should be here?"

I put my hands on my hips. "What are you talking

about?"

"After what you posted on the school Facebook page, I figured you wouldn't show up…"

What?

Immediately, I'm fumbling with my phone, loading the school Facebook page. I see all the notices on Facebook about the auction and the carnival. And sure enough, there's a post from April Masterson:

OMG, you guys, I have never been so sick. I have been throwing up for the last 12 hours! Baking and G.I. bugs don't go well together!

My mouth falls open. "I… I didn't make that post."

Carrie's eyes widen. "Really?"

I click on the name April Masterson. It opens up a Facebook profile set to private. The profile photo is the same as mine, but it's clearly a dummy account. Somebody set it up to make that post. And God knows what else they've posted. I'll have to contact the principal to have the account taken off the school's Facebook page.

"Who would do that?" Carrie says.

I shake my head weakly. "I… I have no idea. I guess somebody thought it would be a funny prank. But I swear, I don't have a G.I. bug. Can you please buy a blondie?"

"Of course!"

Carrie makes a show out of giving me the money for a blondie, then she picks one up from the tray. But I follow her with my eyes and the second she gets away from me, she tosses it in the trash. I guess I can't blame her.

I don't know what to do now. Even if I got the post removed at this point, it's too late. Everyone has already seen it. What am I supposed to do? Put a sign on my table saying "I didn't actually spend the last twelve hours vomiting." I feel like that will only make things worse.

I can't believe I made all this food for nothing.

But it's fine. I enjoy the bake sale, but the real moneymaker is the silent auction. And we're going to clean up on that one. The bidding for the Yankees tickets is really out of control.

After Carrie wanders away, I scan the crowd of children and parents milling around. The bake sale is outside of the gymnasium, but I can see inside if I crane my neck. I've been looking for Maria, but I haven't seen her since I've been here. I haven't seen her since she caught me unearthing Raffey from my backyard. I've been desperate to find a way to apologize for that. I also want to tell her that I spoke to Bobby, who has sworn he didn't have anything to do with it, but she probably wouldn't believe me

Remembering how much Maria liked my apple turnovers at the book club, I put a couple of them in a napkin and head into the gym. I know she's volunteering there. Maybe she'll appreciate it if I bring her some sustenance. After I explain that I don't actually have a vomiting illness.

I find Maria at the table with the raffle bags. She's sitting behind the table, next to Julie. Apparently, they are doing the raffle together. I didn't realize that. And as I approach, I notice they're deep in conversation. Maria says something, and Julie laughs. It's a genuine laugh—not Julie's usual sarcastic laugh.

It's been months—maybe years—since I've heard Julie laugh that way.

I wave to try to catch Maria's eye when I get close enough. She doesn't smile or wave back, but we make eye contact. She looks right at me. Then she lowers her head and says something else to Julie. Julie glances my way, then laughs again.

Are they *laughing* at me?

I lift my chin and stride over to them. I plaster a smile on my face, even though I'm feeling very self-conscious. I should have dressed up more, like both of them did. I thought it would be enough to wear my skinny jeans and a nice cashmere sweater. I mean, I don't want to get chocolate all over my best clothing…

"Hi!" I say brightly. "How's it going?"

Julie frowns at me. "April, I don't understand why you came to the bake sale if you're sick. It's very irresponsible of you."

I grit my teeth. "I'm not sick."

"But you said on Facebook that you've been vomiting for the last twelve hours."

"That wasn't me." I hate the whining edge in my voice.

"Somebody was impersonating me. It must've been a joke."

"Mmm." Julie looks away and fiddles with one of the raffle bags. "Fine. Then maybe you should get back to the bake sale."

"Just taking a break!" I hold out the apple turnovers. "Would you guys like a sample from the table?"

Maria barely looks at me. Julie eyes the turnovers then shakes her head. "No, thank you."

"Um, okay." I stand there awkwardly for a moment with the apple turnovers in my hand. "It seems like the carnival is a huge success though. You did an amazing job, Julie."

If there's one thing I know Julie loves, it's compliments.

"We *all* did an amazing job, April," she says. "It wasn't just me putting this together. I couldn't have done it without help from all the other parents."

And she smiles at Maria. Even though I did half the freaking work for this carnival.

"Well!" My cheeks are starting to hurt from smiling. "I guess I'll get back to the bake sale."

"You do that," Julie says.

My cheeks are burning as I walk back across the gym. I can't believe the way Maria snubbed me. Julie and I used to be so close—she was the one who told everyone in town to watch *Sweet Secrets* and helped me make the show a success. She's been my best friend for five years! But now that Maria is around, it's like I can't do anything right in her eyes.

I can only imagine what Maria has been saying to her about me. I don't know how that stupid giraffe ended up in my backyard. It wasn't Bobby's fault, and it definitely wasn't *my* fault.

Tears are pricking at my eyes. I certainly don't want to go back to the bake sale, where everybody is staring at me like I have the plague.

So instead of leaving the gym, I hang right. That's where the bouncy houses are. Where Sean is doing his second shift, since Teresa backed out. But he doesn't look like he's getting too burned out. He's teasing this little girl about her sparkly pink shoes, and she's giggling. He's really good with kids. And he's such a good dad.

Meanwhile, my husband isn't here at all. He's working. Obviously.

Sean knocks on the door to the bouncy house. "Hey! Sixty more seconds of bouncing then everybody out for the new group! Time to go crazy!"

I take a deep breath and walk over to Sean, who seems taken aback to see me. He *literally* takes a step back.

"Hi," I say.

"Uh, hi, April," he says.

He must think I have the plague, like everyone else. "I guess you saw that post on Facebook," I say.

He frowns. "Facebook? No, I don't have a Facebook account."

Oh, thank God.

"Lucky you." I snort. "So how is it going over here? Looks like fun."

"Yeah…" He rubs at the back of his neck as he avoids my eyes. "It's pretty busy."

"Well, I don't want to interrupt or anything. I just thought you might enjoy a snack." I hold out the turnovers, wrapped in a napkin. "It's those apple turnovers you loved the other night. I saved some for you."

Actually, there's a whole pile of them back at the bake sale table. But he doesn't need to know that.

I had hoped Sean's eyes would light up like they did that night of the book club, but instead, he takes another step back. "I better not."

I look back at the raffle table. Sure enough, Maria's eyes are on my back. I turn back to Sean, my own eyes narrowing. "Did Maria tell you not to talk to me?"

"What? No."

Liar. "So why don't you want a turnover?"

"I just…" He shrugs. "I just don't. I'm not hungry."

"Fine." I almost crumble the turnovers in my hands. "Are you picking up Bobby to go play soccer at the park tomorrow?"

He drops his eyes. "Uh, I was thinking it would just be me and Owen tomorrow. Just some one-on-one time. Sorry about that."

The tears in my eyes are getting dangerously close to

the surface. "I see…"

"Look," he mumbles, "I've got to get back to work…"

And then he turns away from me to deal with the bouncy house. Our discussion is over.

Fine. I'll just eat them myself. Who needs to be able to button my pants?

Nobody stole any food from the bake sale table while I was gone. If anything, it looks like there's somehow more food on the table than there was before. What am I going to do with all this food? I can't even give it away.

"Mom! Mom!" It's Bobby. I haven't seen him in half an hour, because he's been off playing with his friends. The fact that he's returned could mean only one thing. "I need more tickets to go on the bouncy slide!"

I wince. "Bobby, I gave you forty dollars' worth of tickets!"

"Yes, but everything costs so many tickets." He pouts. "I need more. Leo and Owen are going… I don't want to be left out…"

That one tugs at my heartstrings. Especially since I just got left out by Leo and Owen's mothers. So I reach into my pocket and pull out the tickets I had been planning to use to enter the raffles. "Fine. But this is all I've got."

I guess I won't be entering any raffles. Not that I would dare go near that raffle table again.

My heart isn't in this carnival right now. Nobody is buying any of my baked goods, and people look like they're afraid to even breathe the same air as me. I can barely manage a smile. It's not like I'm the sort of person who feels like they need to be loved by everyone. But…

Well, maybe I do feel like I need to be loved by everyone.

Maybe I should go. I'll give Bobby a chance to go on the slide with his friends, then I'm going to abandon my station here and just leave. Nobody will even notice I'm gone. I start to put the money away, and that's when I hear the loud thump from inside the gym.

All of a sudden, there's a hush within the gym. Broken only by the sound of somebody shouting to call 911.

CHAPTER 24

Of course, my first thought is of Bobby.

He's in the gym. I saw him go into the gym. Bobby could be hurt.

It's my only thought as I abandon the bake sale table and race into the gym. I feel the same cold fear I did that day when Bobby disappeared from the backyard. Please, God, let him be okay. Not that I want some other kid to be hurt, but I really, really don't want it to be mine.

And my prayers are answered. As I enter the gym, I see Bobby on the sidelines. He is sobbing, but he's not hurt. He's not part of the mob of parents surrounding the injured party. I race over to him and throw my arms around his skinny frame. He's so shaken that he doesn't even squirm to get away.

"Did you see what happened?" I ask him.

"Leo…" Bobby gulps. "Leo… fell. Off the slide."

He must be talking about Leo Bressler. I follow his gaze to the bouncy house slide. The top of the slide is at least eight feet in the air. There's a mat below, but it's still a big fall.

Owen Cooper is standing nearby as well. He isn't crying like Bobby though. He's looking down at his dirty sneakers. I wonder if the boys were with Leo when he fell. If so, they're probably both traumatized by the whole thing.

Sean emerges from the crowd, looking a little pale. I still feel the sting of humiliation from the way he rejected me earlier, but I push it aside. "Is Leo okay?" I ask him.

He doesn't answer right away, which really scares me. "He has a broken arm," he finally says. "I'm going outside to wait for the ambulance so they know where to find him."

"Did you see it happen?"

He shakes his head. "I was at the other bouncy house." He rests a hand on Owen's shoulder. "Why don't you come outside with me, Owen?"

Owen's lower lip trembles. He looks up at his father and blurts out, "Bobby pushed him!"

What?

"No, I didn't!" Bobby screams through his tears. "*You* pushed him!"

Owen slowly shakes his head. "No. It was Bobby. Bobby pushed Leo off the slide because it wasn't his turn."

"Bobby." I look at my son's tear-streaked face. "Did you push Leo off the slide?"

"No!" He wipes snot from his little nose with the back of his hand. "I didn't! It was Owen. I swear!"

I look over at Sean, who has a weary expression on his face. "It doesn't matter right now whose fault it is. I'm going outside to wait for the ambulance."

I look wildly into the crowd. Quite a few people are staring at us and heard Owen's declaration. But they can't possibly believe Bobby to be the one at fault, could they? Bobby has been going to the school for over two years, while Owen is the new kid. They must believe Bobby over Owen, right?

Before I know what I'm doing, I find myself pushing through the crowd surrounding Leo Bressler. After that little production, people seem willing to part to let me through. After a minute of pushing, I see him. Seven-year-old Leo, lying on the ground, sobbing and clutching his arm.

Well, at least he's alive.

Julie is bent down next to him, stroking his tawny hair. But when I get closer, her eyes snap up to look at me. And they're boiling with hatred.

"Look at what Bobby did," she hisses at me. "He should be expelled."

"Bobby didn't do anything," I say in a tiny voice.

Julie puts a possessive arm around Leo's shoulders as he sobs louder. "I should have you arrested for assault."

"Assault?" I take a step back. "You can't have a seven-year-old child arrested for assault!"

Julie narrows her eyes at me. "Not Bobby. *You.*"

I have made an extremely powerful enemy.

"Julie." I'm trying not to sound desperate, but it's hard. "Bobby didn't do this. You have to believe me."

But my pleas are interrupted by the arrival of the ambulance. The EMTs lift Leo onto a stretcher, and Julie hurries along with them. I watch them leave, keeping my fingers and my toes crossed that Leo is going to be okay. That even if his arm is broken, it will just be something simple that requires a splint or cast—not surgery.

Just as the crowd is dispersing, I see Maria in the corner of the room. She's talking quietly to Owen. I don't know what she is saying, but he keeps nodding solemnly. Then she squeezes his shoulder, and she gives him a hug.

I try to catch Maria's attention. I need to talk to her about what just happened. I wave my arm frantically, hoping she'll notice me. For a split second, our eyes lock. But then she looks away, and the next thing I know, she's gone.

CHAPTER 25

Comment on *April's Sweet Secrets* YouTube video "Making Whoopie Pies with Bobby":

Want to know a secret about Bobby Masterson? He's not so sweet at all.

But I don't know if that's a secret.

Desperate times call for apple pie.

Leo got out of the hospital yesterday, after only an overnight stay, but he still hasn't been back at school. It was the best possible situation though—he did need a cast, but no surgery. That's what I heard, anyway. Not from Julie, of course. One of the other mothers told me at pick-up today from school.

So I decided to make an apple pie for Julie. Aside from

my flourless chocolate cake, she has also commented positively and consistently about my apple pie. I make a really good apple pie. The key is to make a really good crust. My secret is that when I cut the butter into the flour, I stop when the butter crumbs are the size of peas. The little pea-sized pieces of butter melt in the oven and create delicious little buttery air pockets.

Elliot wanders into the kitchen just as I'm pulling the pie out of the oven. Usually, I let it cool for a couple of hours, but it's getting late and I need to get this pie over to Julie, so I take one of my handheld fans and point it at the pie. My dream, when I have the funds, is to get a blast chiller for my kitchen.

"Yum, pie," Elliot comments. "When do I get a piece?"

"Never. I'm bringing this over to Julie."

He groans. "Come on, April. You're not really going over there, are you?"

"Why not?"

"As your attorney, I would advise against it."

I roll my eyes. "Stop it. Julie is my best friend."

"You always say that." Elliot rubs at the back of his scalp. "But from what I can tell, the two of you hate each other. And right now, she's got a good reason to hate you."

"But she's wrong!" I plant my hands on my hips. "She thinks Bobby pushed Leo, but he didn't."

Elliot raises an eyebrow. "He didn't?"

"You really think our son would do something like

that?"

He shrugs. "Maybe. You never played soccer with that kid. He's out for blood."

I glare at him. "Whose side are you on?"

Fine." He reaches a hand for the pie, and I smack it away. "So what do you think happened? Leo just fell off?"

"No." I take a deep breath. "I think Owen Cooper pushed him. And told everybody that Bobby did it."

"So Owen framed Bobby?" Elliot is smirking now. "That's what you think?"

"Yes. It is."

"I see." He nods. "And what about Leo? Who does Leo say pushed him?

"Leo's back was turned. So he didn't see."

"Ah. So there were no witnesses."

I narrow my eyes. "I feel like you're not taking this seriously."

"On the contrary," he says. "I'm taking this *very* seriously. And I'm telling you very seriously that Julie could sue us. So I think you should stay the hell away from her until she cools off. Okay?"

"Fine," I agree. "As soon as I bring her this pie, I'll stay away from her."

"April…"

"Just trust me on this, Elliot."

He shakes his head at me, but he underestimates the power of the pie. Julie and I are best friends, and if I come over with a peace offering and I explain to her my side of the story (or Bobby's side), she'll be reasonable. Granted, Julie does not have a history of being reasonable. But I can talk her around.

After about forty-five minutes, the pie is cool enough that I can carry it over to Julie's house. I walk up the steps to her front door, squinting through the spotless window panes surrounding the entrance. Without a doubt, Julie and Keith have the nicest house on the block. There was a different house here originally, but they tore it down and built a new one from scratch to their specifications. Our house is nice, but it isn't as perfect and shiny and sprawlingly large as the Bresslers' house.

The lights are on inside, and I ring the doorbell, which I can hear chiming throughout their massive house. I wait for a minute, and part of me is starting to get worried that Julie is not going to open the door for me. She finally does, although she doesn't look pleased. Her usually perfect brown hair is looking a little dank and stringy, and there are purple circles under her eyes.

"Hi, Julie!" I plaster on my absolute best smile. "I heard Leo was home and I just wanted to see how he was doing." I hold out the pie. "And bring you this. Your favorite. Well, second favorite."

She looks down at the pie but makes no move to take it from me. "Leo broke his arm. So that's how he's doing."

I pull a sympathetic face. "Poor lamb. Is he in a lot of pain?"

Her lips turn down into a frown. "Yes, he has pain. He broke his arm."

"Oh. Of course, but—"

"Thanks to your son."

I suck in a breath. This is my chance. This is my opportunity to tell her Bobby's side of the story. "Look, Julie. I know what Owen has been saying. But Bobby didn't push Leo. He swears he didn't."

Julie just snorts.

"Bobby wouldn't lie."

"Oh, wouldn't he?" Her voice is laced with sarcasm. "Yes, he's a little angel. We both saw how he almost broke Leo's nose at soccer."

"That was an accident!"

"Well, it does seem like a lot of accidents happen when Bobby and Leo are playing, doesn't it?"

The pie trembles in my hands. This isn't going how I hoped it would. But I push forward. "Look," I say, "I think the kid who pushed Leo off the slide was Owen Cooper."

Her eyes fly open. "Owen? You think that sweet little boy would push Leo?"

"He's not as sweet as you think. He pushed Bobby off the swing and Bobby had scrapes all over him." I glance over at the Cooper house. "Owen's the one who pushed Leo, and then he lied and said Bobby did it."

Julie is staring at me, and I wonder if I got through to her. Bobby and Leo have been friends forever, and Owen has only been around for a couple of months. She has to believe me over them, right?

But then she shakes her head. "You're unbelievable, April. You know, I thought you were coming over here to apologize. But instead of owning up to it, you've got some bullshit story to take the blame off your son."

My cheeks burn. "That's not what I'm doing… It's the *truth*, Julie!"

"Yeah, right." She puts her hand on the door frame. "I don't want Bobby playing with Leo anymore. Tell your kid to stay the hell away from mine, okay?"

I open my mouth to say something more, but Julie has slammed the door in my face.

Well, it looks like I made things worse. I hate it when Elliot is right.

CHAPTER 26

For the last two years and change, I've always walked Bobby right to the front door when I dropped him off at school. There is a drop-off line by the front entrance, but I always parked and walked him to the door. I always wanted to watch him go into the school, and there was the extra bonus of getting to chat with the other mothers.

But today, when I get to school, I don't want to get out of my car.

Leo is going back to school today. That means Julie will be there. And even without Julie, it's been awkward showing up at school since the accident. Everybody seems stiff and uncomfortable when I come over. Like *I* am the one who pushed poor Leo. It doesn't help that they all think I brought a bunch of contaminated food to the bake sale.

"I think we'll do the drop-off line today," I tell Bobby.

He's strapped into his booster seat in the back. He doesn't say anything when I make this suggestion. But he doesn't say *not* to do it. So I pull up alongside the school.

"Okay, honey!" I try to keep my voice as chipper as possible. "Have a wonderful day at school. I love you!"

Bobby doesn't budge.

That's unusual. Most days, he leaps out of the car and is running for the school, and I'm left racing to keep up. But now he is just sitting there in his booster seat, not making any moves to unbuckle himself.

"Bobby?" I don't have much time. This is not a parking area, and if I linger too long, other parents will start honking at me. "Time to get out."

He still doesn't budge. And now his lower lip is trembling.

Right on cue, somebody honks at me. "Bobby, honey, what's wrong?"

I hear another honk. Somebody yells something at me, possibly an obscenity.

"Bobby?"

He's just sitting there. His *Star Wars* backpack is on his left side, stuffed with God knows what. We need to go through that backpack tonight. Last time, I found the *rocks* inside. Like five legit rocks. But that's the least of our problems right now.

There's a rap at the passenger side window. It's a teacher.

"If you're not dropping off a child," the teacher says, "you need to park in a different area. This is the drop-off line."

"I understand that. But my son is very upset and—"

"But this is the drop-off line. We need to keep the line moving. If you're not getting out—"

"All right! I'll move!"

I throw the car back into drive. I pull out of the drive-through line and off to the side. My hands are shaking on the steering wheel. The early bell has already rung and we've got about five minutes before the late bell rings. I'll probably have to walk him in and get a tardy slip.

"Bobby," I say as calmly as I can. "What's wrong? Why don't you want to get out of the car?"

Finally, his little face crumples. Tears start to stream down his cheeks. "Everybody hates me!"

I can't believe what I'm hearing. Bobby has always been very popular. He's one of those kids everybody likes. He gets it from his father. "No, they don't. Why would you say that?

"They think that I pushed Leo. But I didn't!"

"Oh, Bobby…" I'm not sure entirely what to say. People always say "little kids, little problems" but this is a big problem. I don't know what kind of advice to give him when I'm not dealing with it any better than he is. "Listen, the other kids will forget all about it. I promise."

I end up going in the backseat and the two of us talk for another ten minutes. Part of me wonders if I should just take Bobby home for the day. On the other hand, why should he have to stay home? Bobby did nothing wrong.

Owen is the one behind everything.

I finally manage to persuade Bobby to go to school, and I have to walk him inside and he gets a tardy slip. His first tardy in over two years of school.

After sending Bobby off to his classroom, I'm about to leave for home, but then I see Julie Bressler coming out of the nurse's office. My first instinct is to cover my face and make a run for it. But of course, she sees me.

"April," she says. I take it as a positive she didn't ignore me.

"Hi, Julie." I force a smile, which is the hardest thing I've had to do yet today. "How are you?"

She ignores my question. "I need to speak to you."

"Um…" I shift in my flats. "Okay… when?"

"Now, if possible."

"Um, okay…"

I get a sick feeling in my stomach. Is she going to serve me with a lawsuit? How does that even work? Or maybe she believes me about Owen, and she's asking for my forgiveness.

No, not likely.

Whatever it is, I'm not sure I want to hear about it.

———

My legs feel like jello as I follow Julie to her office on the first floor. It's not really an office. It's just a spare room that they let the president of the PTA use for work, but she likes to call it her office, and I'm not going to argue with her. Sometimes I do think Julie ought to go back to practicing law.

The office consists of a small conference table, and Julie sits on one side of the table. She gestures at a chair on the other side. "Sit down," she says.

"No 'please'?"

My attempt at humor is met with silence. I slide into the chair, not a moment too soon because I feel like I can barely stand up. I'm getting upset over nothing though. Julie isn't serving me with a lawsuit—that doesn't make sense. She probably just wants my help with something for the PTA.

Julie leans forward in her seat and folds her hands together. The purple circles she had under her eyes yesterday are gone. She has the best makeup. "I want to talk to you about the silent auction."

My shoulders sag in relief. I knew it had to be PTA related. And the auction went amazing. She probably wants to start planning for the spring. "Yes?"

She pauses, her face a mask. "I was looking at the app you used to record the bids and accept money into the PTA fund. And I noticed that there was a second account recorded. That a percentage of the money was being filtered into an account that wasn't related to the school."

Any relief I had been feeling a moment ago has vanished. "What… what do you mean?"

Her eyes become slits. "I mean, somebody created

another bank account that's been stealing money from the silent auction that was supposed to have been going to the PTA."

I clasp a hand over my mouth. "Oh my God. Who would do something like that?"

"You. You did it."

I feel dizzy. I can't believe this is happening. It's like some sort of a horrible dream. "Do you think I've been stealing money from the PTA?"

Her lips are a straight line. "Yes. I do."

"Julie, I would *never* do that." My words are coming out in a jumbled rush. "You know you can trust me. I would *never* steal from the PTA. Why would I do something like that? Elliot and I have plenty of money. And I get all that advertising money from my show. It's crazy!"

"You're always talking about how Elliot is getting angry at you over your spending," she reminds me. "How you want to buy this or that for your show, but you can't afford it. Maybe you decided to skim a little off the top. I don't know. All I know is that money is missing, and you're the only one who had access to do it."

"But—" Something suddenly occurs to me. "Maria! She and I were working on the silent auction together! She also had access to the account."

Julie lets out a loud huff. "It wasn't Maria."

"How do you know?"

"Because it wasn't."

I nearly asked her how she could be so sure, but then it hits me. Everything suddenly makes sense. "Maria is the one who told you to look at the account, didn't she?"

She's silent for a moment. "I received an anonymous text message telling me to look into it."

My whole body goes cold. My anonymous tormentor has struck again. But now it seems like they have upped the ante once again. My head is spinning.

All I know is my gut is telling me Maria Cooper has something to do with this.

"Look," I say, "Maria set me up. She created this false account, then she 'discovered' it. And now it looks like I've been stealing money! But you have to know, I would *never* do something like that."

"April…"

"Maria is evil!" I spit out. "She… she's been tormenting me for months by sending me threatening text messages."

For the first time since I sat down with her, Julie seems slightly rattled. She's finally taking me seriously. "She has? How do you know?"

"I just do."

She frowns. "What sort of text messages? Can I see?"

I hesitate. "I… I deleted them."

"You deleted them? Why would you do that?"

I open my mouth, but I realize I don't have a great answer to that question. I can't tell her that I deleted them because whoever is texting me is reminding me about things that I would rather they not know. Things that could destroy my career and my marriage if it got out there.

"Look," I say, "you saw that Facebook post saying I had a stomach bug. I didn't make that post! Maria made it to torture me!"

"Hmm," Julie says. But I can tell I've lost her. I wish I hadn't deleted all those text messages. But at the same time, I could never show them to Julie.

There's a lump in my throat. "You've known me for years! You really believe her over me?"

Just like the other night when I came by with the pie, I'm holding my breath. Hoping our friendship holds more weight than Maria's claims.

"Listen, April." A deep groove forms between her eyebrows. "I'm not going to turn this matter over to the police, but I expect you to return the money. If you don't, well, then it will be a police matter."

"Return the money! But I don't have any money to return!"

"That's not my problem." She holds up her hands. "I'll give you five business days to give me a check. Then I'm going to the principal, and we'll be contacting the police. And obviously, you are no longer a part of the PTA. I'll be disabling all your access."

I don't want to cry in front of Julie, but if I don't get out of here quickly, it's going to happen. It's an unstoppable force.

"Julie," I gulp. "This is a huge mistake. Believe me…"

"I'm sorry." She gets to her feet. "The only reason I haven't gone straight to the police is that we're neighbors and I don't want a scandal. But I expect to get that money back."

Then she leaves the room without looking at me again. I'm surprised she left me alone in here. After all, I might steal everything that isn't nailed down.

I thought I would start crying as soon as she left, but now that she's gone, the tears aren't coming. The truth is, I'm not sad. I'm pissed off. Even though Julie denied it, I know Maria is behind this.

And I am going to confront her.

CHAPTER 27

Helena's looks busy, and I almost lose my nerve.

It's the middle of the morning, but apparently, it's peak shopping hours. At least half a dozen women are inside the small store, browsing the overpriced clothing and handbags. I remember how excited I was when Maria mentioned getting a discount to shop here. Back then, that was the most important thing to me.

I've got to get to the bottom of this. Maria has it out for me, and I don't understand why. Does it have something to do with Sean? Obviously, she doesn't like me being around her husband. But this seems rather extreme. And I was getting those text messages before I even met Sean Cooper. Did she just see me on my front lawn when she moved in and think to herself, "Hey, I'd like to ruin this woman's life!"

Or maybe she decided before that. I can't shake that familiar feeling I got when I first laid eyes on Maria.

And that first day, when I found Bobby in her house.

She claimed he had wandered over there, but Bobby said she had invited him. I dismissed it as a lie at the time because she sounded so sincere, but maybe he was telling the truth. Maybe it was all a trick to frighten me. After all, *somebody* sent me that text.

I take a deep breath and stride into Helena's. I catch sight of the row of scarves that I had been coveting for months and shake my head in disgust. I don't want anything from the store anymore. I just want Maria out of my life.

Maria is helping one of the customers. The customer is holding a handbag, and Maria is extolling the handbag's many virtues. She's smiling so that you can see her dimples. She looks sweet. Like the sort of person you would want to buy something from. Someone you can trust.

Ha.

I go over to the desk in the back to wait for her. I noticed her purse is hanging off the edge of the chair where she usually sits. That's when I remember that burner phone I found in her purse the other day. I bet I could find it and prove that she's the one who's been torturing me.

I take one last look to confirm she's distracted by the customer. Then I nudge her purse open, and sift through it with my right hand, all the while keeping my eyes on her. I feel her wallet, a pack of tissues, her regular iPhone, and her house keys. But that's it. No flip phone.

It's gone. Damn it. She must've hidden it away somewhere.

Fine. Maybe I'm not going to find any evidence but I don't need it—I can still confront her. I back away from the desk and walk right up to where she's still chatting up the customer.

I wait a couple of seconds for her to finish up, but I can't wait any longer than that. Now that I'm here and I'm doing this, I want to get it over with. "Maria," I say.

She turns her head and the smile immediately drops off her face. "April," she says. "I'm busy."

"I need to talk to you." I shift between my feet. "Please."

Maria sighs. She smiles politely at the customer. "Can you please excuse me for just a moment?"

Without looking at me, she stomps off to the side so we can have some privacy. I follow her, my stomach full of butterflies. Am I really going to do this? Am I really going to confront this woman?

Maria finally turns to look at me. She folds her arms across her chest. "What do you want, April?"

Somehow, I had expected Maria to be more defensive. I swallow hard. "I want to talk to you about the things you've been saying about me. And about the things your son has been saying about Bobby."

Her expression gives nothing away. "Yes. What is it?"

I frown. "Did you tell Julie I've been stealing money from the PTA?"

"I don't want to get involved in this. Really."

"Bullshit." I feel a vein start to throb in my temple. "You set me up. The same way Owen set Bobby up."

She laughs. "You've *got* to be kidding me. Owen is seven years old. What exactly are you accusing my son of?"

"I just... I know what you're up to. Why do you have it in for me? What did I ever do to you?" The vein starts to throb harder. "All I ever did was be friendly to you. I made Bobby be friends with your weirdo kid. I even got Owen on the soccer team."

"Gee, thanks. That was so kind of you. What a kind, *lovely* person you are."

"Is it because your husband thinks I'm attractive?" I remember the way Sean Cooper looked terrified to even breathe on me. "Is that why you hate me so much?"

Maria's jaw twitches. "Get out of my store."

"You won't get away with this." I jab her in the chest with my index finger. "Believe me, I'm going to make sure everybody knows exactly what kind of person you are."

I spin on my heel and walk away, before she can get in the last word. I head straight for the corner with the silk scarves, and I hide there for a few moments, trying to compose myself. It's not like me to talk to people like that— at all. I'm generally very timid.

But it felt pretty good.

Of course, I don't know what to do next. Maria has it out for me... but why? Did I do something to her?

Maybe the place to begin is with Mrs. Kirkland. I remember what her niece said when she came to visit about that life alert necklace.

She was scared about breaking a hip, you know? I couldn't believe she didn't have it on.

I wonder how bad Maria wanted to live in the house next to me…

Could it really be Maria who has been sending me those text messages and writing all those nasty comments on YouTube? Did she throw the rock through my window? It's so hard to imagine. I only met the woman a few months ago. How could she hate me enough to do something like that to me? Most people like me.

I shake my head. I've got to get out of here. I'm not thinking clearly right now. I'm going to go home, take a shower, and maybe bake some cookies. Something will come to me.

But as I reach the exit, an alarm sounds so loudly, they could probably hear it two stores down. I freeze, looking around, utterly confused.

That was the same sound that went off when the babysitter had that necklace in her purse. But I didn't…

"Ma'am?" It's the big guy who stands by the entrance. I see now that his ID badge says Bill. "Ma'am, can you step back inside the store please?"

I frown, clutching my handbag to my chest. "Okay, but I don't know what this is all about…"

"Ma'am, can you please open your purse?"

The few customers in the store have turned to look at

me. This is *so* embarrassing. And the fact that he keeps calling me "ma'am" is only making the situation worse.

"Of course," I murmur. "But I can assure you, there's nothing inside."

Maria has come to join us at the front of the store. Her eyes are cold, but I see a hint of a smile on her lips. I give my purse to Bill, who rifles through it. I feel so exposed. I just want to get this over with and get out of here. I'm starting to feel like this was all a big mistake. I shouldn't have come here in the first place. This is Maria's turf. I should have confronted her in a neutral place.

Every set of eyes in the store is on me. I recognize one of the mothers from school. This is not good. I remember when Bill nabbed that babysitter for stealing. The same exact thing happened to her. Everybody passing the store was staring at her as he searched her purse, the same way they're staring at me now.

And just like back then, Bill pulls a set of silver earrings out of my bag that is clearly from the store.

My heart sinks. Oh no.

"Ma'am," he says. "I'm going to need you to come to the back with me."

I can barely gasp for air. "But I didn't—"

"I'm afraid our policy is that we prosecute all shoplifters." Maria's voice is without emotion. "Bill, please call the police."

My heart is pounding in my chest. A photograph of me kissing another man is bad for my show, but a shoplifting arrest is even worse. Maria knows how horrible this will be for me. It's exactly what she did to the babysitter—only *I* know what she's done.

"You!" I point a finger at her. "You set me up again! You planted the earrings in my bag!"

Bill and Maria exchange looks. I sound like a crazy person. I'm sure that's what it seems like to everybody in the store.

"Ma'am." Bill places one of his meaty hands on my upper arm. "I'd like you to come to the back with me."

I don't want to go with him, but I don't have much of a choice. So I let him lead me to a room in the back.

CHAPTER 28

The back room is about the size of a large bathroom. It looks like a former storage closet. There's a folding table in the center and two folding chairs. The light overhead is flickering. Bill gestures at one of the folding chairs, and I sit down gingerly.

"I'll be right back," he tells me.

Bill leaves me in this tiny room alone and presumably goes to call the police. As I sit there waiting for him, I hear a buzzing sound from inside my purse. It's a text message. I feel dread in the pit of my stomach as I pull out my phone.

Want to hear a secret? April Masterson is a shoplifter.

A second later, the photograph appears. It's a picture of me standing by the entrance to the store with the security guard apprehending me. The panicked look on my face and the stern look on his makes it obvious what's happening.

The photo was taken from inside the store.

A cold feeling washes over me. I imagine this photograph plastered all over the internet. Who would watch my show if this got out there? I'd be humiliated.

I stare down at the photo, gripped with the urge to delete it to keep anyone from knowing my humiliating secret. But that won't help. Whoever sent me the photo still has it. This text message is my only proof I'm being harassed. I need to save it.

My hands are shaking as I call Elliot. I don't want to tell him what just happened, but I need his help. Not only is he my husband, but he's also my lawyer. He'll know exactly what to do.

Naturally, he doesn't pick up the first time I call. But after I call two more times, I finally hear his voice. "April, I'm really busy…"

"I'm about to be arrested."

There's a long silence on the other line. I've gotten his attention.

"Arrested? For what?"

"Shoplifting. But I didn't do it."

"*What?*"

"They found these earrings in my bag," I say quickly. "They must have… I don't know, dropped inside somehow." I'm not going to tell him my theory about Maria right now. He probably won't believe me anyway. And I can't tell him about the text messages. "And now they've got me in this back room and they're calling the police."

"Jesus, April," he breathes. He pauses for a long moment. "Okay, look, they're not going to arrest you. It's just a pair of earrings. They're just trying to scare you."

A lump rises in my throat. "He's calling the police! I can hear him!"

"Right, but they're not going to take you to jail for shoplifting some earrings. They're probably just going to give you a summons." He exhales loudly. "Whatever you do, don't say anything. Don't sign anything. Just come straight home."

"But what if they take me to jail?"

"It won't happen." He sounds very confident. I wish I felt that confident. "But if they do, just call me right away. We'll figure it out."

"Are you coming home?" I ask in a small voice.

"Yes. As soon as I can."

"Okay, thank you." I squeeze the phone in my hand. "I love you, Elliot."

"I love you too. Remember—don't say anything and don't sign anything."

Bill comes into the room at that moment, so I hang up the phone. He is gigantic. His biceps are straining at the fabric of his button-down blue shirt. He could probably crush me with one hand if he decided to.

"Listen." Bill sits down across from me at the folding table. The folding chair creaks threateningly under his weight. "I spoke to Maria. She's saying we don't have to press charges."

Oh, thank God! "Thank you so much."

"But obviously, you'll be banned from the store permanently." He reaches into his back pocket and retrieves a white piece of paper. "I'll also need you to sign this statement."

"Statement?"

He waves his hand. "It just says that you attempted to take an item, and you understand you won't be allowed to return to the store."

I looked down at the paper in front of me. I skim over the fine print, which seems to be essentially what he just told me. But Elliot *just* told me not to sign anything. "Um…"

Bill puts his hand on the paper and starts to pull it away from me. "If you don't want to sign, I'll go ahead and get the police to come.

I get a flash of panic in my chest. "No, it's okay. I'll sign it."

I'm sure Elliot meant not to sign anything the police gave me. The best thing is leaving the police out of it.

I take the pen Bill offers me and scribble down my name. There. Now I can at least be done with this thing. Two accusations of theft in one day is enough for me, thank you very much.

"Can I go now?" I ask.

"Hold on. Just wait here another minute."

I sit in the room, tapping my feet against the ground. I just want to go home already. I never should've come here in the first place. What was I thinking?

Bill is taking forever to return. I gather up my purse and get to my feet. I did what they wanted me to do—I'm getting out of here. But then I hear the voices outside around.

"Is she in there?"

"Yes. She signed this confession for us."

My hands start to shake. What's going on here?

Before I can get out of the room, they come inside. It's a policeman. My mouth falls open. Why did they call the police? Bill told me if I signed that stupid form, they would leave the police out of it.

Bill was scary, but the police officer is even scarier. Not because he's big, but because of what he represents. He's wearing a dark outfit and there's a gun on his holster. I can see it. And handcuffs. Oh my God, are they going to handcuff me? Am I going to be led out of Helena's wearing handcuffs?

My legs are back to being jello. I feel myself swaying on my feet. I might pass out.

"April Masterson?" the officer says.

I open my mouth to say yes. But before I can get the words out, I start seeing spots in my vision. And the next thing I know, I'm on the ground.

CHAPTER 29

The police officer ends up being very kind to me. It could have been worse at least. Officer Clark helps me into a chair, asks Bill to get me something to drink (water), and most importantly, he doesn't arrest me. Even though Bill hands him my signed confession.

The officer even walks me to my car. He seems apologetic as he writes me the citation.

"It was all a misunderstanding," I tell him one last time, hoping maybe he'll rip it up.

"I'm sure it was." Officer Clark pats me on the shoulder. "Happened to my wife once. She forgot to pay for something at a store. Honest mistake."

I nod. I haven't shared my conspiracy theory with him. I don't want him to think I'm crazy. I know I'm right, but I don't expect anyone to believe me. It's better to pretend I'm just some scatterbrain who forgot to pay for the earrings.

I go straight home with Bobby after I pick him up at

school. Unfortunately, Elliot still isn't home. I send him a text, and he doesn't respond. I'm dreading telling him about the confession I signed. He's going to be furious. He explicitly told me not to sign anything, then I went ahead and did it anyway.

I've thought about it a lot and I've decided to tell Elliot about the harassing text messages. This has gone far enough. Yes, I'm terrified of him seeing that photo of me and Mark Tanner, but I'll have to take that risk. I can't deal with this alone anymore. As soon as he comes home, I'm telling him everything. Then we'll figure out what to do next.

At eight o'clock, I finally get a text from Elliot:

Work is crazy today. I'll be home at nine.

I want to throw my phone at the wall. After everything I've been through today, how could he get home so late? I almost got *arrested*! Is it too much to ask to get to see my husband before bedtime?

Bobby senses something is going on, and he goes to bed without an argument. I think he's getting used to his father not being home at bedtime. After he's tucked in, I go back downstairs and watch television. After the day I had, I just want to zone out with the TV.

At nine-thirty, I finally hear the lock turning in the front door. I sit up straight, preparing to give Elliot a piece of my mind.

My husband stumbles into the living room, looking like he stopped at a bar for a drink or three on his way home. He's got a dark five o'clock shadow on his scalp, filling in the patches where his hair used to be. His tie is partially undone and his shirt is rumpled. He walks into the living room and drops down beside me on the sofa.

"April," he murmurs.

"Looks like you had a shitty day too." I'm not going to make less of my own situation. I mean, I almost got arrested. But I can be sympathetic. "You were right. The policeman just gave me a citation."

He nods, like the information is completely unimportant to him. I'm a little hurt. He sounded upset when I told him about the charges earlier today, but now he doesn't seem to care at all. I guess his career supersedes any of my problems.

"Anyway," I say, "the officer seemed to think it wouldn't be a huge deal. I mean, it was just one pair of earrings. But there's something else I wanted to…"

The words die on my lips when I see Elliot's bloodshot eyes. He looks *awful*.

"Are you okay?" I say.

Elliot rotates his head to look at me. "Brianna is pregnant," he blurts out.

"Oh." That isn't so bad. It's a hassle for him because he'll have to hire a new assistant. But I'm thrilled she won't be around anymore soon—I truly dislike that woman. "So how long will she be working before she goes on leave?"

"No. You don't understand." He rubs his palms against his eyeballs. "She's pregnant and…"

Oh.

Oh no.

I scramble up from the sofa, my heart pounding. "Oh my God. You're joking with me, Elliot. You didn't… not *again…*"

He looks up at me with those bloodshot eyes. He looks like he's been crying. And that he might start again at any moment. "I'm so sorry, April."

"You're *sorry*? You're fucking *sorry*? You got your secretary pregnant and that's all you've got to say for yourself?"

"I…" He shakes his head. "You've got to believe me, it was just a one-time thing. I swear. I never thought…"

"You never thought I'd find out? You never thought you would knock her up?" I clench my hands into fists. "Do you know how bad this is?"

He takes a shaky breath. "I know. I *know*, okay? What can I say? I fucked up."

He tries to reach for me and I shake him off. The thought of touching this man makes my skin crawl. How can I ever forgive him for something like this?

Although it wouldn't be the first time. After that mess with Courtney, I thought…

Oh God.

I start pacing across the living room. There's more

going on here than just his selfish act of infidelity. We've got a *situation* here. This is really bad. I thought being accused of stealing money from the PTA was bad. I thought being cited for shoplifting was bad. But I was wrong. *This* is bad.

"So... what now?" I'm still pacing as I talk. "What does she want?"

He clears his throat. "She, uh... she's saying she wants to keep it."

"What?" I had assumed Brianna was just looking for a quickie abortion and a payout. "You can't be serious?"

He nods miserably.

I look at his face. He's wrecked by this. But part of me wonders if deep down, he's happy. He and I have been trying for a baby for a long time. And now, miraculously, here's a baby. With another woman, of course, but maybe that doesn't matter to him.

Maybe this is the opportunity he's been waiting for.

"So what are you going to do?" I say. "Are you going to run off with Brianna now?"

"No!" Elliot leaps to his feet. "Of course not! April, I love you. You know that."

I snort. "Do I?"

"Of course I do!" He tries to reach for me again, and I jerk away. "I just need to figure out what to do..."

What to do? As far as I can tell, there are two options. He can stay with his wife, or he can leave me for the woman over ten years younger who's pregnant with his baby.

Elliot hangs his head. "Do you want me to stay at a hotel tonight?"

Well, I don't want him in my bed. I can barely even look at him right now. But at the same time, I have a bad feeling that if I tell him to leave, he'll go straight to *her*. And I don't want that right now. I don't want her to be the good guy, while I'm the bad guy. Because the truth of the matter is that as angry as I am, I don't want my family to fall apart. Not like this.

"You can sleep on the sofa," I say.

"Thank you." He pushes his hand against the cushion of our leather sofa. It's a very comfortable sofa. "I just need a pillow and a blanket…"

"Wait," I say.

He raises his eyebrows.

"I don't want you to sleep on the sofa," I say. "I want you to sleep on the floor."

Elliot looks doubtfully at the hardwood floor. "Well, that's fine. I'll just lie on the carpet."

"No. Not the carpet. The *floor*."

He's quiet for a moment. "Okay. I'll sleep on the floor."

"Damn right." Except it's not enough. Not even close.

Elliot chews on his lower lip. "I'm so sorry, April. I know I messed up. But I love you, and I promise, this is going to be okay. I'm going to fix it."

How? How on earth is this going to be okay? I can't even imagine it. But there's no point in arguing. "Good night, Elliot."

I head up the stairs, but there's no chance of being able to sleep. I know Elliot claims he's going to fix this, but I can't figure out a way he could possibly do it.

CHAPTER 30

When I wake up the next morning, I get the surprise of my life: Elliot is cooking breakfast.

He's scrambling some eggs in a frying pan. I didn't know he was capable of such a thing. The other surprise is that Bobby is fully dressed and sitting at the kitchen table, eating the eggs. I feel like I've walked into an alternate dimension.

"Hi, honey." Elliot lifts his spatula and waves at me. "I figured you might need to sleep in, so I got Bobby up and made breakfast."

I get what he's doing. He's on his best behavior because he's trying to get me to forgive him for what he did. Yeah, right.

"Well, thank you," I say stiffly. I look over at the pan, where the eggs have turned slightly brown. But that's okay. I think I might faint from shock if he cooked them perfectly.

"Also," he adds, "I'm going to work from home today,

so I'll be around to watch Bobby when you go to your book club tonight."

My book club. I forgot it was tonight, although I do have the date posted on the refrigerator. I even read the book for a change. But I can't possibly go, given the circumstances.

Although…

I got an email yesterday about a meeting between the administration and the PTA leaders. The meeting is supposed to be tonight. That means Julie won't be at the book club. Which means I'll be there without her and have a chance to tell people my side of the story.

"Okay," I say stiffly. "I appreciate that."

He looks like he's going to lean in to try to kiss me, but then he thinks better of it. Smart boy.

I do the drive-through drop off again with Bobby. I can't even contemplate getting out of my car and standing by the entrance when Julie and Maria will be there. I can't face either of them. So instead, I pull up beside the school, and say to Bobby, "Okay, time to get out."

"How come you don't walk me to the door anymore?" he asks.

The teacher facilitating the drop off is giving me a dirty look. "I think you're old enough to do the drop off now."

Bobby considers this for a moment. "How come Dad slept in the living room last night?"

Somebody leans into their horn behind me. For God's

sake…

"Bobby, we'll talk about this later, okay?"

Thank God he accepts that and gets out of the damn car. I speed away before the person behind me can honk again.

As I drive back home, I tick off all the reasons to try to keep my family together right now. But the reason I keep coming back to is Bobby. When I was growing up, it was just me and my mother. I want something better for Bobby. A mother and father in the same house. If I throw Elliot out, I'm taking that away from him.

I've got to find a way to make this work.

Tonight after book club, I'm going to sit down with Elliot and we're going to figure out what to do next. We've got a really big problem, but there's got to be a way out. We just have to figure it out.

But as I pull into our driveway, I get the surprise of my life.

It's Brianna.

On my street.

And she just came out of Maria's house.

CHAPTER 31

For a moment, all I can do is stare.

What the hell is Brianna doing here? Did she come to see Elliot? That makes some sort of sense, but why was she at Maria's house? That part doesn't make sense at all.

She looks great too. Her blond hair is long and glossy, her legs look long and sleek in her skinny pants, and her face is glowing. She's got a pregnancy glow. A pregnancy glow from my husband's baby.

I can't believe this is happening. How could my life fall apart so quickly?

It's obvious she's headed for our front door. Before she can make it, I kill the engine and scramble out of the SUV. I catch her before she makes it to the front door.

"What do you think you're doing?" I hiss at her. Although the conviction in my words is hampered by the fact that I am slightly out of breath.

Brianna turns to me and gives me one of her

beautifully fake smiles. "Sorry. I just need to speak to Elliot."

She reaches out to press the doorbell, but I step in front of her before she can. "You can't speak to him. You can't see him ever again."

She cocks her head to the side. "*Excuse* me?"

"You heard me." I fold my arms across my chest, partially to hide the fact that they are trembling. "I want you off my property and out of our lives. Permanently. Elliot made a huge mistake, and he doesn't want anything to do with you anymore."

Her eyes take on a sympathetic look. "Oh. So he hasn't talked to you about our plans yet?"

"What plans?"

She lets out a long sigh. "April, you couldn't possibly think he was going to stay with you. We're having a baby. He's been wanting to have a baby for a long time."

"We *have* a baby," I spit at her. "Elliot and I have a child together. We have a family. We have a life together here."

She nods. "Yes, and Bobby will still be a part of our lives—a bit. But you must know how unhappy Elliot has been with you. He can't stand you. All you do is film your little YouTube show and spend his money."

"That's not true."

"Are you completely oblivious?" She snorts. "Why do you think Elliot stays at work so late every night? To *work*? Nobody works that hard, honey."

I grit my teeth. "He told me he regrets what happened with you. He told me it's over."

That sympathetic look again. "He's just trying to find a way to break it to you. I'm sorry, April."

My heart is racing in my chest. Could this possibly be true? Or is she just messing with my head? I don't know what to believe anymore.

"Let me tell you this." I poke her in the chest with my finger. "If Elliot tries to divorce me after what the two of you did, I will take him for every penny he has. I promise you that."

I thought my words would shake Brianna, but it only seems to amuse her. "I don't think so, April."

The way she is looking at me is freaking me out. What does she know? Why is she smiling like that? She has no right to think she has the upper hand. I'm the one married to Elliot. She's just a secretary who got herself knocked up.

Is she the one who has been texting me? Are she and Maria ganging up against me together? I can't even wrap my head around it.

"Get off my property," I say.

Brianna doesn't move.

"Get off my property," I say again.

"Listen, calm down, April…"

My voice grows several notches higher. "Get off my property. Right. Now. Or else I'm calling the cops on you!"

I take a step towards her, and this time she flinches.

Good. She's scared. She should be, because I will absolutely call the police on her and press charges. I'm in no mood to mess around.

"I'll come back later," Brianna says.

"Don't bother."

Brianna walks over to her car, gets inside, and drives away. After her car disappears, I look over at the house next to mine. Maria's house. Why was Brianna at Maria's house?

I have to know the answer.

I march over to Maria's house and dart up the steps to her front door. I press my thumb against the doorbell, and when somebody doesn't answer right away, I pound on the door with my fist. I want some answers, and I want them *now*.

But for some reason, nobody is answering.

I pound on the door a few more times, but I don't hear any sounds from within the house. I peek through the window, but the house looks dark inside. And there's no car in the driveway, although there may be a car in the garage.

Nobody is home.

Was I mistaken about Brianna coming out of this house? I thought for sure I saw her coming down the front stairs, but maybe not. Or maybe she got the address wrong and thought that house was ours. It makes a hell of a lot more sense than what I thought I saw.

I shake my head and return to our house. I stand in the middle of the living room, staring up the staircase. Elliot is upstairs working in his study right now. I should ask him if what Brianna said is true. Was he just biding time yesterday when he told me he wanted to stay together? Maybe he's hiding his assets. Of course, I've got some of my own assets from my show, but it's nothing compared to our joint accounts.

I imagine myself bursting into his study and demanding the truth. And then I imagine him tearfully admitting to me that everything Brianna told me is true. He wants to leave me to have this baby with her. He's going to take everything and leave me penniless.

Suddenly, my chest feels tight. I sink onto the sofa, burying my face in my hands. I'm still furious at Elliot for what he did, but I still don't want him to leave me. I don't want to give up my life here. I don't want to break up my family.

I'll do anything to keep that from happening.

CHAPTER 32

"Mommy, the house is on fire."

I look up from the television and see Bobby standing in front of me. His eyes are wide and he's pointing at the kitchen. And that's when I remember:

The cookies dammit!

I made my famous double chocolate chip cookies for my book club tonight. I did a show on the cookies last year. The secret is using dark cocoa powder for a more fudgy and rich flavor. I made these cookies dozens of times, but I've never burned them before. I must've forgotten to set the timer.

I leap off the couch to retrieve my cookies from the oven. Bobby has flopped down on the floor on his belly. "No, you have to stop, drop, and roll," he says.

Well, at least he was paying attention in that fire safety lecture he got at school last year.

By the time I get to the kitchen, there's smoke pouring

out of the oven. I quickly turn it off and pull my cookies out of the oven. My delicious double chocolate chip cookies have turned into little black hockey pucks. Thankfully, I have enough batter for a second batch, but the kitchen is going to need to be aired out. There's smoke everywhere.

And right on cue, the fire alarm starts going off.

Elliot has been trying to stay out of my way, but the fire alarm brings him into the kitchen. He wanders into the room, coughing into his elbow from all the smoke. "Everything okay in here, April?"

"Wonderful. Just perfect."

"Can I do anything to help?"

I can't say Elliot isn't trying to make nice. During the day, he went out and bought me some flowers. And by "some flowers," I mean that he purchased what appears to be the contents of an entire flower shop. I ran out of vases to put them in.

"It's fine," I say, as I wrench open the sliding door to the backyard. "I just need to air out the kitchen." And throw away a bunch of cookies.

He scratches at his scalp. "When are you leaving for your book club?"

"In about an hour."

"Okay. Um, let me know when you're going so I can come down."

He's a little stiff when he talks to me. Despite his grand gesture with the flowers, the two of us are still acting like a couple of strangers who aren't quite sure how to behave around each other. I am still really angry at him. No, beyond angry. Half the time, I want to reach out and strangle him with my bare hands. (And then strangle Brianna.)

But at the same time, I'm scared he's going to choose her over me. He isn't just having an affair with her (or a one night stand, if that's to be believed). She's *pregnant.* He can't just walk away from that. And Brianna told me that he's trying to let me down easy.

I keep thinking about Carrie's humiliation when her husband left her for the hot, young babysitter. I don't want to be the woman whose husband left her for his hot, young secretary. I just *can't.*

An hour later, I've got a Tupperware container stuffed with double chocolate chip cookies that aren't burned. I call up to Elliot, who comes downstairs to watch Bobby.

"Would you like a cookie?" I ask him. My olive branch.

He eyes the large container of Tupperware stuffed with cookies. "You sure you got enough in there?"

A joke. This is very positive.

A joke and an offer of a cookie are all we've got right now. We don't kiss or hug or even make eye contact as I get ready to leave. I do give Bobby a kiss and hug though. And an extra one for good measure.

The book club tonight is being held at Lucy Miller's house at the end of the block. Lucy has two children, one in middle school and one in high school, so that makes me think she knows nothing of the drama going on between Leo and Bobby. Only a few of the women on the block have kids at the elementary school. So really, I just have to cross my fingers that Maria isn't there.

And if she is? Well, I'm going in anyway. I have a right to be there. I live on this block like everyone else. And I've even read the book for a change, in case the impossible happens and we end up actually discussing it.

I clutch my tub of cookies to my chest as I march up the steps to Lucy's house. Sounds are coming from within the house, which makes me think I'm not the first person to arrive. Good. I press my index finger against the doorbell and then quickly grab the cookie tub again before it falls.

I wait for a moment for the door to open. All the voices from inside have gone silent. Just when I'm about to ring the doorbell again, the door cracks open.

It's Lucy. But she's only opened the door about half a foot. Not enough for me to get inside.

"Hi!" I say brightly. I hold up my cookie tub. "I brought cookies for the book club. That's tonight, right?"

Lucy's lips are set in a straight line so that no color is visible. "We didn't expect to see you here tonight, April."

I keep a smile plastered on my face. "Really? Because I always come to the book club."

"Yes, but with everything going on right now…"

Is she talking about what Bobby allegedly did to Leo? Or the alleged theft from the silent auction fund? Or my shoplifting charge?

Maybe I don't want to know.

"Yes," I say, "I've been having a rough week. I was hoping to just sort of… forget about it for a couple of hours…"

Lucy lowers her voice a few notches. "Listen, April. I just don't think the other women will feel comfortable with you here right now."

I feel my face turning pink. "Maybe you should ask them."

"I did."

I hear a voice in the background. Maria's voice. She's here.

That explains it.

"Fine." Tears are pricking at my eyes, but I don't want to cry in front of Lucy. I can just imagine what she would say to the other women. "I'll go."

Before I can even say goodbye, Lucy has closed the door in my face.

Now I've got two dozen cookies and nowhere to go. I suppose I could donate them somewhere. Is there a homeless shelter around here? I know there's a food pantry because I bring a canned goods donation once a month, but I don't think they accept fresh baked cookies.

That proves I'm a good person, doesn't it? Bad people don't donate huge boxes of canned food every month, right?

I turn back in the direction of my house. I don't know

how to explain what happened to Elliot. He knows about Bobby pushing Leo, but I haven't told him about the PTA theft thing. I don't know how to say those words to him, especially now. And frankly, I'm not looking forward to spending an evening with that man after what he did to me.

So instead of going home, I get in my car. I put the cookies in the passenger seat and take off.

The first place I go to is Taco Bell. Right now, I want some greasy, cheesy processed food. The kind of stuff I would never let Bobby eat, except possibly at a birthday party. I go to the drive-through window and order a quesadilla and two tacos with a large diet soda. Then I park in the lot to eat.

I devour the quesadilla and tacos in under five minutes. And then I eat about ten cookies. After all that food is sloshing around in my belly, I feel mildly nauseous, but I welcome it. Anything is better than that sick clawing feeling in my gut.

I turn on the radio in the car. It's a Maroon 5 song I've heard a million times before. When I first met Elliot, he sort of reminded me of Adam Levine. That was back when he had hair. I almost laugh at the memory.

I was so happy when the two of us got married. Then soon after, we had Bobby. He was the man I had been looking for my entire life. We were just so in love. I know a lot of people say they're in love, but Elliot and I were *really* in love. The kind of love where we wanted to be together every second of the day. I couldn't stop thinking about him. From the moment I first met him, I knew he was going to be my husband and we would be together forever.

Well, there's no point in dwelling on the past. It doesn't matter how in love Elliot and I were back then. The only thing that matters is now.

Now we've got a problem.

Brianna.

CHAPTER 33

I stumble home about two hours later, after eating a bunch more cookies in the parking lot of Taco Bell, then taking a mind-clearing drive. There's so much to think about, it helped to cruise along the empty streets, letting my mind wander.

I try to fit the key into the lock to our front door, but it doesn't go in. I try a second time, but it still doesn't seem to fit. I get a flutter of fear in my belly. Did Elliot change the locks while I was gone? Is this his way of telling me we're through?

But then the door swings open and Elliot is standing in front of me. His dark brown eyebrows knit together. "April, are you okay?"

I hold up my keyring, the offending key between my thumb and forefinger. "My key won't fit."

He smiles crookedly. "That's because you're using the mailbox key."

Oh. "Oops."

"April," he says, "have you been drinking?"

"No." I slip past him into the foyer. Bobby is clearly in bed, because the living room is completely silent. "I haven't been drinking. I've been *thinking*."

He raises his eyebrows. "What have you been thinking?"

"About you, mostly." My words come out flirtier than I intended. But I don't regret it.

"Oh?" His smile widens. "And what have you been thinking about me?"

I open my mouth to answer, but before I can get any words out, I find myself throwing my arms around his shoulders and pressing my lips against his. He stumbles backward, shocked. But after that initial surprise wears off, he pulls me closer to him and kisses me back. It's a long lingering kiss that guarantees we'll end up in the bedroom.

"You're incredible, April," he breathes in my ear.

"Don't you forget it."

He squeezes me tight to his body. "I didn't think you'd be up for this anytime soon."

"Well, there's a lot you don't know about me."

"Is there now?"

"There sure is."

Elliot shakes his head at me, and then we're making out again. And for the first time in a very long time, we can't even make it up to the bedroom. We do it right on the couch, ripping each other's clothes off like when we first got together.

CHAPTER 34

I find myself singing out loud as I cook breakfast the next morning.

No, the Brianna situation isn't resolved. But that's okay. I've solidified my marriage and that's the most important thing.

And no, I haven't forgiven Elliot—not even close. I'm not a *complete* pushover. I still expect him to do a massive amount of groveling. I may make him sleep on the floor a few more times. But I want to give him a hint at what the reward will be.

"Why are you singing, Mommy?" Bobby asks as he walks into the kitchen.

"Why can't I sing?"

Bobby thinks about this a moment, but can't come up with an answer. "What's for breakfast?"

"Chocolate chip pancakes."

Bobby couldn't have looked happier if I told him that

we were having an early Christmas tomorrow. But he's had a rough week. He deserves chocolate chip pancakes. And so do I. I've had a rough week too.

I've just finished mixing the batter when the doorbell rings. I lower the flame on the stove and race to get the door. I don't check the peephole before throwing it open, which turns out to be a mistake.

Because there's a squad car parked in my driveway. And what I presume is a plain-clothed police officer standing at my door.

My heart sinks. Is this about the shoplifting thing? Because my court date isn't for another couple of weeks. I haven't done anything else wrong. I've barely left the house!

"Mrs. Masterson?" the officer says in a thick New York accent.

He's in his early forties with red-tinged brown hair and he's solidly built, with a scar running through the stubble on his left jawline. He has pale blue eyes that make him look non-scary—he's actually pretty cute. He's the sort of officer I'd see in the community and bring him some baked goods to enjoy on his break, and maybe flirt a bit for fun.

But right now, I'm scared out of my wits.

"Yes, I'm Mrs. Masterson," I manage.

"I'm Detective Hanrahan." He flashes a badge at me. "Is your husband home?"

He wants to talk to Elliot. That's a good thing, I assume. It means at least I haven't allegedly done anything else wrong.

I go to the base of the stairs. Elliot was in the shower when I came down to make breakfast, but I don't hear the shower anymore. He must be getting dressed. "Elliot!" My voice cracks. "Could you come down here please?"

A few seconds later, Elliot emerges from the upstairs bedroom wearing a dress shirt and slacks, his head freshly shaved. He's got a tie loose around his neck that he's expertly tying. But when he sees Detective Hanrahan at the door, his fingers freeze.

"Mr. Masterson?" Hanrahan calls out.

Elliot looks around, like he's hoping there's another Mr. Masterson the officer might be talking to. "Uh… yes…"

"My name is Detective Hanrahan. Could I have a word with you?"

Elliot makes his way down the stairs, nearly tripping on the final step. "How can I help you, Detective?"

Hanrahan's expression is grim. "I'm afraid I have some bad news."

When a policeman comes to your door and tells you he's got bad news, you can't help but think the worst. I wonder if something happened to one of Elliot's parents. It can't be my mother—the nursing home would have called me.

But why would a *detective* be coming if something happened to one of Elliot's parents?

"Yes?" Elliot says.

Hanrahan hesitates for a split second and bows his

head. "I'm afraid I gotta tell you that your receptionist, Brianna Anderson… was found dead last night."

Brianna is… dead?

Elliot looks like he's about to choke. He grabs onto the banister of the stairs, and it's the only thing holding him up. All the color has left his face.

The detective squints at him. "Are you okay, Mr. Masterson?"

He nods, but it looks like he's barely keeping it together. My head is spinning. Brianna was found *dead*? What does that mean? She's so young… People in their early twenties don't just die for no reason.

"What… happened to her?" Elliot croaks.

"I'm afraid…" Detective Hanrahan pauses for what seems like an eternity and a half. "I'm afraid she was murdered."

Murdered. Oh my God.

But I suppose that makes sense, considering there's a detective at our door.

Elliot's eyes widen. My husband might have a heart attack right now. "Murdered?" he gasps. "How?"

"Blunt trauma to the head. Basically, she was beaten to death. We found her in an alley a block away from her house"

"She was…" He sinks onto the steps. "Someone *beat her* to death? That's… Jesus Christ, I can't…"

"I'm very sorry for your loss."

He sounds like he means it. He doesn't sound suspicious of us at all. It sounds like he's just letting us know, by the way, Elliot's receptionist is dead.

I wonder if he knows Brianna was pregnant. He's going to know sooner or later, I assume. They do an autopsy on anyone who gets murdered. That's the sort of thing that would show up on autopsy. And then he might not seem quite so friendly.

"This is so sad," I speak up. There's no need for him to know that I hated Brianna with a passion. "I can't believe somebody would do that to poor Brianna. She was such a nice girl."

He nods. "Yes, it's very sad." His eyes dart between the two of us. "I'm afraid I gotta ask you both a few questions. You have time to talk?"

Elliot raises his face to look at the detective. He reaches out for the banister and shakily gets back to his feet. "Of course. Whatever we can do…"

Hanrahan clears his throat. "Can you tell me where you were during the late evening last night?"

Elliot rubs his neck. "I was home. I was here the whole night. With my son."

"Me too," I quickly add. "We were here together."

Hanrahan raises his eyebrows. "So you two were together here the whole night?"

"Well," Elliot says, "except for the time when April went to her book club."

Why? Why would he say something like that?

"You went to a book club meeting last night?" Detective Hanrahan asks me.

"Yes," I say. Technically, it's true. I did go to the book club meeting. But Lucy wouldn't let me in the door.

I flinch as the officer studies my face. "What book?" he says.

"Excuse me?"

"What book were you reading for your book club?"

"Oh!" My smile feels so phony. He must see through it. "We were reading *Life of Pi*."

He gives me a crooked smile. "I always meant to check that one out. Any good?"

I did read the book, but that doesn't mean I have anything intelligent to say about it. "Yes. I enjoyed it very much."

He nods, like this is a key piece of information. "And the other members of the book club could vouch for you that you were there?"

"Yes."

My stomach feels like it's full of rocks. Why did I lie like that? Nobody at the book club will vouch for me. I have no alibi at all for last night. It will take the detective five minutes to walk over to Lucy's house and find out I was lying through my teeth.

My head starts to spin as I realize what is happening here. Brianna has been murdered, and I have both motive and a lack of an alibi.

I look over at Elliot, who seems like he's going to throw up. I wonder if we should just tell this detective everything. Admit to him that Elliot was having an affair with Brianna. She was pregnant. It was his. And then admit to him that I wasn't at the book club last night.

Of course, that last bit of information is damning. I can't bring myself to hammer that nail into my own coffin.

"Mr. Masterson," the detective says, "do you have any idea who might have done this to Miss Anderson?"

Elliot shakes his head slowly. "No... No one I can think of."

"Did she have a boyfriend?"

He runs his hand over his skull. "Um. Maybe. I don't know. We didn't discuss things like that."

"Her roommate said she was seeing someone." Detective Hanrahan reaches into his pocket and pulls out a little notebook. He consults it for a moment, then looks back up at us. "She said Miss Anderson was seeing a married man. You got any idea who that could have been?"

He shrugs helplessly. "I don't know."

The detective stands there for a moment, scratching at his reddish-brown hair. Does he know Elliot was the man Brianna was seeing? He must at least suspect. Or maybe he doesn't. He doesn't seem like he thinks one of us is a murderer.

"Do you have any other questions?" Elliot finally says.

Detective Hanrahan shakes his head. "Not at this moment. Thank you for your time. But if you could make yourself available in the future, I'd really appreciate it."

"Of course." Elliot manages a half-hearted smile. "I want to cooperate in any way I can."

The detective turns around and heads for the door. I feel a rush of relief. He's leaving. He hasn't accused me of anything. He doesn't even seem that suspicious of us. But then, just before his fingers touch the doorknob, he turns around.

"One more question," he says.

Elliot raises his eyebrows. "Yes?"

"Who was Courtney Burns?"

I feel all the blood rush out of my face. That is the last question I wanted to hear right now.

"Courtney Burns?" Elliot repeats. He's stalling for time. He knows very well who Courtney Burns is.

"That's right."

"She, uh…" Elliot squirms. "She used to be my receptionist. About five or six years ago."

"And what happened to her?"

"She, um…" I can almost hear him swallow. "She killed herself. It was very… unfortunate."

"Wow." Detective Hanrahan shakes his head. "Two dead secretaries in five years. That's pretty bad luck."

"Right." Elliot drops his eyes. "Like I said, it was unfortunate. But Courtney had… a lot of problems."

"I'm sure she did." The detective's light blue eyes are locked on my husband. I get this horrible sinking feeling in my chest—that nice guy routine from a few minutes ago was just to get us to let down our guards. The detective thinks Elliot killed Brianna. It's so obvious. "Anyway, I'll leave you to your breakfast. But don't go anywhere. In case we have more questions."

After the detective leaves, I shut the door behind him. My fingers are shaking so badly I can barely turn the deadbolt. I rest my forehead against the cool plaster on the door.

"April?"

I feel Elliot's hand on my shoulder, and I instinctively jerk away. I turn around to face him, and I'm shocked by how pale his face is. Bobby is at the doorway to the kitchen, watching us. We need to keep our voices down.

"I can't believe this," Elliot murmurs.

Despite everything, I feel a surge of rage. "Why are you so upset? Brianna was threatening to destroy our lives."

"No, she wasn't."

I snort. "Of course she was. She wanted you to leave me."

He doesn't deny it. I remember Brianna's conviction that Elliot would leave our family to start over again with her. She seemed so sure. Maybe she was sure about it because he told her he would.

"I didn't want her dead," he says in a low voice.

Well, I did.

Elliot glances back at the kitchen—Bobby is gone. "And I'm screwed—a seven-year-old is my only alibi. At least you were at your book club."

I take a deep breath. I couldn't work up the nerve to tell the detective, but I should tell Elliot. He's my husband and my lawyer, after all. "I never went to the book club."

His brown eyes fly wide open. He takes a step back. "You… what?"

I don't want to tell him the story about how they kicked me out. So I tell him a portion of the truth. "After everything that happened with Bobby, I just didn't feel like being judged. So I didn't go."

"So where were you for over two hours?"

"I went to Taco Bell. I drove around."

"You just drove around? By yourself?"

"Who else would I be with?"

He's staring at me, a strange look on his face. "April…"

Oh my God, he thinks I killed her. I see it all over his face. I've got a motive and no alibi. I am so screwed. Whoever did this set me up good.

"Elliot." I'm trying to hide the hysteria I'm feeling inside. "I didn't kill Brianna. You have to believe that."

He just shakes his head. "I… I better get to work…"

I try to reach for him, but this time he's the one who jerks away.

I see it all unfolding. Detective Hanrahan finds out Elliot got Brianna pregnant. He discovers my alibi is bullshit. He takes my picture around Brianna's neighborhood, and maybe somebody thinks they recognize it. And that's all it will take.

I look out the window at the house next door. The lights are on inside and I see a silhouette in the window. Maria. She's been watching. She saw the police come to my house. She knows they were questioning us.

She's behind this. My life was perfect until she showed up in our neighborhood. Brianna was talking to her just yesterday, and now she's dead. I should let Detective Hanrahan know about Maria's friendship with Brianna. I would have told him all about that burner phone she's got hidden in her purse, except I didn't think he would believe me. He'd think I was making it up to take the suspicion off myself. And in the meantime, Maria would probably throw that phone in a dumpster where nobody would ever find it.

I just wish I understood. Why is she doing this to me? I never did anything to this woman. And ever since I met her, it seems like she's been determined to ruin my life. I bet she really did lure Bobby to her house the first day, like he said she did. She's been wanting to scare me.

She hates me. She's been targeting me.

And the only way to prove it is to get that burner phone.

CHAPTER 35

I can't seem to focus on anything today. I wanted to record an episode of my show—I figured snickerdoodles would be an easy one, because I make those all the time. But I burned my first batch, then when I tasted the second batch, they tasted terrible. I think I forgot the salt. My heart wasn't in it today.

I just keep thinking about what happened to Brianna. And that stupid burner phone.

Maria must be responsible for what happened to Brianna. And if I could get that phone, I could prove it. But how could I get my hands on it?

In the early afternoon, I see Maria take off for her job. She'll probably be gone until the evening. Shortly after, Sean's truck leaves their driveway. The Cooper household is empty.

It would be a perfect time to look around. I looked in Maria's purse the other day, and the phone wasn't there.

Granted, Maria may have the phone in her pocket, like she must have when she snapped a picture of me being apprehended by the security guard. But this morning when she left, she was wearing a dress. There was nowhere for her to put a phone. I would guess with the police asking questions, she might not want to be carrying it around. And even if I can't find her phone, there's got to be some other evidence around of her connection to Brianna. I'm convinced I can find something.

Anyway, it can't hurt to have a look around.

I have just slipped my feet into my ballet flats when the doorbell rings. I race over to answer, but I check the peephole first this time.

It's Detective Hanrahan again. Oh God. I'm not in the mood for this.

I take a second to compose myself. I pat my blond hair, which feels disheveled, but there isn't much I can do about it. I plaster a smile on my face and throw open the door.

"Hello, Detective!" I say brightly. "How can I help you?"

He returns the smile, and the fine lines around his light blue eyes crinkle. "Could I come in for a minute, Mrs. Masterson?"

"Of course!" I exclaim, like I'm absolutely delighted that this man who is investigating the murder of my husband's mistress is entering my home. "Can I offer you some coffee? Or maybe some homemade cookies?"

"Oh right." Hanrahan snaps his fingers. "You got that

cooking show. Something Secrets…"

I get a sick feeling in my chest. How does he know about my show? Has he been investigating me? I'd prefer he knew nothing about me. "*Sweet Secrets.*"

"Right. *Sweet Secrets.*" He nods. "I saw the one where you were making chocolate chip cookies. That was a good tip with the sea salt. If I ever find myself making cookies, I'll go ahead and do that."

I swallow. "Could I offer you a cookie, Detective?"

"No, thanks, Mrs. Masterson." He pats his gut. "Watching the waistline, you know?"

"Right." I force a smile. "Unfortunately, Elliot isn't here at the moment. He went to work."

"Well, that's okay. Actually, you're the one I wanted to speak to."

I have to grab onto the banister to keep from collapsing. He wants to speak to me. That's not good. "Sure. What about?"

"Well, here's the thing…" I feel the detective's pale blue eyes studying my face. "I spoke to the woman who had the book club last night, and she said you weren't there. She said you came for a minute, but then you left."

"Right." There's no point in denying it. There were too many witnesses. "I just came for a very short time."

"Huh. Interesting. So tell me…" He cocks his head to the side. "Where were you last night when your husband thought you were at the book club?"

"I just…" I take a step back. "I went to get some dinner at Taco Bell. Then I pretty much came right back."

"Okay, I see," he says. "And how long did that take?"

"About half an hour. Then I came home."

Half an hour couldn't possibly be long enough to have killed Brianna and make it back home. Granted, the actual time was more like two hours. But Elliot will vouch for me. We can be each other's alibis.

Unless they think we killed her together.

He nods at the front door. "Is that your SUV out front?"

"Yes…"

"It's just interesting." He shrugs. "We have a witness who noticed a white SUV driving around Brianna's neighborhood late last night."

I swallow. "Well, it's a very common color. I mean, there are probably three or four white SUVs on this block alone. Even my next-door neighbor has one. We all have big cars because we've got kids, and SUVs are very safe. And white is the safest color, because you're more visible."

He smiles again but it doesn't touch his eyes. "Yeah. You're probably right."

Well, I *am* right. White SUVs are very common. That's not enough to lock me away for murder.

"Is that all?" I say, a touch coldly.

"I think so." He starts to turn around just like last time, but once again he pauses. "Wait. One more question."

God, no more of this. Please. "Sure."

"What were you and Brianna fighting about yesterday morning in front of your house?"

A sick feeling comes over me. I should have known one of my nosy neighbors would have witnessed that fight. "Fighting?"

He smiles almost apologetically. "Your neighbor said she saw the two of you fighting. I was just wondering what it was about."

My "neighbor." I'm willing to bet any amount of money that this helpful neighbor was Maria Cooper.

"It wasn't really a fight," I say quickly. "It was more like… it was too early and… that's all."

Hanrahan blinks at me. "Was it because Brianna was pregnant?"

My legs wobble beneath me. If I weren't gripping the banister, I might collapse. "What?"

"Sorry, let me say that more clearly. *Were you fighting over Brianna being pregnant?*"

I'm starting to dislike this detective. "I… I didn't realize she was pregnant."

"Oh." He nods thoughtfully. "Interesting. Because I was just thinking if Brianna was pregnant and you thought the baby was your husband's, that would be a pretty good reason for you to be fighting. Don't you think so?"

I can't even bring up the breath to answer his question. For a moment, we just stand there staring at each other. I'm still gripping the banister to keep my legs from giving out underneath me. He thinks I killed her. He thinks I killed Brianna, and he probably also thinks I killed Courtney.

I should tell him about the text messages. I can prove someone has been harassing me. But if I do that, he'll see the photo of me being arrested for shoplifting. A photo of me kissing a man who isn't my husband. Those text messages are a catalog of every bad thing I've ever done. I don't think any of that will help my case.

"Well," he finally says, "I guess that's it for now. But I may come back later and talk to you and your husband together again. Maybe we'll go down to the station and have a little chat over there."

He wants me to go down to the station. That is not a good sign.

"Sure, I'll help in any way I can," I say. My voice sounds unnaturally high, and he has to notice it. He's a detective, after all.

I've got to get that burner phone.

CHAPTER 36

I wait until the cop car is out of sight. But I don't want to wait too long, because I don't know how long Sean will be out of the house. And also, I've got to pick up Bobby from school in an hour and a half. I've never been late before, and today won't be the first time.

I cut across Maria's front lawn from my own, to reduce the chances anyone will see me. Of course, nobody will think anything of it if they do see me. What are they going to think—I'm breaking into my neighbors' house? Unthinkable.

I keep my fingers crossed as I look under the potted plant by the front door. I know Sean gave Maria a hard time about keeping the spare key there, so it's very likely it's not there anymore. But to my relief, when I move the plant, the key is exactly where it was before. I pick it up and fit it into the lock.

Maria's living room is just as it always is. Clean, but

slightly cluttered with Owen's toys. Photos all over the walls of the family. My eyes fall on one photo over the fireplace— a Christmas photo based on the sweaters they're wearing. They look so happy. You would never guess Maria wasn't Owen's biological mother—they look so much alike.

That's when it hits me. What has always bothered me about this living room. There are no photos of Owen's mother.

Not that Maria is obligated to have a photograph of Sean's first wife in her home. But you would think if the poor woman was the mother of her son and died tragically, they would want *some* memory of her to be in their home. Especially considering how many photos there are. Why isn't there even *one* of Owen's biological mother?

I wonder how Sean's first wife died. People that age don't just drop dead. Something terrible must have happened to her.

Well, I'm not going to let anything terrible happen to me.

I've got to find that burner phone. I'm convinced it's the key to everything. She probably used the phone to communicate with Brianna. And now the detective is claiming people saw a white SUV in Brianna's neighborhood. Except Maria's car is almost identical to mine. Maybe that wasn't unintentional. Maybe her plan all along was to set me up.

I noticed that when I cut across the lawn, I got mud all over my shoes. It won't do to leave my muddy footprints all over their house. So I slip off my flats and walk across the living room in my bare feet. It will be quieter this way.

I check the obvious places. The desk in the living room. I search around the kitchen, trying to be as thorough as I can without making a mess. After twenty minutes of frantic searching, I've come up with nothing. My best bet is to look upstairs. Of course, if somebody came in while I'm on the first floor, I would hear the door and be able to slip out through the back. If I go upstairs, I'll be trapped up there.

But I won't be up there long. Twenty minutes at the most.

I walk up the stairs quickly. They creak a lot compared with our stairs. Mrs. Kirkland lived here forever, and she probably never got them repaired when they needed it. They creaked back then too.

I know exactly where the master bedroom is after last time. I step inside, quickly scanning the room for hiding places. There are about six dresser drawers. A drawer in the nightstand. And then there's the closet. This could take a long time.

I look down at my watch. I still have an hour before I have to get Bobby. I'm going to find that phone if it's here.

I pull open one of the dresser drawers. It's full of Sean's large T-shirts. I run my fingers over one of them. I still don't understand how Maria ended up with a guy like him. He could do so much better. He doesn't even seem to realize it.

Maria was there at the right time and the right place after his wife died. Almost like she planned it.

That's when I hear the noise from downstairs. The lock turning.

Oh no. No no no no…

In my surprise, I stumble backward and knock into the dresser. A hardcover that was balanced on top of the dresser slips off and lands on the ground with a resounding thump.

This just got so much worse.

"Sean?" It's Maria's voice from downstairs. "Is that you?"

I freeze, not sure what to do.

"Sean?" she calls again.

And then she's quiet for a moment. I don't hear footsteps though. I would know if she was coming up the stairs. She's just standing there. What is she doing?

Then I remember.

My shoes. I left them by the front door.

I stand there, trying to be as quiet as I can, wondering if I should attempt to hide. The closet is wide open and there's enough room for me to slip inside. She can't be here for long.

And then I hear my phone buzz inside my pocket.

My hand is shaking so badly, I almost drop the phone before I take it out. Once I get it safely in my hand, I look at the words taunting me from the screen:

I know you are inside the house, April.

And then I hear the creak of footsteps on the staircase.

CHAPTER 37

JULIE

Want to know a secret?

April Masterson is the evilest woman you'll ever meet. Everything she has told you has been a lie.

I should know. She's my best friend.

FIVE YEARS EARLIER

My heels clack noisily on the hardwood floor of my new house that was only erected one month earlier. The chimes of the doorbell echo through the living room, which still has a few boxes I haven't unpacked yet. I'll get to them tonight—I absolutely hate stacks of boxes.

I look through the peephole, because I'm still used to

living in Manhattan, where there's just as likely to be a burglar standing on the other side of the door as a neighbor holding a plate of cookies. But today, it's the plate of cookies. A woman is standing there, smiling brightly at my closed door.

I throw open the door and force a smile, even though my head is still aching from being on hold with the cable company for two straight hours. "Hello…"

The woman standing at my front door is extremely pretty. Pretty in an open, friendly way, with her blond hair pulled into a perfectly messy bun, earnest blue eyes, and a smattering of freckles across the bridge of her nose. She's the sort of woman everybody instantly likes.

"Hi!" she chirps. "I'm April! I live two houses down the block. You must be Julie!"

"Uh, yes…"

She beams at me. "I brought you some cookies."

"Oh." I have to admit, her cookies look delicious. I could use a cookie right now. "Won't you come in?"

"I'd love to!"

April follows me into my house, clutching her plate of chocolate chip cookies. Her lips part slightly as she looks around the living room. It's extravagant—I know. Keith drew up the plans for the house, and I didn't realize quite how big it was until I saw it being built. And then it was too late. Now I'm in this ridiculously large house for God knows how long. Probably at least until the boys are in college.

"You have such a beautiful house," April says as she puts the plate of cookies on our kitchen island. "I was so excited when I saw it being built."

"Thanks," I say. "Have you lived here long?"

"A couple of years," she says. "We moved here right after my son Bobby was born."

My heart leaps. "I have a son about the same age. Leo is two. He's napping upstairs."

"Same age as Bobby!" April is practically glowing. "And coincidentally, Bobby is also napping right now. At our house, of course."

I furrow my brow. Wait, if her son is napping, who's watching him? Is her husband home in the middle of the day? Does she have a babysitter with him?

She couldn't have left him *all alone*, could she?

No, I'm sure someone is watching him.

"This is so exciting!" April is gushing. "We'll have to get them together for a playdate!"

"Yes, absolutely," I say.

A playdate. Even though I have two sons, the concept is still strange to me. Up until six months ago, I'd been working in the DA's office. It was what I had been doing since I graduated from law school, and it was what I was born to do. But after Leo came along, I felt stretched thin. Keith started pushing me to cut back on work, but that was impossible. So then he started pushing me to leave entirely. Move out to the suburbs.

And now here we are.

April prattles on about life in our town while I take a bite of one of her cookies. It's incredibly delicious. Maybe the best cookie I've ever had in my life. So good that I can't stop eating them, and before I know it, I've demolished half the plate, while April hasn't even had one.

"These are good!" I say. "Are you a professional?"

Her cheeks color. "No. Well, not exactly. I have this little YouTube show where I give out baking tips, but hardly anyone watches it."

This woman is so sweet. At least, she seems sweet. If I were still back in the DA's office, I would have trouble getting a jury to convict April Masterson. You would think looks don't matter in a courtroom, but let me assure you they do. When you look at April, you believe her. Nobody with a face like that could be a liar.

It's funny, because I'm the opposite. Dark hair, penetrating dark eyes that a few people have told me are "scary." It served me well in my job. I'm not sure how well it will serve me now that I'm a housewife and stay at home mom.

While we're eating the cookies, my older son Tristan wanders downstairs. Of my two children, he looks the most like me, with his pale skin and dark hair and eyes, but more than that, he reminds me a lot of myself. He's very focused and disciplined. And honest. He's only four years old, but sometimes he acts forty.

"I'm just getting my Thomas engine," Tristan explains, as he pulls his Thomas the Tank Engine toy from the toy box in the living room.

"Tristan!" I call to him. "Come meet April Masterson, our new neighbor."

He hesitates for a moment, then comes over to the kitchen table, clutching his blue train. "It's nice to meet you, Mrs. Masterson."

April throws back her head and laughs. "Oh my, so polite! You can call me April, Tristan."

Tristan looks to me for approval, and I nod in my head. "Okay," he says.

"Have a cookie!" She pushes the plate of chocolate chip cookies in his direction. "They're chocolate chip."

I frown. I don't like the fact that April offered my son a cookie without asking me if it was okay. The convention is you always ask the parents first, isn't it? Then again, I hate to be the cookie police. And it's hard for me to throw stones, considering I've eaten half a dozen cookies myself. They're addictive.

Tristan again looks at me for approval. I nod, and he reaches for a cookie. "Can I take it up to my room, Mommy?"

"Yes. As long as you don't make crumbs."

Tristan takes a paper towel and gently rests his cookie on top of it. Then he goes upstairs to his room with his train and his cookie.

After he's gone, April looks at me with an expression I

could only describe as curious amusement. "What a well-behaved child!"

It sounds like a compliment, but somehow there's an edge to her voice. Like she's silently judging me. "Thank you," I say anyway.

"I must introduce you to everyone in our playgroup," she says. "You'll love it."

I look at her blankly. "Playgroup?"

She laughs. "For the kids. They play together, and we moms… we drink wine."

"Oh," I say. "Sure."

This is going to be my life now. Playgroups for adults.

I miss putting people in jail.

"Also," April says, "in March, you're going to want to put in your application for Sunshine preschool. It's the best one around. *Very* selective."

I frown. "Tristan is at Rosa's Preschool. I think they're really good."

"No, no, no." She puts her hand on mine—I'm shocked by how smooth her palms are. "You *must* get Leo into Sunshine. It's too late for Tristan, but trust me on this."

"Uh, sure," I say.

She beams at me again. That edge has vanished, and her face is warm and open. "I'm just so happy to have met you, Julie. I know we're going to be great friends."

―――――

Six months later, April and I are carpooling together to Sunshine Preschool.

No, we haven't gotten in yet. But the applications are due today. Unlike other preschools, there's no waiting list for Sunshine. You have to show up on March first and hand in your application, and then they decide whether or not you get in. God knows what sort of qualifications they're looking for in a three-year-old child. It makes me sick to my stomach to think Leo might not pass muster.

Then I feel like a fool for being so worked up over what preschool my kid gets into. *What have I become?*

April is fiddling with the radio from the driver's seat. She has, as she predicted, somehow become my best friend. The first close friend I've ever had. I always wanted friends, but I found it hard to get close to people. Everyone thought I seemed aloof, and it became a self-fulfilling prophecy.

But April wanted my friendship—badly. My husband Keith sometimes jokes, "She acts like she's campaigning to be your best friend. I keep expecting her to show up with buttons that say 'April and Julie forever.'"

I always defend April: "She's really nice."

"Sure," he would say. "She just needs to cut her caffeine intake by about fifty percent."

There are, unfortunately, some strange rumors about April. One of my neighbors told me there was a whole mess about six months before I moved here when April's husband's assistant killed herself. The poor girl, Courtney Burns, apparently took a bunch of pills. But the rumor mill claimed that Courtney had been having an affair with April's handsome husband.

There are quite a few people in the neighborhood who think Courtney's suicide was a little fishy. A little too convenient for April.

But of course, that's insane. I know from my years in the courthouse that anyone can end up being a murderer, but I know April very well now. The idea that she might have tried to harm someone is out of the question. Anyway, the whole mess had died down by the time I moved to the neighborhood.

I have both our applications to Sunshine piled in my lap. The application was nearly an inch thick, but paperwork is something I'm great at, so I helped April with hers. I even wrote her essay for her. Yes, the application included an essay. I'm so embarrassed.

Five minutes later, April has pulled up in front of Sunshine Preschool. I have to admit, it's a darling little school. It's painted with bright colors that make it look like something out of a Dr. Seuss book. Even though I find the whole thing a little ridiculous, at this moment, I desperately want Leo to be at this school.

Before we go in, April pulls a compact out of her purse and gives herself a once over. April always wants to look perfect. While she's doing that, I take my phone out of my purse. To my surprise, there's a text message on the screen. It's from a detective I used to work with pretty closely, Riley

Hanrahan.

Are you coming back to work soon? It's hell without you.

I get a rush of nostalgia, thinking about the good old days. But no. I made this choice for my family. I type in: **Sorry, no. But I do miss it.**

Three bubbles appear on the screen for a few seconds before I see Riley's response. **I miss you.**

I suck in a breath. I quickly delete the text messages, then smile over at April. "You ready to go in?"

"Yes, let's go!"

I recognize Heidi at the front desk from when I picked up the applications for me and April. She flashes me a tight-lipped smile that gets on my nerves. You would think a preschool would have somebody friendlier at the front desk, not this sour-faced woman.

"Hello!" April says. "My name is April. I was hoping to drop off my application for the preschool."

And then I see a genuine smile from Heidi. "Of course! Hand it right here!"

April beams. "You must be Heidi. I think we talked on the phone."

"Yes! We did!"

And then April spends the next several minutes charming Heidi. I'm impressed and even a little jealous. How is she so good at that? God, I hope it helps.

We finally walk back outside together, sans applications. I start to walk to April's car, but then she puts her hand on my arm. "No," she says. "Wait."

After a few minutes, a car pulls up in front of the preschool. A woman with a three-year-old strapped into the back of the car as well as a newborn comes out of the car, looking overwhelmed at the idea of getting both of her kids free. But before she can attempt it, April approaches her.

"Hi!" April says. "You can drop your application off right here! I can take that for you."

"Oh, thank you so much!" The woman gratefully plops the application into April's waiting hands. "Getting the kids out of the car is such a hassle. "

"Believe me, I know!" April says.

And then as the woman drives away, April winks at me.

What the…?

And then she does it again. And again. We stand there for another twenty minutes and accept a dozen more applications. I know I should stop her from doing this, but I can't. I just keep watching her in fascination. She's so sweet. She even handed one of the women a tissue to wipe up some drool on her baby's face.

Then when we each have a stack almost too heavy to carry, she motions to me and we walk back to her car. She tosses her applications in the back and nods for me to do the same.

"April," I say. "What are you doing?"

She winks again. "Improving our odds."

"Yes, but…" I look up at the preschool, then at all the applications littering the backseat of April's SUV. "This isn't right. We should bring them to the school. Everyone should get a fair shot."

That makes her throw back her head and laugh. "Come on. Let's go get some coffee."

We go get a cup of coffee. But not before April stops at a dumpster and throws all the applications inside.

CHAPTER 38

ONE YEAR EARLIER

"Do you want to hear some incredible gossip?" Kathy Tanner asks.

I hate myself for how excited I am about this. A piece of good gossip? That's the highlight of my week. This is what my life has become. It is ten o'clock on a weekday morning, and I've been sitting in Kathy's kitchen for the last fifteen minutes, drinking coffee and complaining about having stepped in a pile of dog crap right outside her house.

(Although honestly, what sort of psychopath lets their dog crap right on the sidewalk and then doesn't clean it up? We live in a *society*, for God's sake!)

"Of course," I say.

Kathy flashes me an evil grin. "Are you sure? It's about your BFF April."

It doesn't surprise me that the gossip is about April. People love to gossip about April, maybe because she's the closest thing we've got to a celebrity in this town, thanks to her little YouTube show. It isn't even that popular, which goes to show how little we have to talk about.

Also, Kathy doesn't like April. It's not entirely clear why, but it likely has something to do with the way her husband Mark is always flirting with April and staring at her breasts. To be fair, my husband always stares at April's breasts too. Yet somehow it doesn't bother me as much.

"Tell me," I say.

Kathy giggles. "Okay, this is a good one. So you know how April sometimes talks about how she went to culinary school, but she decided it wasn't for her?"

"Yes…"

"Well," she lowers her voice, "I heard from a very reputable source that April did not leave culinary school voluntarily. She was kicked out."

I clasp a hand over my mouth. "No…"

"Yes!" Kathy squeals. "And this is the best part. It's because she was having an affair with one of her professors!"

I take a sip of my coffee, letting this little detail percolate in the back of my head. Somehow, it doesn't surprise me that much. It seems like the sort of trouble April might get herself into. Maybe not now, but when she was younger.

Or maybe now. Hard to say.

"God, I can't wait to tell everyone," Kathy muses. "April acts like she's such a big deal. This will totally put her in her place."

I pick up my spoon and stir my coffee, even though it's black. When I worked at the DA's office, I got into the habit of drinking a cup of bitter black coffee every morning to wake me up, even though I hate the taste. And now I can't break that habit. "Maybe you shouldn't go around telling everyone."

She rolls her eyes. "Come on. April deserves it. She's awful. You know it better than anyone."

I have some idea what she's talking about. Obviously. That incident at the preschool—which we both got into, incidentally—was just the tip of the iceberg. April has an edge. Most people who know her well enough find out about it. Although most people just think she's very sweet.

"I just think," I say, "it's better not to mess with April."

Kathy snorts. "Please. If there were anything she wanted to do to me, she'd be doing it. I'm not worried."

I can't help but think that she's wrong. She *should* be worried.

———

Today April and I are on our way to see her mother at the nursing home.

I met Janet Portland a few times before she became ill. She reminded me a lot of April. Very sweet and friendly and pretty for her age, with a similar build to April, even though she was thirty years older. One night a few months after I moved to the neighborhood, April and I went for drinks while Janet stayed behind to watch our boys, and I completely trusted her. She seemed very sensible and trustworthy.

That's why I was surprised when barely six months after I moved in, April tearfully told me she had to put her mother in a nursing home. "The doctors diagnosed her with early-onset dementia," she says. "She just can't be alone anymore. I had to get power of attorney."

April ends every single episode of her show by telling her mother goodnight. It's very sweet. It even melts my own icy heart a bit.

Now Janet lives at Shady Oaks, a nursing home about forty minutes away from where we live. We're driving down there because April got the brilliant idea to include her mother in an episode. I have to admit, she has a lot of clever ideas. That's why her show has taken off as much as it has, although it's not nearly as successful as she likes to pretend it is.

"You remembered the extra butter, right?" April asks as we merge onto the highway.

"Check," I say. April cooks with a horrifying amount of butter. It's one of the reasons why I try not to eat her delicious treats anymore. Just because I don't go to work anymore, it doesn't mean I'm okay with not fitting into any of my suits.

She turns the radio down a notch as she glances at me. "Have you heard the horrible rumor Kathy Tanner is telling everybody about me?"

I toy with a loose thread on my blouse, debating whether I should tell the truth. "Yes. I heard it."

April lets out a huff. "The nerve of her! It's not true you know."

"Uh-huh."

"It's not," she says more firmly. "It's pure fiction Kathy made up just to make me look bad."

"Right. I assumed."

She flashes me a grateful smile. "I knew you wouldn't believe it. Honestly, I don't know why Kathy hates me so much."

"She's jealous," I reply honestly.

"Well, she's horrible." April speeds up a bit to pass an SUV. "I don't understand what Mark sees in her. She's so vile, and he's such a hottie. Don't you think so?"

"I guess so." Vaguely, I'm aware that Mark Tanner is attractive. At least, I know all the other mothers think so. But it's not something I think about.

April is silent then for the rest of the drive, lost in her thoughts. It makes me a little nervous to wonder what she's thinking about.

Shady Oaks is surprisingly dreary and depressing. In the past, April has gone on and on about how lovely the nursing home where her mother lived was. But the reality is nothing like that. The walls of the home have peeling paint and flickering lights. If my parents ever needed to be in a home, I *never* would put them in a place like this.

Of course, Keith and I are far wealthier than the Mastersons. Keith is a partner in his law firm in Manhattan, whereas Elliot works for a dinky firm on the island, where he's been for the last decade, and they won't promote him after the mess with Courtney Burns. According to Keith, that incident has left an indelible mark on his reputation, even though he was never charged with anything. Surely this is not the life April imagined when she married an up-and-coming lawyer.

When we get inside, I get another shock when I see Janet.

She looks like an entirely different person than she had when she had watched Bobby and my boys only a few years ago. For starters, she looks twenty years older. Her honey-blond hair is now completely gray, although presumably it had been dyed the last time I saw her. She has a vacant look in her blue eyes. There's a big glob of drool in the corner of her mouth.

"Hi, Mom!" April encircles her mother in a giant hug. Her mother seems only vaguely aware she is being hugged. "How are you doing?"

Janet doesn't answer. She just stares distantly at a wall.

The filming is being overseen by a nurse named Peggy. It's quite obvious from the moment we walk in that Peggy despises April. It's strange. Most people like April, at least at first. And Peggy seems like one of those nurses who truly cares about her patients, and April is quite doting on her mother.

We record the episode without any difficulties. I have to say, it was a brilliant idea on April's part. The whole thing is incredibly heartwarming—April concludes the episode by throwing her arms around her mother's shoulders and planting a kiss on her cheek. I find myself tearing up.

Yes, even the ice queen can cry sometimes.

After we're done filming, April disappears somewhere and I'm briefly left alone with Janet. Peggy is also no longer in sight, so I feel I should stay with Janet and make sure she's all right. She was fairly spaced out during most of the episode, but now she is happily eating one of the cookies April made.

"Did you enjoy seeing April today?" I ask Janet.

Janet looks up at me with her bleary blue eyes. She seems like she's trying to place me.

"I'm Julie," I say. "I'm April's friend."

"April," Janet repeats. Her gray eyebrows knit together. "You need to tell April to let me out of here."

I frown. "What?"

"Please…" A tear trickles down her right cheek. "Tell her to let me go home. I won't tell anyone. I *swear*. I'll say she was with me the whole night."

"I… I don't understand…"

"The night that girl died." There's a spark of clarity in the older woman's eyes. "I won't tell the police she wasn't with me. I promise. I won't tell a soul."

"Um, Janet…"

Janet reaches out and wraps her bony fingers around my forearm. She seems old and frail, but her grip is like a vise. I couldn't escape if I wanted to. And I'm no weakling—I do Zumba twice a week and kickboxing once a week. And I run every morning.

"Tell her!" she shrieks.

Before I have a chance to panic, April comes running over. And then Peggy also joins us. The two of them manage to wrench my arm from Janet's grip. And then a moment later, Janet seems to calm down. Her shoulders sag and she allows herself to be led away.

April apologizes to me profusely, and she chews Peggy out as well. As I'm gathering up our supplies from the kitchen, I hear April's voice float down the hall.

"Peggy, is she having episodes like this a lot?"

"Not a lot. But she's been talking a lot about somebody named Courtney. She goes on and on about it."

"And what do you do?"

"Nothing. She's just talking."

"No. That's not acceptable. I can't believe you wouldn't tell me about this, Peggy. I'll have to contact Dr. Williams directly to adjust her medications."

"Mrs. Masterson, I don't think she needs more medication. She's already so out of it as it is."

"Well, you're not the doctor, are you?"

Peggy is quiet after that. April comes back to help me get cleaned up, but my thoughts won't stop racing. I can't get that haunted look in Janet's eyes out of my head. Janet knows something. She knows something April doesn't want anyone else to know.

I remember all those rumors about Courtney Burns. Elliot Masterson's secretary, who killed herself years ago. It was ruled a suicide, anyway. But was it?

I used to be a prosecutor. My job was to put guilty people in prison. If April did something terrible, it doesn't matter if she's my best friend. She needs to pay the price.

CHAPTER 39

I call Riley Hanrahan.

I haven't talked to him in years. He's a detective who I worked with very closely when I was a DA. All right, we didn't *just* work together—we also had a little fun on the side. What can I say—I was so busy those days, the only men I met were through work. But that was a long time ago. Before Keith. And then just once after Keith. When I first moved out here, he sent me some text messages and tried to call me to convince me to come back to work. I was tempted, but I did what was right for my family. I stayed.

In any case, he hasn't changed his cell phone number.

"Riley," I say when he answers the phone. "It's Julianne... Abrams." He would only know me by my maiden name. I had always said I would never change my name after getting married, but then it just... happened. I wanted to have the same name as my children, after all.

"Jules!" Riley's boisterous Queens accent rings out on

the other line. Nobody but Riley ever called me Jules. "It's been… Christ, how long? You back at the DA's office?"

"No," I say quietly. "I'm not."

"Yeah? Where are you working now?"

"I'm still… I'm staying at home with my boys." I had said that when Leo started kindergarten, I would look into going back. But he's already been in kindergarten nearly a year, and I've made no moves to apply for jobs. In my defense, kindergarten is just half-days. How could I possibly work with that schedule?

"Huh. Well, how you been?"

We spend the obligatory two minutes catching up on our lives. I tell him a little bit about my boys, and he confirms he's still single. Married to the job, yadda yadda yadda, same way I used to be. As we talk, I feel that deep ache in my chest, remembering everything I gave up when I moved to the island.

"Riley, I'm wondering if you could help me out," I tell him. "I'm looking for some information."

"Just tell me how I can help you, Jules."

I looked up online all I could find about Courtney Burns, but there isn't much. Her obituary was scarce on details. Her social media pages are long gone. Her death has long since been ruled a suicide. "I'm looking for details about a woman named Courtney Burns. She committed suicide about four years ago."

"And what's this for?"

"Just… curiosity." I pause. "Will you do it, Riley?"

There's a long silence on the other line. What I'm asking Riley to do isn't exactly kosher, but he's done it for me before. "Okay," he says. "Give me a couple of days."

A few days later, Riley sends me a text, asking if I would meet him out in Queens. At a pizza place where we used to eat a while back. Dino's. Great crust, oily cheese. I haven't eaten a slice of Dino's Pizza in almost ten years. These days, if somebody brought a pizza pie into my house, I would yell at them. That's the sort of woman I have somehow become.

Ironically, I have to ask April to pick up Leo so I can meet Riley. The kindergarten day ends at noon. The boys get in a whopping three hours of school, then it's all over. April is so cheerful about agreeing to pick Leo up, I feel a stab of guilt.

I show up at Dino's ten minutes early. Ever since I can remember, I've been a stickler for promptness. Nothing upsets me more than when somebody can't be bothered to show up on time. So it pleases me when I walk in the door of Dino's and find Riley already waiting at a table.

"Julianne Abrams." He stands up to greet me. "It's been a while."

It *has* been a while. A long while. I feel suddenly self-conscious in that way you always feel when you're in the presence of somebody you used to have that sort of relationship with a long time ago. Worrying if my hips have gotten too wide or if the makeup has concealed the crow's feet. To make matters worse, Riley looks *great*. Still so solid and muscular. Same reddish-brown hair, now a little gray at the temples, but it suits him. There's a scar on his right jaw that I don't remember from the last time I saw him. And he still had those unassuming light blue eyes that make people trust him—a valuable commodity for a detective.

"It's Bressler now, actually," I say as I sit down across from him.

"Right." He nods. "Keith Bressler. That was the guy you gave it all up for."

"Right."

He grins at me. "I've gotta be honest, Jules. I never got what you saw in the guy."

He always says that. The God's honest truth is I never liked Keith the way I liked Riley. But Keith was who I was expected to marry. You don't move out to Long Island and become president of the PTA if you're married to Riley Hanrahan. That would be a very different kind of life. At the time, picking a man like Keith seemed like the right thing to do.

"Really," I say, "it's none of your business."

That only makes Riley grin wider. "Funny. That's exactly what I expected you to say. That's your answer whenever you don't have an answer."

I just roll my eyes.

"And what about the DA's office? When are you coming back?"

"I don't know," I say quietly. Every time I mention the idea to Keith, he's unenthusiastic. He says if I go back, it should be on the defense side. Better money to be had. But I never liked the defense. From what I could see, almost everyone who walked into that courtroom was guilty.

"You need to come back," he says. "The guy who took your place? He sucks. They need you."

I try not to let on how pleased his words make me. I've been doing a lot of things with my life since I quit my job: motherhood, the PTA, volunteer work, far too much time at the gym. But nothing ever seems to fill that void.

We each get two slices of cheese pizza with pepperoni on top. At first, I start counting calories, but then I say to hell with it. Today, I'm going to have two slices of greasy pizza. And I'm going to enjoy it.

"So this chick Courtney Burns," Riley says, when his mouth is stuffed with cheese. He always seems to have something to say when he has a mouthful of food. "That was an interesting one."

I raise an eyebrow. "Really? How so?"

He puts down his pizza slice. "This is between us, right? This information doesn't leave Dino's."

"Of course."

"Well..." He takes a drink of soda. I watch him, wondering how he got that scar on his jaw. "Officially, it was ruled a suicide, but they were investigating it as a homicide. The woman was hot and heavy with her boss, some big shot lawyer. And from what I gathered, she was pressuring him big-time to leave his wife and kid. He didn't want to. But she wasn't rolling over easy."

"I see."

"And then all of a sudden, she takes a bunch of pills and offs herself? No, that doesn't make sense to me."

I agree with him. But I keep my mouth shut.

"But the lawyer had an airtight alibi," Riley says. "He was at work at the time they estimated Burns took the pills. Lots of witnesses. And the lawyer's wife—they looked into her too—she was home the whole night with her baby and also her mother was visiting. So again, there was a witness."

I think back to the other day at the nursing home. Janet's words: *I won't tell anyone. I swear. I'll say she was with me the whole night.*

"Maybe they put the pills in her food?"

"Nah, sounds like they checked for that. And anyway, it wasn't like she swallowed a few drops of cyanide. It was a huge overdose of one of her own prescription medications—she never would've done that by accident. They found the empty bottle of Ativan in her medicine cabinet. And you want to hear the other crazy part?"

I swallow a glob of pizza. "What?"

"She hacked off all her hair before she killed herself." He makes a snipping motion with his fingers. "With a knife. It was all over her bathtub. Disturbing stuff."

"Was there a note?"

Riley shakes his head. "No note. And her family and

friends also swore there was no way she would do something like that. But you never know. People do crazy stuff. You know it better than anyone."

"Yes…" That was, after all, how Riley and I first met. He was assigned as a detective on a murder trial where some guy killed and buried his girlfriend in the backyard. I'm the one who made certain the guy was locked up for life. But we wouldn't have had a chance of nailing the guy without Riley's solid detective work.

"So." He picks up his pizza again. "Why the interest?"

I consider telling a lie, but Riley stuck his neck out for me. The least I can do is be honest. "The wife of the lawyer is my neighbor."

He laughs. "Figures—that's the suburbs for you. Anyway, if I were working the case, I'd bet odds the wife killed Courtney Burns. So, you know, be careful."

"Don't worry about me."

"Except I do." The smile drops off his face. "You know, if you got a problem, you can still call me."

"Right."

"I mean it."

"I know." My eyes meet his, and somehow the thought pops into my head that Keith and I haven't had sex in six months. At some point, he stopped asking for it, and I was never one to bring it up. He probably has someone like Courtney on the side, and the crazy part is, I don't care. "I better go, Riley."

He doesn't try to stop me, although part of me wishes

he would. I have too much to think about. Maybe I'm not working, but I have a lot going on in my life. And I just found out my neighbor and best friend might be a murderer.

CHAPTER 40

Now that I have this information, I'm not entirely sure what to do with it.

Maybe April killed Courtney Burns. Maybe her mother was her alibi, and she stuck her in a nursing home when she threatened to go to the police. Maybe all of that is true. But if that's the case, what can I do about it? It's not like Janet is in any condition to testify right now.

There's the added complication that April is my best friend. Do I really want to investigate her? Do I want to risk ruining her life, especially if she might be innocent?

Yes, April has a dark side. But that doesn't mean she would kill somebody. She is, in many ways, exactly what she seems to be. She's the sort of person who would bend over backward to help her friends. If somebody is going through a tough time, she is the first one there with a casserole. It's hard to believe she would kill a woman just because she was sleeping with her husband.

Back when I was a prosecutor, I spent a lot of time investigating cases. I was extremely meticulous. I wanted to make sure nothing could come up in court that would surprise me. I am equally meticulous in planning my children's extracurricular activities and the PTA events. It isn't quite the same though.

When April and I were recording her *Sweet Secrets* episode, there was very little time for me to spend with Janet. I had no chance to get the real story out of her. If I were to go to the nursing home alone, I could spend as much time as I wanted.

So that's what I do.

A couple of weeks later, I find time to head over to Shady Oaks by myself. I already knew April was recording one of her shows that day, so there's no chance I might run into her there. If I do, it would be difficult to explain myself.

Fortunately, it's incredibly easy to gain entrance to the nursing home. I simply inform the woman at the front desk I'm there to see Janet Portland and that I am a "friend" and she waves me in without hesitation. I do have to sign my name in a roster in the front, but I write as illegibly as I possibly can.

When I reach the nursing station of the dementia unit, that nurse from the other day is there. Her ID badge is flipped around, and I'm thankful for my photographic memory. "Peggy," I say.

She lifts her eyes. She has the sturdy build of a woman

who has been lifting heavy patients for many years. It takes her a moment, but then she seems to place me.

"You're April Masterson's friend," she says.

"Right." I hold out my hand to her. "Julie Bressler."

Peggy takes my hand. Hers is strong and calloused, but I have quite a strong handshake myself. "What are you doing here? Are you filming another show?"

Her voice is dripping with disdain. Apparently, she isn't a fan.

"Actually," I say, "April asked me if I could check in on her mother. She was just worried about her with all the episodes she's been having lately. And April has been so busy herself."

I pray Peggy won't call April to confirm my story. I doubt it though. It seems like Peggy speaks to April as little as humanly possible.

Peggy looks me up and down, her eyes narrowing. After a moment, she nods and gets to her feet.

I follow Peggy down the hallway to Janet's room. The lights keep flickering as we walk and there's an awful stench I can't identify—it's almost overpowering. I try to imagine what it might be like to live in a place like this. It seems horrible. I would rather be dead.

When we finally come to the end of the hallway, Peggy nods at the last room on the right.

"You might not be able to wake her up," she says. "She's heavily medicated."

I nod and clutch my purse a little tighter.

Janet Portland's room is small. There's barely enough room for me to slide between her bed and a small dresser. She has one tiny window, and it's littered with tiny cracks. Janet herself is lying on a twin bed, her wiry gray hair disheveled. As she sleeps, her lips make rhythmic smacking movements.

"Janet?" I whisper.

Her eyelids flutter.

"Janet," I try again. "Could you wake up for a moment? I'm April's friend, Julie. I want to talk to you about something important."

She doesn't acknowledge me in any way. It's like she's in a coma.

"Janet!" I use my tone for when the boys disobey me. "Wake up!"

This time, her eyelids flutter and her eyes crack open a few millimeters.

"Janet." My face relaxes into a smile. "Hi. It's Julie."

She mumbles something unintelligible.

"Can I talk to you?" I ask. "It's about… well, I heard you've been talking about somebody named Courtney. Courtney Burns?"

I can just barely make out her mumbling the word "Courtney."

"Right." I nod vigorously. "I just have a few questions about her. About… April."

And then Janet shuts her eyes again.

I've questioned hostile witnesses, but none of them were nearly as challenging as Janet Portland. She did fine for the video, but today she can't seem to keep her eyes open. I try for a good fifteen minutes. At one point, I reach out and shake her shoulder. But it's no use. Janet is out for the count.

"Maybe I'll come back again later," I tell her. As if she cares.

As I turn to leave the room, I nearly run right back into Peggy. As it turns out, she'd been standing at the door to the room. Watching me. For God knows how long. My heart skips in my chest.

"Why the interest in Courtney Burns?" Peggy asks.

I take a breath, trying to come up with a reasonable answer to why I would be asking these questions. I decide to go with the truth. "I want to know what happened."

"You want to know what happened," she muses.

"Right."

"Well," she says. "How about if I just tell you what happened?"

I raise an eyebrow. "Tell me…?"

"Janet Portland was her daughter's alibi for murder," Peggy says. "Then a year later, Janet decided to stop being her alibi anymore. And now she's here. On enough medications to kill a horse. You can connect the dots from there."

I lift my chin. "If that's true, why don't you go to the police?"

"For what?" She snorts. "Do you think that woman in there is any kind of reliable witness? And I'm not in charge of her medications. If I questioned it, I'd be gone. Just like that." She snaps her fingers.

I look back at the room, where Janet Portland is sleeping quietly. I understand what Peggy is trying to say. As awful as it is, April is going to get away with what she has done. She has already gotten away with it—it was years ago. There's nothing we can do at this point. Better to accept it.

But I can't accept it.

Most states have a statute of limitations on crimes—for fraud, armed robbery, assault. But there's never a statute of limitations on murder. If you kill somebody, it's never too late to prosecute you for that crime. Because the person you killed will never stop being dead.

"Listen," I say to Peggy, "don't tell April I was here."

"You got it," she says. She looks into Janet's room and a shadow comes over her face. "And if you want to talk to her again, let me know. Maybe a couple of her pills could fall down the toilet that day."

I thank her again and head out. I'm going to come back here and I'm going to take Peggy up on her offer. I'm going to get to the truth. I'm going to get justice for Courtney Burns and Janet Portland.

As I'm signing myself out in the lobby, I hear a voice behind me: "April's friend, right?"

I whirl around, my heart pounding like it did when Keith walked in on me responding to Riley's text messages. I come face-to-face with a familiar-looking middle-aged man with sexy silver hair.

"Hello," I say. "Have we... met before?"

His eyes crinkle when he smiles. "I'm Joe Williams— April's mother's physician here at the nursing home. We met at her Christmas party."

"Oh," I say. "Yes. I remember."

I feel distinctly uneasy, because I remember this guy very clearly now. I remember how I saw him and April talking together in the corner at the party. Her hand was on his shoulder. And at one point, she leaned in and whispered something in his ear, and he laughed.

Peggy might be willing to keep my visit here a secret, but this man is sure to tell her.

But then again, is it so wrong that I'm here visiting Janet? The poor woman is demented (or so April proclaimed). It stands to reason I might visit her to brighten her day.

"What brings you to Shady Oaks?" Dr. Williams asks.

I consider making up a fake relative, but all he would have to do was ask me the name and my cover would be blown. Better to stick close to the truth. "I thought I might pay Janet a visit. Brighten her day."

"Well, how kind of you!" he exclaims. But the look in his eyes tells me otherwise. His eyes tell me he knows I'm full of it. It's not just April who needs to protect their ass.

"People with severe dementia like Janet really benefit from seeing familiar faces."

"Yes, that's what I was thinking. And I had some free time, so…"

"If you decide to come back," he says, "let me know. We can have Janet arrange to meet with you in the dining area."

"Will do!" I say cheerfully.

I get the feeling if I ever tell this man I'm returning, he'll make sure Janet is so snowed with medications, I won't be able to wake her up. And it occurs to me maybe that is the eventual plan. More and more medications until one day, she stops breathing.

The thought of it makes me ill.

CHAPTER 41

More than anything, I need to get to the bottom of this.

I didn't even realize until I'm driving home how good it feels to be investigating a murder. Ever since I gave up my job at the DA's office, it was like I had been in some sort of fog. Always trying to find more and more activities to substitute for the job I missed so badly. The one I was born to do.

I don't know what to do next about April. I have to find time to return to the nursing home when Dr. Williams isn't around. Peggy will help me. Next time I'll record my visit, and I'll call Riley if I manage to find out anything. Maybe there's no chance of getting justice for Courtney Burns. But if I can get Janet Portland out of that nursing home, it will be worth it.

I stop off to get groceries on the way home. I still have some time before the boys' karate class ends. April is supposed to be picking them all up and bringing them home. But I'm not comfortable with that anymore. I don't want that woman near my kids.

I call her while I'm driving home from the grocery store, but the call goes to voicemail. I'll have to intercept her at the karate school. Maybe I should call the karate school and ask them not to release the kids to her.

I walk into my kitchen through the back door with my bags of groceries. I'm carrying four bags, so I drop them on the kitchen counter and extract the handles from my wrist. Then I get out my phone and call the karate school. I look at my watch. Still twenty minutes left till pick up time. Just enough time for me to drive over there.

The karate studio answers after a couple of rings. A slightly accented female voice answers, "Hello? Teraoka karate studio."

"Hi!" I say. "This is Julie—Leo and Tristan Bressler's mom. I just wanted to talk to somebody about their pick up today."

"Oh, yes, yes!" the woman says. "Your friend April already picked them up. No problem."

"But… the class isn't over yet…"

"She explained… there was a party…?" She sounds confused. "It was okay for her to pick up, right?"

"No!"

"But…" she sputters. "She always picks them up… I thought…"

"Don't *ever* let her pick them up again," I snap into the phone. And then I slam it down on the kitchen counter.

Why would April pick up my kids twenty minutes early? There was no reason for her to do that. Unless…

Unless she already knows I was at the nursing home with her mother. Maybe Dr. Williams called her right after I saw him.

I get a stab of panic in my chest. Oh my God, what is she doing? What is she planning to do to my children?

Okay, I need to calm down. So what if April has my kids? It's not like she's going to run off with them. I know where she lives—practically next door. And it's not like she's some sort of monster who would murder two young children.

Is she?

I call April's number yet again. Again, right to voicemail. This time I punch in a text message:

Please give me a call back as soon as possible. I really need to talk to you.

I don't know what to do. I can't call the police. I gave April permission to pick up the kids. She would have been negligent if she hadn't gotten them. The karate studio has written permission from me to allow April to pick them up. If I call the police, I'll sound like a nut job.

I call Keith, but he doesn't answer. Naturally. And then I call him again. And again. On the fourth try, he picks up the phone.

"What's going on, Julie?" he barks into the phone.

"I…" I bite my lip, trying to figure out how I'm going to tell him what happened. "April has the kids—"

"So?" he interrupts me before I can get the rest of the sentence out.

"I'm worried they might be… in danger."

"From April?" He snorts. "What's she going to do—bake them into a pie?"

"I just… I'm worried she might hurt them."

"Julie, have you been drinking?"

"No!"

"Look, I don't have time for this." Keith's voice becomes muffled as he talks to somebody in the background. "Julie, I'm going. I'll be home late tonight."

Before I can even attempt to explain, he has hung up on me.

I pace back-and-forth across my kitchen. I try calling April again, and I send her three more text messages. As much as Keith was a jerk, he was probably right. April won't hurt them. It's crazy to think otherwise.

But April not picking up her phone is unusual behavior. Not answering text messages is even more unusual. April's standard reply time is fifteen seconds.

This goes on for almost two hours. I even walk over to her house and peer through the window, but the Masterson house is empty. By the end of the two hours, I'm going out of my mind. April knows what she's doing. This is no accident. At the two hour mark, I punch in the following text message:

Please. I'm sorry. Bring them back.

Still no response. That bitch.

Fine. I'm not just going to stand here and let April torture me all night long. I go to my recently dialed numbers list and select Riley's number. It rings twice, then I hear his reassuring voice on the other line. "Jules? What's wrong?"

I tell him everything. It all comes out in a rush of words, but he doesn't interrupt me. He listens to the whole awful story, and waits until I'm done to remark, "Jesus."

"What should I do, Riley?"

He's silent for a moment on the other line. "You really think she might hurt them?"

"I don't know. Look what she did to her own mother."

He heaves a sigh. "Okay, give me your address. I'm coming over."

I recite my address for him, but before we end the call, I hear a noise. It's the front door. The lock is turning.

And there is April. With my boys.

"Never mind," I mumble into the phone. "She's here."

I don't wait to hear Riley's response. I toss my phone on the kitchen counter and rush over to hug the boys tightly to me. April is standing behind them, her usual sweet smile plastered on her lips. I want to scratch her eyes out.

"Oh my gosh!" she cries. "You weren't *worried*, were

you? I just took them out to McDonald's after karate."

I swipe at the tears forming in my eyes. "I called you."

April raises an eyebrow. "Did you? I think I left my phone in the car. *So* sorry about that."

I straighten up to stare her in the eyes. The thing is, I was a prosecutor. I have stared into the eyes of a lot of horrible people who have done a lot of horrible things. But when I look into April Masterson's pretty blue eyes, I get a chill. She isn't just horrible. She isn't just a murderer.

She's evil.

And she's making her message to me very clear. If I try to hurt her in any way, she will destroy me and everything I care about. And unlike back in my prosecutor days, when I was single and childfree, I have a family I care about now.

That night, I send Riley a text message, telling him I have made a terrible mistake. It turns out my neighbor hasn't done anything wrong after all.

CHAPTER 42

FIVE MONTHS EARLIER

It's a beautiful spring day, and Bobby and Leo are playing soccer out in the backyard.

Yes, April and I are still friends. She still calls me her best friend. Even though I despise her.

I can't seem to cut her out of my life though. She's just so *nice*. And our kids still go to the same school, and somehow they ended up in the same class yet again even though I *specifically* requested Leo to be in a different class than Bobby. She still goes to the PTA meetings, despite my efforts to assign her all the most unpleasant tasks to do. But she always does it. With a smile.

I've been trying to dodge her every time she asked for a playdate, but she begged me this time. *Bobby misses Leo so much. Why do you have Leo in so many activities?* She doesn't seem to get that I put him in the activities to keep him away from Bobby. April aside, I'm not a fan of Bobby Masterson. He's a bad influence.

While the boys are kicking around the soccer ball, I'm doing the incredibly exciting task of putting away a load of laundry. We have a cleaning woman who comes once a week, but there's too much laundry so I always do an extra load mid-week. There's nothing wrong with doing laundry. I've probably done hundreds—nay, thousands—of loads in my life. But it bothers me that I invested so many years and so much pain in my education, and somehow laundry is the highlight of my day today. My brain feels like it's rotting away.

Don't laugh, but I used to have this fantasy about being the U.S. Attorney General someday. I wrote an essay about it when I was in grade school, and even though I kept it to myself after that, it was always in the back of my head. My dream job.

Of course, now it's outright laughable. I'm so far off from my dream, it seems completely out of reach.

As I throw a load of Keith's underwear into the top drawer of our dresser, my fingers touch something cold and metallic. I frown and sift through the underwear, looking for the object. I pull out a little flip phone. It's one of those burner phones people use when they want to talk to somebody without it going to their main phone.

What is my husband doing with one of those phones?

Of course, I'm not stupid. The answer is pretty obvious. He's cheating on me. It's not like my husband is some kind of spy.

I flip it open and I see a string of text messages. Some are from Keith and some are from the other party. I take a second to scan through them.

Do you want to meet tonight?

I can't wait.

Is your wife around? Can you get away?

I'm on my way to see you.

I want to be furious, but somehow, I'm not. I'm not even surprised. But then again, I can't exactly let him get away with this. I calmly type into the text message screen:

This is Keith's wife. You're busted. Don't contact him again if you know what's good for you.

I get distracted from the phone by the sounds of shouting coming from outside. I shove the phone into my pocket, then I rush to the window, where I see Leo and Bobby in the backyard, screaming at each other. Then I watch as Bobby picks up the soccer ball and hurls it right at Leo. It smacks him right in the face, and my son lets out a howl and clutches his cheek.

I go running.

By the time I get to the backyard, Leo is sobbing. Bobby is standing nearby, shifting between his little legs. I ignore him and pry Leo's hand off his cheek. I can see right away there's going to be a bruise there.

"He threw the ball at my face on purpose!" Leo sobs.

"No, I didn't!" Bobby says. "It was an accident. We were playing soccer and it accidentally hit him."

I whip my head around to look at Bobby. His blue eyes are wide and earnest. If I didn't see the whole thing myself, I would swear he was telling the truth. Like mother like son.

"It was an accident," Bobby says again. "It wasn't my fault!"

"I saw you," I snap at him. "I was watching through the window upstairs."

Bobby opens his mouth again like he's going to protest my eyewitness account, but then he thinks better of it and hangs his head.

"Say you're sorry," I hiss at Bobby.

"Sorry," Bobby mumbles.

It's the least sincere sorry I've ever heard, and I'm raising two little boys. I can't even look at Bobby right now, so I send him into our house to watch TV while I stay out in the backyard with Leo, who is still crying.

"I hate Bobby!" Leo sobs. "I don't want to play with him anymore. He's always mean to me and taking my

WANT TO KNOW A SECRET?

I know about the latter. At first, I thought Leo was just misplacing his things. But then I found one of his toy trucks that we had been looking for days in a drawer at April's house. Bobby clearly took it from him and hid it. As I said, that kid is not a good influence.

"You don't have to play with him anymore," I tell Leo. "I promise."

Leo wipes his eyes and winces at the pain in his cheek. Keith's burner phone buzzes in my pocket—an apology from his mistress? I don't want to know. "If you tell him that," Leo says, "he's going to make everybody gang up on me at school."

My heart is breaking for my son. I wish I had never moved into this neighborhood. I wish I had never met April Masterson.

Maybe she's going to get away with killing Courtney Burns. But she's not going to get away with terrorizing my son. I'm going to have a talk with her about Bobby. And she's going to listen.

CHAPTER 43

I know I have to go talk to April the next morning, but it's hard to work up the nerve.

Instead, I take far too long rearranging the huge display of flowers Keith brought me last night when he came home from work. Clearly, he found out that I discovered his phone and decided to be proactive. The flowers are very beautiful. He got my favorite—lilacs in several different colors. He handed them to me last night, smiling nervously as he waited to see if I would confront him about the phone.

I decided not to say anything. After all, if he's messing around with another woman meant I didn't have to touch him, that was fine with me. But I kept the phone.

Finally, I grab my purse and head over to April's house. She's surely back from school by now, so she'll probably be looking for something to do. We'll have a cup of coffee, and I'll talk to her about Bobby. I'll try to be nice.

I'm not going to outright say her kid is a monster. Even though that's what I think.

I cut around the back to get to April's house. She and I have a back door sort of relationship right now. April always says friends come in through the back. Of course, maybe I should come in through the front then. Maybe that will be a message.

Except when I get outside the kitchen, I see April isn't alone. She's got a man in her kitchen.

It's Mark Tanner. And oh my God, they're kissing.

No, not just kissing. They're making out. She's got his arms wrapped around him and he's got his hand sliding up the back of her tank top. This is a prelude to sex. April is going to have sex with Mark Tanner.

Well, I guess she got back at Kathy Tanner for telling everybody she got kicked out of culinary school.

I reach into my purse and pull out my cell phone. I point the camera at the window to the kitchen and snap a couple of photos. It seems like it might come in handy.

Before April can see me, I hurry back around the side of her house, in the direction of my own house. I'll talk to her later. Much later.

"Julie!"

My breath catches in my throat at the sound of my name. I turn around and see Mrs. Kirkland, standing on her lawn by her mailbox, staring at me. Mrs. Kirkland is a tiny old lady who lives in the small house between mine and April's. She has been there for decades—long before either of us was living here.

I'm not going to lie. Mrs. Kirkland is not the most pleasant woman I've ever met in my life. But somehow, I like her. She's lived a long time, and she just says whatever the hell she wants to say.

April can't stand her.

It's fairly mutual. Mrs. Kirkland doesn't like April. She thinks Bobby is a little brat, and she doesn't much care for Elliot either. April is equally vocal in her dislike of Mrs. Kirkland. It seems like they're always at each other's throats. More than once, I have come out of my house to find the two of them shouting at each other. Although to be fair, that was partially because Mrs. Kirkland is so deaf.

"You saw, didn't you?" Mrs. Kirkland says. "You saw her and *that man*."

"Um," I say.

She shakes her head in disgust. "It's been going on for *months*. Sometimes I can *hear* them. Horrible stuff."

April has been sleeping with Mark for months? Oh God. Poor Kathy.

"She's a disgrace," Mrs. Kirkland rants. "The worst person I've ever met in my whole life. You should stay away from her, Julie."

"Mmm," I say.

"The way she carries on." Mrs. Kirkland shudders. "I should tell her husband about it. I really should."

My thoughts start to race. If Elliot discovers April is

cheating on him, maybe they'll break up. And move far away. "Have you spoken to April about it?"

"Not yet," Mrs. Kirkland says. "But I plan to. Honestly, it's horrible what she thinks she can get away with."

"Yes," I say. "It is."

———

I'm still thinking about my conversation with Mrs. Kirkland a few days later during my morning jog.

I'm up to five miles a day. I never, ever skip a day. When the weather turns too cold, I've got a treadmill in our finished basement. I tell everyone that I'm trying to keep fit, but the truth is, the adrenaline I get from running is the only thing close to what I used to feel when I was in the courtroom. If I ever stopped running, I would probably have to start taking speed. I love pushing myself as hard as I can.

I also do my best thinking when I'm running. Not that I have a lot to think about these days, but I plan out events for the PTA or dinner menus for the week. I think of fun things to do with the kids on the weekend.

And today I'm thinking about Mrs. Kirkland.

She's going to tell April she knows about her and Mark. I may be scared of April, but Mrs. Kirkland isn't. The question is, how will April react to it? Will she stop the affair? Will she deny everything?

Of course, I have proof on my phone. In case I need it.

As I turn the corner to get back to my house, I see a

police car and fire engine parked on our block. I feel a surge of panic. But no—there's no reason to freak out. The boys are at school. Keith is at work. This can't be for us.

I jog over to the police car, which is parked in front of Mrs. Kirkland's small house. A policeman is standing by his vehicle, a somber look on his face. Even though I'm in shorts and a sweaty T-shirt, I want him to take me seriously, so I throw back my shoulders, putting on my prosecutor's face.

"Excuse me," I say. "My name is Julianne Bressler and I live next-door. Can you tell me what's going on here?"

The officer looks me up and down, then he shrugs. "The old lady who lives in this house—your neighbor—she took a bad tumble down the stairs."

I have to struggle to compose myself. "Is… is she all right?"

He hesitates for a moment. "No. I'm sorry, ma'am. She didn't make it. Looks like she's been lying there at least a day."

I clasp a hand over my mouth and back away from him. Doris Kirkland is dead. Only a few days ago, she and I were standing on her lawn, chatting. And now she's dead.

And the last thing we were talking about was April. But that couldn't have anything to do with it. Could it?

At that very moment, April's car pulls up into her driveway. I watch her get out of the car, the measured expression of surprise on her pretty features. She jogs over in those stupid ballet flats she always wears.

"Oh my God!" she cries, a stricken look on her face. "What happened?"

"I'm afraid your neighbor took a fatal tumble, Miss," the officer says to her. "They just took her away."

"Oh no!"

April's eyes fill with tears, and it looks so real. Even the police officer starts trying to comfort her. *There, there. She was very old. Sometimes old people fall.*

But just as she's wiping the tears from her eyes, I see it. So quick, if I had looked away, I might have missed it.

She winks at me.

CHAPTER 44

TWO MONTHS EARLIER

I'm all alone in the house today.

Keith took the boys to see his mother. I stayed behind because I had a headache. *What a surprise*, Keith remarked. He has rightfully noted that I seem to get headaches a lot when he suggests visiting his mother. And now that I'm not going, the headache has miraculously cured itself. Look at that.

Last summer, we built a little porch coming off of our bedroom, and I'm sitting up there, enjoying the fall weather, while I read our latest book club selection. It's this beautiful book about a man and his bird. I know everybody thinks the books I pick for book club are too long and boring, but it's not like I pick the books to torture them. I try to pick books that I think are meaningful. Something we could have a great discussion about.

Then, for some reason, everyone just wants to talk about their husbands.

While I'm taking a sip from my iced tea, I notice Bobby Masterson playing in the backyard behind April's house. I have a very good view of her backyard from my little porch. And I can see Bobby throw his ball on the ground, walk around to the gate, open it up, and leave.

I put down my book entirely and lean forward to watch. Bobby walks off all by himself and goes right to our new neighbors' front door. I watch as he knocks on the door, speaks with the neighbors, and then goes inside.

April is probably inside, filming one of her YouTube shows. She undoubtedly has no idea her son just left the backyard and is at her neighbors' house. She's going to flip when she realizes he's missing. I've got to let her know.

I go back into the bedroom and get out of my phone. I already texted her before I came out here to remind her about the PTA meeting, because she tends to let it slip her mind. I start to text April that Bobby left the backyard, but then I stop myself.

Why should I tell her? If anyone deserves a few minutes of panic, it's April. She deserves a hell of a lot worse than that.

And then I get an even better idea.

I've still got that burner phone Keith was using to communicate with his girlfriend. I've got it tucked away in one of my drawers. I pull it out. It's out of juice, but the charger is the same one as the one I have for my phone, so I plug it in and wait for it to charge. When the screen lights up, I start typing.

Want to know a secret?
Your son isn't where you think he is.

I stare at my message on the screen for a moment. Is this too mean? She's going to panic when she sees this text. Then again, she kidnapped my kids for two hours. She let me think she was doing God knows what to them. And she may have killed two women.

I press send.

CHAPTER 45

I'm addicted to torturing April.

I keep sending her messages on that burner phone, and I also start posting comments on her YouTube videos. I even toss a rock through her window one night, although I immediately regret it. Anyway, I can tell it's getting to her. She doesn't look as put together as she usually does. It's petty. Sending her these text messages won't bring back Courtney Burns. It won't get any sort of justice.

But for instance, after her monster of a son almost breaks Leo's nose and we are traveling to the hospital in an ambulance, I can't help but text her the picture I have of her and Mark. I'm only sorry I can't see her face.

Meanwhile, I've gotten to know our new neighbors a little better. Sean and Maria Cooper. And they have a lovely son named Owen. Owen is *actually* lovely, not fake lovely like Bobby.

But Maria is the one I get very close to. She's

everything I thought April was when I first moved in. She has this great infectious smile with deep dimples. She can't bake like April does, but she's a nice person. I feel like Maria and I are becoming friends in the same way April and I used to be. Before I knew what April was really like.

One Sunday in October, Maria and I are sitting together in her kitchen, having some wine I brought over while the boys play upstairs. I love how close Leo and Owen have gotten. And when they're playing together, I don't have to worry that Owen is going to give my son a black eye or steal his favorite toy. Even Tristan has gotten in on the fun, even though he's two years older.

"This is so nice," Maria comments as she swirls the wine around in her glass. "You… you're not the way I thought you were when I first met you."

I know the impression I give when I first meet people. I don't have April's warm smile. "Really? How did you think I was?"

"I don't know. That email you sent about not allowing phones at the PTA meetings was pretty intense."

That might be true. I wouldn't have to do it if not for all those meetings where three-quarters of the women in the room were too busy talking or texting to listen to anything I had to say. It's so incredibly rude.

"Also…" She giggles. "Who picks James Joyce for a book club?"

I laugh along with her. "Hey, I love Joyce. It gives me

an excuse to read it. I'm always hoping maybe we'll have a discussion about it. But April always makes sure to turn the conversation around."

Maria traces a line along the rim of her wine glass with her finger. "You don't like April, do you?"

At that moment, I want to tell her everything. I want to tell her how evil April is. I want to confess about my secret burner phone, and how I've been using it to torment her. But can I trust Maria? After all, I thought I could trust April and look at what happened. So I simply shrug. "She's okay."

"You know, she thinks you're her best friend."

"She doesn't really think that."

Sean has been doing some work out in the backyard and he comes into the living room with his fingers still slightly embedded with dirt. "Hey," he says. "I'm going to get the grill going in the backyard. Julie, you staying for dinner?"

"Um…" I glance at the stairs. Leo and Tristan will want to stay for sure.

He holds up his hands and grins at me. "Don't worry, I swear I'll wash my hands before I get started."

Sean and I got off to a bit of a rocky start. He was pissed off about some notes I left on their door about how they were parking their car incorrectly. But I explained to him that the parking rules were there for a reason. Two years ago, a fire truck couldn't get through our narrow street because of the way people were parked. I'm not going to be responsible for somebody *dying*. So I organized the rules about how to park the cars, and we haven't had any issues since.

Sean understood after I explained it to him. Now we're good friends. Although he's not going to be happy when I send him the rules about dogs. After one of our neighbors kept half the block awake with his dog barking all night for months on end, I've done what I can to keep that situation from happening again.

I return his smile. "Okay, sure."

"And Keith?" Maria asks.

I wince. "No, just me. Keith won't be joining us."

I don't have to ask my husband to know he'll be staying late at work. And even if he weren't, he wouldn't want to have dinner with the Coopers. They aren't his kind of people.

"Now, Julie," Sean says, "before I get started, you gotta tell me if there are any specific *block related grill rules* that I need to know. Like do I have to get you to individually approve every piece of meat I use...?"

He's still grinning at me though. Teasing me. Sean is a good guy. You can see it all over his face and in everything he does. And he loves his family.

As promised, Sean washes his hands and then goes out to the backyard to get started on the food. Soon enough, the tantalizing smell of ground meat wafts into the house. Keith was never interested in grilling.

"Do you guys grill a lot?" I ask Maria.

"Constantly." Maria rolls her eyes. "I think there might be pure ground beef flowing through my veins right now. But Sean loves it. And so does Owen. If your boys weren't here, they'd be grilling together."

"He's so great with Owen," I say. "I'm surprised you don't have six or seven children."

"Yeah." Maria takes a sip of wine. "The truth is, I can't have children. I had these horrible fibroids and one of them ruptured. They had to do a hysterectomy to save my life."

I cover my mouth. "Oh my God, I'm sorry. That was after Owen was born?"

She shakes her head. "Owen is … He's Sean's son from another marriage. His first wife… She died of breast cancer when Owen was a baby."

I don't know what to say. "That's terrible. So much tragedy."

"It was a long time ago." She smiles distantly. "Actually, it's how Sean and I met. He had all these hospital bills to pay, even though his wife died, and he had to drive an Uber to make extra money. He was the one who drove me to the hospital when I started having pain from my fibroids, and he kept so calm when I started bleeding halfway through the ride. He made sure I got to the right place and waited with me until the doctor came. He was a complete stranger, but he was so kind." She takes another sip of wine. "And then a couple of weeks later, he called me to check on me. We got to talking and… well, you know."

Maria's story makes me think of when I went into labor with Tristan. Keith started freaking out about the possibility of my water breaking in his precious BMW. He put down a tarp on the backseat before he would let me get in.

There's no doubt that Sean Cooper is a good guy. But even good guys sometimes do bad things.

―――――

The only reason I ever go over to April's house anymore is to talk about PTA stuff. Years ago, I used to be there all the time. We used to have coffee together almost every morning. Now I do whatever I can to avoid her.

Today I need to talk about a few details about the upcoming fall festival. Admittedly, she has been invaluable in getting things set up. Everything I have asked her to do, she has done without question.

But when I come in through her back door, I find her in the living room, but she's not alone. And she's not with Mark either. I haven't seen Mark skulking around here in months—maybe she ditched him after that mess with Mrs. Kirkland. Maybe she thought it was too risky. Or maybe she just got sick of him and figured she had taught Kathy Tanner her lesson.

No, the person in April's living room is Sean Cooper.

I'm not going to lie. Sean is a very attractive man. Attractive in that sort of hot blue-collar laborer way, with the beard and the muscles—the kind of guy who doesn't even know or care that half the women on the block are slobbering over him. Not that I personally find him attractive. I never liked that type particularly. Also, I might be dead inside after so many years of plotting to get out of my wifely duties with Keith.

April finds him attractive though. It's painfully obvious. Now that she's done with Mark, she's set her sights on Sean. She's always giving him that coy smile and forcing her various fattening treats onto him. It's sickening, considering the man is her neighbor's husband and she's married herself.

Anyway, I don't catch Sean and April in a liplock. Thank God. He's standing on a stool in her living room, changing a lightbulb while she watches him. But then he sees me walk in, and he gets this sheepish, guilty look on his face. He knows this doesn't look good for him.

And April, of course, winks at me. Every time that woman winks at me, I want to strangle her.

"Sean is helping me with the lightbulb," she explains to me. "He's so much taller than me. It's much easier for him… I don't want to break my neck."

"Of course," I mutter. Even though I am only an inch taller than April, and I've changed every single lightbulb in our house dozens of times.

Sean finishes screwing in the bulb, and the living room lights up. April reaches out to touch his shoulder. "Thank you so much. You're my hero."

Sean glances at me and rubs the back of his neck. "It's just a light bulb."

"Let me get you those brownies I promised you before you go."

April hurries off to the kitchen, leaving me and Sean alone in the living room. He shoots me a look. "I was just changing her lightbulb."

"Sure," I say.

He grits his teeth. "Don't look at me that way, Julie. You know I love Maria. I would never—"

"Right," I say. "Except I'm not the person you need to convince."

He heaves a sigh. Part of me is hoping he'll refuse April's brownies, but he takes them from her before he leaves. I'm disappointed in him. One day it's brownies, the next they'll be in April's bedroom. It's a slippery slope. He just doesn't know it yet.

CHAPTER 46

Maria notices something going on between Sean and April too.

At first, she laughs it off. But about a week after the blown lightbulb, I come over to Maria's house in the morning and find her fuming mad. "Sean is over there *again*. At April's house."

Even I'm angry at Sean now. Why can't he just say no to her? "Why?"

"She thought she saw a mouse." Maria lifts her brown eyes. "Am I being paranoid? I feel like she's just making things up to get him over there."

She is absolutely not being paranoid. I don't want to fan the flame though. "April's husband doesn't help her much."

"Yeah…" She squeezes her hands together. Maria is attractive, but not as attractive as April. April is beautiful. And several years younger than Maria too. "But she could hire an exterminator. Sean doesn't have to come running over there every single time. I mean, do you think she would… Do you think it's possible…"

"Well," I say slowly, "you trust Sean, don't you?"

"Yes," she says firmly.

"So there you go."

But it's clear Maria still feels anxious about the whole thing. I can see it on her face. She trusts Sean, but maybe not more than she mistrusts April.

"Why don't we go over there?" I suggest. "We can make up some excuse."

She must be truly suspicious, because she agrees to go over to April's house. As we walk next-door, my stomach turns to butterflies. I'm not even sure what I'm hoping we'll find. Part of me wants her to discover Sean and April going at it, so she'll see what April is really like. But mostly, I don't want Maria's marriage destroyed. She's had a hard life, and she doesn't deserve that. And I also want to believe Sean is a good guy.

As we approach the front door, I can hear the voices coming from the backyard. Sean and April talking. Even from far away, I can hear the flirtatious tone in April's voice.

Maria looks pale, and I get a sinking feeling in my stomach. This doesn't sound good.

We don't end up knocking on the front door. I motion to Maria, and we walk along the side of the house so we can hear directly into the backyard. We can make out every word perfectly.

"I don't know how to thank you, Sean." April's voice is dripping with suggestion. "You have been so kind. I don't know what I would do without you."

"Uh, well, no problem."

A long pause follows. I imagine April running her hand along his biceps. I look at Maria and know she's imagining the same. "If there's anything I can do for you. Anything at all…"

"It's fine."

"I have an idea. Why don't we go inside and have a beer together? I got this amazing beer from Amsterdam. You would love it."

"April…"

"Oh, come on. Maria won't mind. One beer."

Maria's eyes are wide as her husband contemplates following his sexy neighbor into the house. I want to reach out and hug her.

"I better go," Sean says. "It's getting late."

"Don't be silly. It's still early. And I made cupcakes too. Come on."

"No, I really… I have to go."

Maria and I barely have time to scramble out of the way before Sean bursts through the gate out of the backyard. His own eyes widen when he sees us standing there. All the color drains from his face.

"Maria," he murmurs. He looks mortified. "I…"

She just blinks at him. She's holding back tears.

"I'm not going over there anymore," he says firmly. He glances at me, then picks up Maria's limp hand. "Okay?"

She nods silently.

He runs a hand through his messy hair, and I notice his hand is shaking. "I'm sorry," he says softly.

Of course, Sean hasn't done anything wrong. He was just trying to be a good neighbor and April was the one who tried to lure him over. He turned her down although I suspect part of him was tempted. In any case, I don't think he's going to eat any more of her brownies.

Oh, and Maria *hates* April now.

———

Like me, Maria can't cut April from her life. After all, the two of them are working on the silent auction together. Every time Maria goes over to April's house, it seems like she has a new piece of gossip.

"She claims that she and Elliot are trying to get pregnant," she tells me one morning in my kitchen, "but guess what? I found *birth control pills* in the closet in her downstairs bathroom."

It's almost not even a surprise. April isn't maternal, except for the cooking part. And she's more into cooking for her show than her family. She mentioned to me how much she hated gaining weight when she was pregnant with Bobby. I did the math and realized April must've been pregnant when she got married. I wonder if she needed that to seal the deal.

But Elliot wants another baby. I know that much. He'd be very interested to know his wife is sneaking birth control pills.

April sure has a lot of secrets.

"Also," Maria adds, "I caught her going through my purse!"

I gasp. "No!"

She nods. "I was in the bathroom, and when I came out, she had my other phone in her hand."

Maria fishes into her purse and pulls out a flip phone. It looks a lot like the one I've been using to torment April. Why would Maria have a phone like that? "What's that for?"

Her cheeks color slightly. "I volunteer for a nonprofit center to help battered women. After my first marriage, well… I wanted to give something back. When I'm 'on-call' women can call me at this number at any time. We arrange a safe place to meet."

I frown. "Maria, I had no idea you went through something like that…"

She waves her hand. "It's in the distant past. Having Sean… that makes up for it all."

Her voice breaks slightly, and it makes me hate April even more for trying to split up her new family. A thought occurs to me though. If April was going through her purse and saw that phone, was it possible she might think *Maria* was the one sending her the text messages?

If that's the case, is it possible Maria could be in danger?

But I quickly dismiss that thought. April probably just thought Maria was messing around on her husband. And anyway, Maria can take care of herself. I heard what she did to Carrie's babysitter and I know she's tough stuff. And she has Sean to protect her. I have nobody. Well, technically I have Keith, but he's equal to nobody. Maybe worse.

CHAPTER 47

I feel terrible for Owen when Raffey goes missing.

Maria told me he sleeps with that toy every night. His biological mother gave it to him when he was a baby. Even though he doesn't remember her, he's very attached to the toy because it's all he has of her. Sometimes I wonder if that must bother Maria, but it doesn't seem to.

"Sean's first wife was a good woman," she has told me. "I'm sad for her that she never got to see her son grow up."

Sean and Maria launch an all-out search to find Raffey. They ask Leo if he's seen the stuffed giraffe, and he says no, but he's holding back. A mother always knows. So after they leave, I question him.

"Leo," I say, "do you know where Raffey is?"

My son chews on his lip. "No…"

"Leo. What did I say about lying?"

He drops his eyes. "Bobby will be mad if I say anything."

Great. I should have known Bobby Masterson is behind this. "Leo, tell me where Raffey is."

Leo looks me in the eyes, then promptly bursts into tears. My stomach sinks—I'm not going to get any information out of him right now. I've dealt with enough witnesses on the stand to know when you won't get them to crack. Although most witnesses have a lot less snot coming out of their noses.

"Mom."

Tristan has been sitting on a sofa, listening to the entire interaction. He stares at me with eyes that are so much like mine, it's like looking into a mirror.

"Yes?" I say.

My older son lets out a sigh that makes him sound like he's ninety rather than nine. "Owen's toy is buried in Bobby's backyard. I heard them talking about it."

I nod. I can always count on him to tell me the truth. "Thanks, Tristan."

Leo's eyes fly open. "What are you going to do?" He wipes his eyes with the back of his sleeve as he tugs on my shirt with his other hand. "Don't tell him I told. Please, Mom!"

"Don't worry," I say through my teeth. "I'm not going to let Bobby Masterson hurt you." He'll have to go through me first.

After calming Leo down, I reach for my phone to tell Maria where to find Raffey. Except just as I'm texting the message, I get another idea. Maria and I are going over to April's house later today to discuss the fall carnival. The timing is perfect.

So just before I meet Maria outside on the way to April's house, I send a text message from my burner phone:

There's a surprise buried in your backyard.

I can't wait to see the look on her face…

———

A few days later, I knock on Maria's back door to say hello and ask if she wants to have some coffee and chat, and I catch her sitting at the kitchen table, watching something on YouTube. It's only after I knock that I realized she's watching April's show. *Sweet Secrets.*

She looks embarrassed that I caught her. Not only that, but she has a plate of cookies sitting on the kitchen table next to her. I could recognize April's cookies a mile away.

"Sean loves these cookies," Maria explained to me. "April brought them by last night to try to make up for the whole fiasco with her son stealing Raffey. I'm trying to replicate the recipe, but I have a feeling they won't come out as good."

I stare at April on the screen. *The secret to chocolate chip cookies is that you never use chocolate chips. You take a high-quality chocolate bar and slice it up.*

"She does have a gift," I admit.

"And," Maria adds, "she's really pretty."

It's true. Part of the reason April's show is so popular is because of how she looks. She's pretty, but also very photogenic. She looks great on camera.

"You don't have anything to worry about," I say. "I promise. Sean is a good guy."

"Maybe." Maria shoves a cookie into her mouth. "I can't stop eating these cookies. These are, like, insane. What does she put in them that makes them so good?"

"Poison," I joke.

Her eyes widen. She stops chewing and puts her hand over her mouth.

"I'm joking," I say. "April wouldn't poison you. You don't really think that, do you?"

I watch her face, waiting for her response. Because the truth is, I believe April is perfectly capable of poisoning someone. These cookies probably aren't poison. But I've become very wary of eating anything she's made. Everybody else gobbles up her treats, but I steer clear.

"No, I don't think that," Maria says. "But I do think she hopes I'll get fat from them. And that's just as bad."

I put my hand on her shoulder. "You know what will make you feel better?"

Maria raises her eyebrows, and I go to the comments on the YouTube video. I quickly type in: **I'm worried if I make these cookies, I'll gain a lot of weight like you have.** Maria snickers as I post the comment.

"Oh my God, that's awful!" she cries. "You should take it down."

"Oh, come on," I say. "She deserves it."

On the screen, April is pulling a tray of cookies out of the oven. She inhales deeply and smiles at the camera. *There's nothing like the smell of fresh-baked cookies.*

"You're right," Maria says. "She does deserve it."

CHAPTER 48

A few days before the fall carnival, I'm driving home from my morning kickboxing class when I see a young woman on the Mastersons' doorstep.

She's in her twenties, with blond hair similar in color to April's. Actually, she looks a *lot* like April—same build, height, and even similar facial features from afar. For a moment, I thought she *was* April. They could be sisters, except April is an only child. Perhaps a long lost sister?

I pull into my driveway and watch her from the car for a little while. I'm not quite sure what to make of it until I see her peering through the dark windows into the Masterson house. As the block captain, I recognize this is unacceptable behavior. I could call the police, but she looks harmless. So I go outside to talk to her.

"Excuse me." I clear my throat. "May I help you?"

The young woman jumps away from the window. She's only about ten or fifteen years younger than me, but somehow she seems decades younger. She blinks a few times. "Oh, I… I was just looking for Elliot."

Somehow, I'm reminded of Courtney. I saw Courtney's photo in the paper, and this woman is a dead ringer. Of course, they both look a lot like April.

"I'm his assistant," the woman explains hurriedly. "And I came to bring him…" She looks down at her bare hands. "I have some papers in my car."

"Do you?"

"Yes." She nods vigorously. "I just need to… to…"

And then she bursts into tears.

Of course, I invite her inside. I sit her down at her kitchen table and make her a cup of tea while the story unfolds. Her name is Brianna Anderson. She is, as she said, Elliot's assistant. She is also pregnant. And it is his.

Oh, and she's keeping it.

By the end of the story, my mouth is hanging open. I've forgotten about the tea sitting in front of me. I can't even believe what I'm hearing.

"Does Elliot know?" I manage.

She shakes her head miserably. "He'll flip. I mean, this was supposed to be a casual thing. Fun, you know? A break from that evil witch he's married to."

"Right…" I chew on my lip. "But you have to tell him. If you're keeping the baby."

"Yes, but…" She frowns. "He's just going to insist I get rid of it."

"I don't think it's up to him."

"He won't leave April."

I wonder about that part. Despite everything, Elliot does seem devoted to his family. But he has to know what April is like. Maybe he's looking for a way out. "I wouldn't be so sure."

Brianna takes a sip from her tea. "This is really good, Julie. Thank you for listening to me."

"Of course." I take a drink from my own cup. This is the special Thai milk tea that I ordered from overseas. "I'm happy to do whatever I can to help."

"So…" She lifts an eyebrow. "You're not friends with April, I take it."

"No," I say. "I wouldn't say so."

I study Brianna sitting across the table. She looks so young. I think about what happened to Courtney all those years ago. April wouldn't dare try something like that again, would she? Two assistants in a row? She has to know that would look very suspicious. Even so…

I get up and find my purse. I fish around inside until I come up with what I was looking for.

"Take this, Brianna," I say.

She stares at the bottle of pepper spray. "What is it?"

"It's pepper spray. Just in case. Keep it with you at all times."

She cringes as I lay it down on the kitchen table beside her. "You're scaring me. What do you think is going to happen?"

"I just… I think it's good to be prepared." And then I scribble down my phone number on a piece of paper. "Call me anytime. I want to help you."

She manages a smile. "I may need help finding a good lawyer. One who isn't too expensive."

"You're in luck. I'm a lawyer. And I'm not too expensive."

I want to help this girl. And I know exactly how to do it. Enough messing around. I have that photo of April with Mark Tanner. All I had to do is show it to Elliot—that will be the end of their marriage. He won't understand about her cheating, even if he has done it himself.

I can stick it to April and give Brianna a happy ending.

CHAPTER 49

The day of the fall carnival was just about the worst day of my life.

In the ambulance, Leo told me what happened. Bobby wanted a turn on the slide, and when Leo told him it was *his* turn, Bobby pushed him off the edge of the bouncy house.

Leo could have died. I could have lost my son that day, thanks to April's little monster. The teacher told her repeatedly that he should be in some sort of therapy. But she won't send him. In her eyes, he's perfect. Like mother like son.

I keep reliving that moment when I saw Leo drop off the top of that bouncy castle. I thought for sure he wouldn't survive. I thought I was going to run over there and find him dead on the ground. But by some miracle, he survived. He had a broken arm, but he was okay. He didn't even need surgery—just a cast.

That night, I'm saying a prayer of thanks that Leo is

still with us. Every time I think about it, I feel sick. For a long time, I'm going to see Leo plummeting off that slide every time I close my eyes.

I give Leo an extra squeeze when I put him to bed, being careful of his broken arm. I thought after all the excitement of the day, he might have trouble falling asleep, but his eyes are drifting shut before I even close the door to his bedroom.

I go to Tristan next. He's lying in bed, his eyes so big and wide that I can almost see them glowing in the moonlight. It looks like he might need an extra squeeze too.

"Is Leo going to be okay?" he asks in a tiny voice that makes him seem younger for a change.

"He's fine." I lean in to kiss Tristan on his smooth forehead. "I promise."

His lower lip juts out. "Bobby pushed him. I saw it. *Everyone* saw it."

"I know."

Tristan gives me a hard look with his dark, penetrating eyes. I swear, he's going to be a prosecutor someday just like I used to be. "So what are you going to do?"

Great question.

"I'm not going to let anything like that happen again," I promise him.

My conversation with Tristan has gotten me fired up. After I kiss him good night, I go downstairs and start ranting to Keith. Unfortunately, that proves a bit frustrating. Keith is upset too, but he wasn't there. There was never a moment when he thought our son might be dead. He just got a call from me saying Leo had a broken arm. So he's not as fired up as I am. Or even as fired up as Tristan.

"I think we should sue them," I say to Keith, as I pace across the living room. "Don't you think so?"

He's sitting on the couch, doing something on his phone. He doesn't even look up. "Sue who?"

"April and Elliot!" I nearly scream at him. He never listens to me.

"For what?"

"Parents can be held civilly liable for any minor child's willful misconduct."

Keith lifts his eyes just long enough to roll them at me.

I plant my hands on my hips. "Why? Am I wrong?"

"You're not wrong. But what are we going to do? Sue your best friend? Anyway, everyone will take April's side."

My mouth falls open. "Why do you say that?"

"Well, you're not exactly Miss Congeniality, Julie."

"*Excuse* me?"

"I'm just saying…" He shrugs. "Everyone loves April. She's very likable."

"And they hate me?"

He shrugs again.

"Well, gee," I say. "If I'm so goddamn unlikable, why did you marry me in the first place?"

"Beats me."

I glare at him.

He rolls his eyes again. "I'm just kidding around. Relax, Julie. Leo's fine. Just let it go."

But I can't stop fuming. Moreover, I'm starting to wonder what I'm doing here, in this marriage. It isn't like I haven't thought about leaving. I mentioned it to my mother, and she quickly shot the idea down. *Keith is the man you chose.* That's true, but I'm worried I may have made the wrong decision.

And I can't help but think about Riley Hanrahan.

I got together with him a few weeks before my wedding. One thing led to another... and yes, I was unfaithful that one time. But I couldn't help myself.

Afterward, while Riley and I were lying in bed together, me curled in his muscular arms, he said to me, *You're not really going to do it, are you? You're not really going to marry that guy?*

His words irked me. He knew we were getting married. Everything was nonrefundable. *Well, who am I* supposed *to marry? You?*

He jerked away from me, hurt in his light blue eyes. *Good to know where I stand,* he muttered under his breath.

I didn't say it to be mean though. I didn't think there was any chance Riley would ever ask me to marry him. But at that moment, I wondered if I was wrong.

But no. He wouldn't. And I didn't want to wait any longer. As my mother constantly was reminding me, my biological clock was ticking.

I don't regret the decision I made. After all, I've got Leo and Tristan. I wouldn't trade them for anything else in the world. And anyway, that's the least of my problems right now. I've got to figure out what to do about April.

———

The next day, when Elliot is leaving his office for the evening, I'm waiting for him outside my car.

He comes out at nearly eight o'clock at night. I made up some story for Keith about a friend I'm going out for drinks with. Keith gave me a look. He probably thinks I'm cheating on him, but he didn't try to stop me.

Elliot is wearing a gray suit and tie, and carrying a briefcase stuffed to the brim as he strides in the direction of his Tesla, parked right next to my SUV. Elliot Masterson is a handsome man. You can't deny that fact. Unlike my husband, who managed to gain an impressive eighty pounds during the time we've been married, Elliot has kept in shape. He started to lose his hair a few years ago, and then he just shaved it all off. But it works for him. Before Sean Cooper came along, he was easily the sexiest guy on the block.

"Julie?" Elliot looks surprised to see me. "What are you doing here? Is everything okay with April?"

"Not exactly." I shift my purse with the incriminating photograph inside. "Can we talk?"

"Uh… sure." He rubs at his bald scalp. "You're kind of

scaring me, Julie."

I'm scaring him? He's married to April and *I'm* the one he's scared of?

Elliot follows me into my car. In the moonlight, I can just barely make out dark circles under his eyes. He looks exhausted and he doesn't even know that his secretary is pregnant. I dig around in my purse until I come up with the photograph I had printed—I told Brianna I would be delivering the news tonight. I hand the photo to him, watching his expression. I could have made sure he got it some other way, but I want to see the look on his face. I deserve that, after what happened to Leo.

Elliot frowns down at the photo. "It's April and Mark Tanner."

"Right. You see what they're doing, don't you?"

"Yeah. I'm not stupid." He hands the photo back to me. "Is that it?"

My mouth falls open. "You don't care?"

"Oh, I *care*, but…" He lifts a shoulder. "Look, I'm not clueless. I know April messes around on me. You think you're the first person to talk to me about it?"

"And you're just going to *stay* with her?"

Elliot narrows his eyes at me. "Aren't you supposed to be April's best friend?"

I stare at him. This isn't going how I expected it to go *at all*. I expected him to be furious right now. I thought he'd drive right home and tell April it was over.

He nods down at my purse. "I would get rid of that

photo if I were you. You better hope April never finds out what you tried to do to her."

And all of a sudden, I get it. Elliot is scared of April too. Maybe not scared enough to keep it in his pants, but scared enough that he would never ever leave her.

Right after Elliot leaves my car, I get out my phone and text Brianna:

Don't tell Elliot anything yet. It didn't go like I thought it would.

A second later, my phone starts to ring. It's Brianna's number. I glance out my window to make sure Elliot is gone, then I accept the call. "Brianna. You can't tell him yet."

"Julie, I have to." Her voice is shaky but firm. "I'm three months pregnant. I can't wait any longer. He's going to figure it out."

"Yes, but—"

"I have to." She's silent for a moment. "If he stays with her, then… that's just the way it is. But he has to know."

"April is dangerous," I blurt out. "You have to be careful."

Another long silence on the other line. "I know about that other secretary. But you don't think April is the one who…"

"Yes. I think she is."

I hear something that sounds like a sob on the other line. "I have to tell him, Julie. I'll be careful."

I grip the phone tighter. "Look, whatever happens, I'm going to get you a fair deal. I'll be your lawyer. I... I haven't practiced in a while, but I'm pretty tough."

Brianna's laugh sounds strangled—ugh, bad word. "I can imagine."

"Be careful. If you have any concerns, call me. Or the police."

"I will."

But when I hang up, I still have a terrible feeling. This isn't going to work out well. April got rid of Courtney, and Courtney hadn't even been pregnant. What will she do to Brianna?

CHAPTER 50

With Leo home from school for a few days, I distract myself by throwing myself into PTA work. We earned a ton of money at the fall carnival, and I have some catching up to do, since I was in the emergency room with Leo most of the evening of the carnival.

The biggest fundraiser by far was the silent auction. I have to admit, April does a good job with it.

Except as I'm looking at the bids, it doesn't seem to add up. The winning bids seem greater than the amount deposited in the PTA account. I finally get a calculator and do the math. It turns out I'm right. There's a big discrepancy.

There's money missing. A *lot* of money.

I spend the next hour on the phone with the bank. It takes some investigating, but it turns out some of the money was being filtered into a second account. One that isn't affiliated in any way with the PTA.

Meaning somebody stole the money.

And then I do something really sickening. I go back to last year's numbers. To my horror, there was a discrepancy last year too. How did I miss it? I thought I was so careful and organized.

Somebody stole money from the PTA account for the last two years. And there's only one person who could have done it.

April.

I can't believe it. After everything else she's done, she also stole money from her child's school? What is her encore going to be? Is she going to set an orphanage on fire while poisoning puppies?

The worst part is, I'm not sure how to handle it. I would love to turn this over to the police. I would love for April to go to jail for this, if nothing else. I mean, this is a lot of money. We're talking grand larceny. That's a felony.

But at the same time, I'm afraid of the scandal. The PTA has been my life for the last few years. If people found out that money was being stolen, we're never going to be able to raise money again in the future. My best bet is to try to get the money back and sweep it under the rug.

I have to confront April.

The next morning, after Leo returns to school, I call April into my office at school to talk to her about the silent auction. My heart is thudding so loudly, April must be able to hear it. She has to know how terrified I am of her.

And now I'm going to confront her for the first time. I have no idea how she's going to take it.

She doesn't even look nervous when she sits down across from me at the conference table. April is never nervous. Not really. She sometimes tells people she's nervous about this or that, but she isn't really. I wonder if she ever feels any real human emotions or if she's faking everything.

"Sit down," I tell her.

"No 'please'?"

There's an edge to her voice that makes a chill go down my spine. I lift my eyes and her own eyes are boring into me. Do I really want to do this?

I take a deep breath. *Be brave, Julie. You've brought down worse people than her.* "I was looking at the app you used to record the bids and accept money into the PTA fund. And I noticed that there was a second account recorded. That a percentage of the money was being filtered into an account that wasn't related to the school."

She blinks innocently. "What do you mean?"

Okay, she's going to play dumb. "I *mean*, somebody created another bank account that's been stealing money from the silent auction that was supposed to have been going to the PTA."

She clamps a hand over her mouth. "Oh my *God*. Who would do something like that?"

But of course, she knows. And she knows I know. She's still going to make me play this game though.

"You," I say. "You did it."

"Julie, I would *never* do that." She reaches out and before I can yank my hand away, her hand is on mine. "You know you can trust me."

Her hand is gripping mine, applying an uncomfortable pressure. I take another deep breath and yank my hand away. "I'm sorry. But I know you did it."

"But—" Her eyes light up. "Maria! She and I were working on the silent auction together! She also had access to the account."

"It wasn't Maria."

I can see the wheels turning in her brain. "Maria is the one who told you to look at the account, didn't she?"

Oh God. She must have seen that burner phone in Maria's purse, and now she thinks Maria is the one tormenting her. I can't let her believe that. "I received an anonymous text message telling me to look into it," I lie.

April's face turns pink. This might be the first time I've ever seen her lose her composure. "Look," she says, "Maria set me up. She created this false account, then she 'discovered' it. And now it looks like I've been stealing money! But you have to know, I would never do something like that."

"April…"

"Maria is evil!" she cries. "She's been tormenting me for months by sending me threatening text messages."

My stomach sinks. She's convinced Maria is the one doing this to her. This isn't good. Especially since I know what April is capable of. "How do you know?"

"I just do."

"What sort of text messages? Can I see?"

April sits there a moment, quietly gnawing on her thumbnail. Finally, she says, "I deleted them."

And then I feel a rush of relief. She has nothing on me. Nothing on Maria. She's too scared of her secrets coming out. "That's unfortunate," I say.

"You've known me for years! You really believe her over me?"

"Listen, April." I use my courtroom voice—no emotion. "I'm not going to turn this matter over to the police, but I expect you to return the money. If you don't, well, then it will be a police matter."

Her eyes fill with tears. Is it all an act? I can't tell with April. But I've shaken her. I hope she returns the money so I don't have to go to the police.

"Julie." She stares across the table at me. "This is a huge mistake. Believe me."

I get that chill down my spine again. I wonder if she's right. Maybe I'm making a mistake by crossing her. But I have to take the chance.

I can't let her get away with it anymore.

CHAPTER 51

After confronting April, I go to Helena's to see Maria.

Unfortunately, she's busy with customers. She tells me she's got a break coming up in about half an hour, so I wait in the back, browsing merchandise. Maybe I'll buy something, get Maria a nice little commission.

And that's when April comes into the store.

Instinctively, I hide behind a rack of dresses. I feel like an idiot, camped out behind the dress rack, watching April. But I can't look away. She's looking through Maria's purse. Is she searching for that phone? Whatever she's looking for, she doesn't seem to find anything.

And then I watch her march over to Maria, and the two of them have it out. I want to leap to Maria's defense, but something tells me my presence will only escalate things. I don't want to get Maria in trouble at work. So I hang back.

And then I watch April storm off while Maria goes to help another customer. But the next thing I see, I can hardly believe.

April takes a pair of earrings off a rack. She glances around to make sure nobody is watching her, but she can't see me crouched behind the dress rack. She expertly removes the tags from the earrings, then drops them in her bag. She does it like somebody who has stolen many things in her lifetime—that doesn't surprise me one bit. And then she strides purposefully toward the exit.

I nearly leap out of my hiding place to warn Maria that April is about to steal some earrings. But it turns out it's unnecessary.

The alarm that goes off is almost deafening. My first instinct is to cover my ears, but that isn't what I do. Instead, I take out my phone and snap a photo of April being apprehended by the security guard.

That should give her something to think about.

Maria is fuming mad when the security guard takes April away into a back room. I come out to talk to her, and her face is pink. "Can you believe that woman?" she rants. "She tried to steal two-hundred-dollar earrings!"

"I believe it," I say. April has stolen far more than that from her own son's school.

"What a mess." She shakes her head. "Now we've got to deal with the police coming over. And I'm sure she'll pretend it was all a mistake. The police officer will probably end up taking her out for coffee."

She's probably right.

"Wait." I grab her arm. "Before the police come, have her sign a confession."

Maria freezes. "What?"

"If she signs a confession," I say. "Then you use that in court."

"She won't sign a confession!"

"Of course she will." I shrug. "Just tell her you won't call the police if she signs a confession."

"I have to call the police. It's our policy to prosecute shoplifters."

"Right. But you don't tell her that."

Maria narrows her eyes at me. "Okay... But where do I get a confession?"

"Do you have a computer? I can type one up for you. It's not rocket science."

I have seen enough signed confessions before, so I'm able to have one typed up in five minutes. And just as I predicted, April is only too happy to sign—Elliot will go nuts when he finds out. Any good lawyer will get it thrown out of court, but I want to stick it to April.

Maybe this will teach her a lesson.

CHAPTER 52

The next night, while the boys are in bed and I'm watching television on my sofa, I get the phone call.

It's Brianna.

"Julie." Her voice is a whisper. "April is following me."

Last night, Brianna told Elliot everything. She told me he just seemed dazed. Tried to convince her to get rid of the baby. She told him no, and he said he had to think about it. Obviously, he told April everything. And this morning, she came to my house looking for me, and she ended up running into April and they had a huge confrontation in front of her house.

"Are you sure?" I ask.

"Yes." I hear the screeching of wheels. "I'm driving home and her white SUV is right behind me. I tried to make a few turns down empty streets, just to make sure. She's definitely following me."

"Did you call the police?"

There's a long silence on the other line. "If I call the police, Elliot is going to hate me."

"Brianna." I stand up from the couch and start pacing. "You have to call the police."

"I'm almost home," she says. "I see a parking spot. I'm going to pull in."

"Call the police," I repeat. My knuckles are turning white as I grip the phone. "Brianna, you have to call the police. She's dangerous."

"Look, we're in the middle of the street. She's not going to do anything to me out here. I'll be home in a minute."

I glance out the window. "But it's dark."

"I'll call you as soon as I get inside."

"Brianna—"

But the line is dead.

I stare down at the phone. I'm itching to call the police, but I don't know what I would say. I don't even know where Brianna lives. *A woman is being followed by another woman, but I'm not sure where she is.* Yeah, they'd get on that right away.

I sit back down on the sofa, but I can't relax. I keep waiting for Brianna's call.

And I wait.

And wait.

Thirty minutes later, it's painfully obvious I'm not going to hear from Brianna. I dial her number, but nobody answers. She never made it home. April got to her first.

I have to tell the police, but what can I say? I wish she

had told me where she lived. I get the feeling it isn't a great neighborhood.

I look in my phone contacts. There's only one person I could call at this hour who could help me. I select Riley Hanrahan's number.

I hesitate for a moment, feeling a little awkward about calling him. A year ago, after he helped me get that information about Courtney Burns, I then told him everything was fine and I didn't want to pursue it further. He realized something was up, and he sent me a few more text messages to make sure I was okay. He even tried calling. But I didn't take the call.

Still, there's nobody else I can talk to about this.

"Jules?" His voice sounds muffled. "Is that you?"

"Um, yeah…"

"Geez, it's been a while." He yawns. "What's up?"

"I… I'm sorry. Were you sleeping?"

He hesitates. "A little. What's wrong?"

It's such a relief to tell somebody else the entire story. I start at the beginning and ramble on for several minutes. It sounds crazy, even to my own ears. But Riley is silent on the other line, listening. I get to the part about Brianna being followed by April, and then the purpose of the call: "I think April did something to her."

"Jesus Christ, Jules," Riley mutters. "You really took the law into your own hands. I think you need to get back to work. Or else… I don't know… get a dog or something."

I feel a lump in my throat. "You don't believe me…"

"Of *course* I believe you. I just wish you would've called me sooner."

My shoulders sag. "Will you help me?"

"Yeah, I'll do my best." He grunts on the other line. "This isn't my… you know, jurisdiction. But I'll work it out. Just hang tight. Don't do anything stupid. I'll call you later tonight."

"Thanks, Riley."

But I have a horrible feeling it's too late.

———

The phone wakes me up at one in the morning.

I'm lying in bed next to Keith, but I'm not asleep. I'm lying awake, staring at the ceiling. Keith is about three feet away from me, as far as he could possibly be while still in the same bed, and he's snoring up a storm. He has horrible sleep apnea, but he refuses to wear the CPAP machine that his doctor prescribed. Most nights, I sneak into the guest room and sleep there. Besides snoring like a chainsaw, Keith is also a bed hog. I prefer to sleep alone.

But tonight, I want company. I can't stop thinking of Brianna's last phone call to me. What happened to her? I called Maria to see if April had shown up to the book club, and apparently, they had turned her away. God knows where she went after that.

Keith rolls over in bed and the phone starts ringing. His eyes spring open. "Who the hell is calling in the middle of the night?"

I snatch up the phone before Keith can see the name on the screen. He knows exactly who Riley Hanrahan is, and he won't be happy to see that name pop up on my phone. "Sorry. I'll go to the other room."

Keith grumbles something and punches his pillow with his hand. I take the phone outside before I press the green button.

"Riley?" I whisper.

"Hey, Jules." His voice is low, almost a whisper like mine. "Sorry it's late."

"Did you find her?"

"Yeah." He heaves a sigh. "She's dead, Jules."

The room starts to spin. I lean against the wall and sink onto my knees. "What happened to her?" I manage.

"I shouldn't be talking about this," he murmurs. "I'd get in a lot of trouble."

"I've stuck my neck out for you too," I remind him.

"Yeah, I know." Back when I was at the DA's office, we worked together a lot. We shared information not everybody got to know. I trusted him. He trusted me. "We found her lying behind some trash bins. It looks like she was hit repeatedly in the head with a blunt object, but we won't know for sure until the autopsy."

"Oh my God," I breathe.

"Look," Riley says, "I gotta be honest with you. I know you think April Masterson did this, but I don't know. It would have taken a lot of force. That Masterson woman doesn't look like she has it in her."

I bite the inside of my cheek. "She has it in her. Trust me."

"I don't know." I imagine him scrunching up his brow, the way he always did when he was deep in thought. "Anyway, like I said, I could get in a lot of trouble for calling you like this. So this is the last time. But we'll probably have you come in tomorrow to talk to us on the record about your phone call with Brianna."

"You're staying on the case?"

"Yeah. I got approval."

"Good."

There's a long silence on the other line. "Be careful, will you, Jules?"

"I will."

"Don't do anything crazy. Your part is done. You're not a prosecutor anymore. We got this."

"I know."

He lets out a sigh like he doesn't entirely believe me. "Good night, Jules."

"Goodnight, Riley." I grip the phone tighter. "Thanks... for..."

"Yeah," he says.

We hang up the phone, and I just sit there on the floor, shaking. I sit there so long, I drift to sleep in that position.

CHAPTER 53

I'm not going to lie. I'm not blameless.

Maybe I am partially responsible for what happened to Brianna. Maybe I drove April crazy with my text messages and the comments on her videos. Maybe sending her that photograph of her shoplifting was what drove her over the edge.

I regret a lot.

I spend most of the morning sitting in the kitchen, contemplating what I've done. I thought I was serving justice to April. But that's not what I've done at all. And now there's nothing I can do to fix it. Riley is right—I'm not a DA anymore. I'm a housewife who is completely out of my element. I need to stay out of it. All I can do is sit here and hope Riley has enough to pin the murder on her. So she doesn't get off scot-free yet again.

I've opened up a pint of ice cream. It's this ice cream with little blondie bits in it and a core inside of salted caramel. It's one of the best things I've ever tasted. I've already eaten half a pint. Each spoonful has about five-hundred calories. I don't care.

"Julie?"

Keith is standing in the middle of the living room. I look up in surprise. I can't remember the last time I've seen my husband in the middle of the day.

"What are you doing here?" I ask.

Keith is dressed for work in his gray suit. He bought that suit about a year ago, and it's already too tight. "I had a dentist appointment," he says. "But I'm heading to the office now."

"Oh." I listlessly scoop ice cream into my mouth. "Okay."

"Watch the ice cream, Julie. You don't want to weigh five-hundred pounds."

I shoot him a look. "Or else what?"

He shrugs. "Or else maybe I get myself a new wife."

I toss the metal spoon on the table. Ice cream splatters all over the marble counter. "That sounds like a great idea. We're through."

Keith's eyes widen. "Hey, don't get all bitchy. I didn't mean it."

"Well, I do." I put the lid back on the ice cream and shove it in the freezer. I shut the door with a slam. "I'm done here. I don't want to be married to you anymore."

"Come on, Julie." He frowns at me. "Look, I'm sorry. You can go back to eating whatever you want and doing whatever you want and spending my money whenever you want."

I grit my teeth. "You're making this really easy for me. So thank you."

"Julie…"

"When you come home tonight, the boys and I will be gone." I raise my eyebrows at him. "Not that you would even notice."

"Right. And how are you going to pay for all the things you like without me?"

"I'm going back to work." As the words come out of my mouth, it feels so good. I can't believe I didn't do this ages ago. I miss my job so much. "And also, there's alimony."

I can't wait to take Keith to the cleaners. I know every single woman he was unfaithful to me with.

Keith's face darkens and he takes a step closer to me. "Does this have to do with Riley Hanrahan?"

I freeze. "What?"

"I saw his name on your phone last night." He narrows his eyes. "Are you messing around with that guy again?"

"Absolutely not." I plant my fists on my hips. "This has nothing to do with anyone else. This is about you and me. I don't want to be married to you anymore."

A muscle twitches in Keith's jaw. He stares at me, his face turning pink, then red, then almost purple. I wonder if he's going to try to hit me. Well, let him try. I've got years of kickboxing under my belt while he gets out of breath walking up the steps to the second floor of our house.

"Fine," he snaps at me. "Do whatever you want. It'll be good to be rid of you."

With those words, Keith turns around and storms out of the house. I hear his BMW revving to life outside, and then he zooms off. And he's gone.

Despite everything, I feel wonderful. I didn't realize how much I hated my life with that man until I called it quits. It's like a horrible weight has been lifted from my shoulders.

I'm free. Thank God I'm free. And I'm getting the hell out of Long Island.

I race up the stairs to our bedroom. I yank my large brown suitcase out of the closet, and I start packing. I'll have to stay with my parents for a little while, until I figure out the shelter and job situation. But I don't want to live here another minute. The boys will be upset at first, but they'll get used to the idea. It's not like they saw Keith much anyway. It's better for them if I'm happy. And I'm not happy here. I haven't been happy for a long time.

As I'm throwing shirts and pants in the bag, my eyes are drawn to the window. Maria's master bedroom is right across from ours. Close enough that I could almost reach out and touch her if I had extremely long arms. Well, it's at least within throwing distance. A few times, they left their blinds open, and I got an eyeful of Sean walking around with his shirt off.

There's somebody in the bedroom now. But it's not Maria and it's not Sean.

It's April.

I stand there, staring out my bedroom window. April is in Maria's bedroom. What is she doing in their bedroom?

I step to the side so she doesn't see me and let the curtains fall closed. I peek between the curtains to get a closer look.

April is searching through the bedroom furiously. She's yanking open drawers and sifting through them. At one point, she looks in the closet. She's desperate to find something.

Oh my God, I bet she's looking for Maria's burner phone.

I walk over to the drawer by my nightstand. I reach behind a couple of books and pull out my little flip phone. This is what she's looking for. But she won't find it in Maria's bedroom.

Fine. Let her look.

I peek through the curtains again. April is still searching the room. She won't be there for long though. She'll have to head to the school soon to pick up Bobby. When I see Maria I'll have to warn her.

Except my eyes are drawn to movement at the front of the house. It's Maria. She's unlocking the front door.

No no no no…

I feel a surge of panic as Maria steps inside her house.

I've got to warn her that April is in there. I don't know what April is capable of. No, actually, that's not true. I know exactly what April is capable of. This isn't going to end well.

But I left my phone downstairs. All I've got up here is my flip phone and that doesn't have Maria's number plugged in. The only number I've got is…

April.

My hands are shaking as I type on the screen:

I know you are inside the house, April.

There. That should frighten her off.

I peek through the curtains again. I see April freeze. She feels around in her pocket and pulls her phone out of the purse on her shoulder. Her eyes widen as she reads my message.

She puts her phone back in her purse. I watch her sifting through the purse for a few seconds, and I wonder what she's doing. And then I see her pull something out of her purse.

It's a knife.

Oh God.

I've got to do something.

I consider calling 911, but it seems like by the time I get through to the police and explain the whole thing to them, and tell them how urgent it is, it will be too late. So instead of the police, I click on Riley's number.

He answers after one ring. "Jules? What's going on?"

"April is at my neighbor's house," I manage. "She's upstairs in the bedroom with a knife. I… I think she thinks my neighbor knows something and is going to turn her in."

"Got it. I'll be right there."

I stare across the way, into Maria's window. April is still standing there with the knife. Any second, Maria will go upstairs. "How long?"

"With the sirens? Maybe… ten minutes."

"No. Somebody has to come right now." I squeeze the phone until my fingers tingle. "Right this minute."

"Okay. I'll get a squad car to go."

I try to look in the windows downstairs, to see if Maria is still on the first floor. I don't see her. "I've got to go over there."

"Jules, *no*." I hear the siren going on the other line. He must've gotten on the road. "Don't go over there—it's too dangerous. I'm getting a squad car to go. Don't move. We will take care of this."

"I have to…"

"I mean it, Julianne. Don't even think about—"

I hang up the phone before he can say anything else. I know he wants to try to talk me out of it, and he might be right. It might be stupid to go over there. But it's my fault this is happening. I've got to do something.

I've got to go over there.

CHAPTER 54

APRIL

Courtney Burns.

You want the truth about Courtney Burns? Here's the truth:

Bobby was two years old. He wouldn't stop crying that day. While we were at the department store, he threw himself onto the ground and had an all-out tantrum, his legs and arms flailing around, his tiny face turning pink. I can't even remember what the tantrum was about. Maybe because he wanted to wear his diaper as a hat and I wouldn't let him. Maybe because I wouldn't let him eat sunscreen. Who knows. But at the end of a very long day, I finally got him to bed. He passed out in his crib and I went to the kitchen to make some dinner before Elliot got home from work. It smelled wonderful.

But Elliot wasn't interested in dinner. He got home from work and he said, "April, we need to talk."

I didn't look up from the meat sauce I was stirring on the stove. I didn't want it to burn. "About what?"

"I…" I could feel Elliot's presence behind me. "I've met someone else."

I put down the spoon and turned to look at him. This was before he started shaving his head, and his hair was receding a lot, but he still looked very handsome. He still sometimes turned heads. "What?"

"I'm sorry." He dropped his eyes. "It's Courtney. My assistant at work. I… I didn't mean for it to happen."

Elliot was cheating on me. I was hurt, but not entirely surprised. Men cheated. That was just what they did. I would make him grovel, but ultimately, I would forgive him. "Is it over then?"

"April." His brow furrowed. "I… I'm in love with her."

And then I realized what he was saying to me. He wasn't confessing an affair. He was telling me he was leaving me for her.

I saw my entire life falling apart. My son growing up without a father in the house. Scrounging around for money. I could never afford to live in this neighborhood as a single mother. Where would we live? What would I do?

All because of Courtney.

So I kept it from happening. Dr. Williams was so wonderful about that. Joe was my primary care doctor back then, and I always felt like he had a thing for me, even though he was happily married. He was able to look up the name of Courtney's doctor and call in an Ativan prescription under his name. I picked up the prescription and I went to Courtney's house. I got in through the back door, which was hanging right open. It wasn't even locked!

And I waited for her.

Ultimately, what the police determined was true. Courtney did take all those pills herself. So technically, it was suicide. But she probably wouldn't have taken them if I wasn't holding that knife. I explained to her the way I would slice up her beautiful face first, then the rest of her if she didn't do what I said. She was resistant at first, but when I cut off her pretty blond hair, she became much more compliant.

And Elliot stayed, of course. Although he never looked at me quite the same after that. But you can certainly understand why I never wanted to get pregnant again. He started up with her when I was still padded with about fifteen pounds of my baby weight from Bobby, when I was too tired for the kind of enthusiastic performance I'm sure Courtney put on in bed. Elliot claims he wants another baby, but look what he did to me after the first one we had. You can't blame me for taking birth control pills.

My mother was my alibi for the night of Courtney's death. I explained to her the way it would look. I swore to her I didn't kill Courtney, but I needed an alibi. I needed her to help me. And she did it.

A year later, she changed her mind. She decided I probably did kill Courtney after all. Can you believe that? What kind of loyalty is that to her daughter? Yes, she was right. But still.

Luckily, Joe helped me again. He was her doctor too by then—I made sure of that—and it was almost too easy to label her with a diagnosis of early-onset dementia. I took her to court and became her health care proxy and power of attorney. Joe pulled some strings to get her into Shady Oaks, where he was able to give her enough medications to make sure nobody doubted the diagnosis.

He's been great. But to be fair, I've made it worth his while.

That's one of the tenets of life. Some people get pushed around, and some people do the pushing. I don't let myself get pushed around. I'm successful. My husband is an attorney, although granted, he isn't around as much as I'd like and his career has been in the toilet a bit lately. And I've got a successful YouTube show with tons of subscribers. And I have a beautiful and intelligent little boy, who has some minor anger management issues that everyone blows totally out of proportion.

If anyone tries to push me around, I make sure they're sorry.

For example, Mrs. Kirkland.

She came to my house, ranting and raving about how she saw me and Mark together. How she was going to tell everybody in town. How I was a disgrace. She even called me a…

Well, I don't like to use bad language. But she called me something that rhymed with "poor" and started with the letter W.

Can you imagine? We were neighbors for *years*. I mean, yes, I hated her. I did let Bobby trample her roses on purpose a few times. But that sort of language was *uncalled for*.

She was so old. I barely even pushed her down the stairs. It was more like a nudge.

I do what I have to do. Yes, I took money from the PTA account. But it wasn't much. Is it my fault my husband has torpedoed his career because he can't keep his junk in his pants? I can't even buy the basic stuff I need for my show. I hardly took any money. Julie didn't even notice last year.

Maria Cooper has also been trying to push me around. I can't imagine why. I suppose she may know my secret about Courtney. But why would she care? Maybe she's jealous because she sees the way her husband looks at me. But that's not my fault.

She should thank me. Because if I wanted Sean Cooper, I could have him. *Easily*. Men are so weak. If I gave him a serious invitation, he would be in my bed in an hour. She's lucky I've kept my distance.

But I'm done being pushed around by Maria. Now she's going to get what she deserves. The same way Courtney did. The same way my mother did. The same way

Mrs. Kirkland did.

That's why I brought the knife with me.

———

I'll make it look like a robbery. Somebody was burglarizing Maria's home, and she came home unexpectedly in the middle of the day and surprised them. I'll have to take a few things from the house to make it realistic. Some jewelry. Maybe her laptop. It's not like the Coopers have anything worth stealing. Any logical burglar would go next-door to the Bresslers. That house has the motherlode. I've almost been tempted to burglarize them a few times.

I do feel sorry for Sean and Owen. This will be hard on them. Sean will probably be the one to find her. Lying in a pool of blood in the middle of their bedroom. I hope Owen will be spared that. Maybe I should pick him up from school today to make sure he isn't around when the body is discovered.

See? I'm not heartless.

I hide behind the door to the bedroom, as the sound of Maria's footsteps on the stairs grow louder. And then a pause, when she gets to the top of the steps.

"Sean?" she calls again.

I don't understand why she keeps asking for Sean. His car isn't here. And she already texted me that she knows I'm in here. I grab the handle of the knife tighter in my right hand. My knuckles are white.

I wonder if she has a weapon. Not a gun—I heard Sean ranting about how dangerous it is to have a gun in the house—but she could've grabbed a knife from the kitchen. That said, she doesn't know where I am. I have the element of surprise.

And I don't think Maria Cooper has it in her to stab somebody. She's all talk.

The footsteps start up again. She's right outside the bedroom door. I hold my breath. "Sean?" she says one more time.

And then she comes into the bedroom. She doesn't have a knife. She has no weapon at all.

I step out of the shadows, the knife raised in my hand. Maria sees me, and she takes a step back. I hear the sharp inhalation of air. "April?" she gasps.

Now that I see she has no weapon, I can take my time. Well, not a lot of time because I have no idea when Sean will be home, but I can get what I came here for. The timing could not have been better. "Give me the phone," I say.

Maria blinks at me. "I… I don't understand. What are you talking about?"

"I want the phone. Now."

Her eyes dart around the room. "I… I left my phone downstairs. In my purse. Where I always keep it."

"Quit playing dumb." I take a step toward her, the knife still tightly gripped in my right hand. "You know what phone I'm talking about."

Maria takes a step back. "I… I don't know."

"Bullshit," I say through my teeth as I take another step forward. "We both know what you've been doing. I want that phone."

Maria tries to take another step back, but she hits the wall. I see the fear in her eyes. That's exactly how Courtney looked when I sliced through her hair.

"April," she whispers. "Please don't do this. Please, I—"

"Wait a minute," I say. "Shut up for a minute."

I heard something just now. It sounded like… steps on the creaky stairs. Is someone else in here? It couldn't be Sean—his truck is so loud, I can hear it coming all the way down the block.

And then I hear my phone buzz inside my pocket.

I keep one eye on Maria as I reach into my pocket and pull out my phone. I drop my eyes and read the words on the screen:

I'm right behind you, April.

Oh God.

I look up at Maria. She's just staring at me, with those wide, terrified eyes. I look down at the screen again. **I'm right behind you, April.** It wasn't Maria. It couldn't have been.

Slowly, I turn around.

Maria's closet is behind me. I squint into the dark

depths of the closet, my heart pounding. Is there somebody in there?

And then I feel something hit me from behind. A vase shattering against my scalp, and I collapse onto the ground, the knife falling from my grasp. I realize nobody was in the closet at all. I was tricked.

My head is spinning. I touch the back of my scalp and my fingers come away red. I roll over and look up, expecting to see Maria standing over me. But it's not Maria. It's *Julie*.

My best friend.

CHAPTER 55

JULIE

I look down at April lying on the floor, the broken pieces of the vase from my house splayed out around her head. She's still moving, so I didn't knock her out, but I knocked her down. I've never hit anyone that hard in my life. Zumba doesn't quite prepare you for that.

"Julie!" Maria's brown eyes are wide. "Oh, thank God!"

The knife April had been holding fell out of her hand when she collapsed. I see it on the ground, and before my brain can even react, my hand is reaching for it. I pick it up and grab it in my right hand.

April rolls over, clutching her head. There's a drop of blood running down her temple. "Julie," she murmurs. "What…?"

In the distance, I can hear sirens. It's been about five

minutes since I called Riley. He got someone here quickly. But it wouldn't have been quick enough.

"Go downstairs," I say to Maria. "Let the police in."

"Are you sure you'll be okay up here?" she asks.

I nod. "I'll be fine."

More than fine. I look over at my hand holding the knife. It's steady as a rock.

April watches Maria leave the room as she clutches her head where I clocked her a good one. The second Maria is out of sight, her eyes lock with mine. "Thank God she's gone, Julie. She's crazy. You have to believe me."

"Yeah, right."

"Julie…" April tries to stand up, but I shake my head at her and point to the ground. "Julie, you're my best friend. You have to believe me. She… she murdered Elliot's secretary and she's framing me for it."

"No, she didn't."

"She did!" April's eyes fill with very real-looking tears. "She's out of her mind. She's been… torturing me. She has it out for me!"

I almost feel sorry for her. Does she really think she's going to convince me? "I saw what you were about to do to her."

"I was just defending myself!" She swipes at her eyes. "Because I thought she was going to kill me!"

"I'm sure."

We can hear the sound of the front door opening. April's blue eyes widen with panic. "Julie, please. Look at what she sent me."

She fishes around in her pocket and pulls out her cell phone. It still has the message I sent her on the screen:

I know you are inside the house, April.

"It's all been sent from a burner phone I found in her purse," April says hurriedly. "She's out to get me. Don't you believe me?"

"Maria didn't send you that message," I say quietly.

There are footsteps on the stairs. Men's voices. The cops. "Yes, she did!" April cries.

"No, she didn't," I say. "I did."

April's mouth falls open just as the police burst into the room.

———

It's a good thing Riley is there to explain everything to the police who show up, because it doesn't look great for me. I'm the one holding the knife. But between him and Maria, the truth quickly comes out. April broke into the house. She was threatening Maria. And I'm the hero.

"We have an eyewitness who can place April at the scene of the crime," Riley explains to me after April is taken away in handcuffs. "They saw her white SUV following Brianna's car, and they saw them both get out of the car. They didn't see the attack itself, but considering she has a motive, no alibi, and there's a witness who saw her there, we've certainly got enough to charge her."

As I watch the police doing their job, all I can think about is how I wish I were the one trying this case. I can't wait to get back in the courtroom. I'm itching for it.

But I'm not there yet. My old life is still very much in the present. "Do you need me here?" I ask. "I've got to pick up my sons from school." I should probably also pick up Bobby Masterson. God knows April won't be doing it.

"Well, it would be good if you could stay..." He hesitates. "Any chance your husband could go pick up the kids?"

I snort. "Definitely not. And I'm not excited about calling him to ask any favors right now considering..." I take a breath. "I just told him I want a divorce."

God, it feels so good to say those words out loud. I want to scream it from the treetops.

Riley's eyebrows shoot up. "Really?"

"It's been a long time coming."

He cocks his head to the side. "I can't say I'm sorry. Like I said, I never got what you saw in the guy."

Me either.

"Maria! Maria, are you okay?"

Sean came home and saw all the police cars in front of his house—and was understandably panicked. He sees Maria and runs over to her. I watch as he wraps his arms around her and holds her while she starts to cry. He whispers in her ear, and she clings to him. It makes me ache for what could have been if I had married a decent guy like Sean.

Of course, maybe things would've been different for April too if she had married a decent guy. But she didn't. And now Elliot has to live with the mess he created.

"Go get your kids," Riley says. "Call me later today, when you have a chance to come down to the police station. We'll want to get your official statement on the record."

"Okay," I agree. "And… thanks. For your help. For rushing over here."

"It's my job." Except it's not really his job. His precinct is all the way over in Queens, for God's sake. "Talk to you later?"

I nod. "Looking forward to it."

CHAPTER 56

JULIE

It feels so strange to be sitting in Maria's kitchen after everything that's happened.

April is in jail. In *jail*. I still can't wrap my head around that one. When I texted her with that burner phone months ago, I never thought this would be the outcome. Of course, it's not because of that phone. It's her own damn fault.

Maria is checking on something in the oven. She looks pretty today. Her hair is pulled back in a ponytail. And her eyes look less haunted than they have for the last couple of weeks. You almost can't see the circles under them anymore.

"Two more minutes," Maria announces.

"I can't wait," I say. Although that's a lie. The last time I tried Maria's cookies, they tasted like hockey pucks. I figure I'll take one bite to be polite.

Maria slides into the seat next to me at the kitchen table. "I still can't believe you left Keith."

"It's the best decision I ever made." I take a sip of my coffee. "And I've got my resume out there. I can't wait to get back to work."

"So no regrets?"

"Absolutely none."

Just the opposite. It's like being free from shackles. And Keith decided to let me stay in the house, so I didn't even have to move. Although I will eventually. I'll be as relieved to get rid of our ridiculously extravagant house as I was to get rid of Keith.

"I've got to get Sean to go back to work," Maria says. "He's so scared to leave me alone after what happened."

I can't blame him. But with April in jail, we're safe.

"I think," I say, "I'm done with men for a while."

A tiny smile plays on Maria's lips. "Even that cute detective I saw checking on you the other day?"

Riley did come by yesterday. And the day before that. And so forth. He's been checking on me regularly since the whole thing happened. He comes in, we chat for a little while, then he leaves. Nothing has happened. Nothing is going to happen—I'm not ready for anything like that now. Not yet. But it's nice to know a detective is looking out for me.

The timer goes off. Maria leaps up from her seat and

pulls the tray of cookies out of the oven. They don't look too bad. They're not black like her last batch.

"That looks promising," I say.

"It's April's recipe."

We exchange looks. We have made a pact not to discuss April anymore, but we break the pact on a daily basis. It's hard not to talk about her. The woman murdered three people. She got her own mother locked up. How could we *not* talk about that?

I've only seen Elliot a couple of times since April was arrested. He looked awful. He mumbled something about going to stay with his parents for a little while, and also he's selling the house. I can't blame him. I don't think he intends to stick by her through this whole thing, but you never know. They do have a child together.

"I wonder how she's doing in prison," Maria murmurs.

"She hates orange," I say.

"I'm sure that's not the worst part about being locked up."

"You want to hear the crazy part." I lower my voice. "Riley told me she's still insisting she didn't kill Brianna. I mean, it's not like she's cooperating. But she confessed to killing Courtney Burns. Why wouldn't she admit to killing Brianna? What's the point of lying about it?"

"Well…" Maria sits back down next to me. "Maybe she didn't kill Brianna."

"Of course she did! I told you, Brianna said she was

following her. Then an hour later, she was dead."

"Right." Maria nods. "But you told me it was a white SUV that was following her. I mean, think about how many white SUVs there are out there. Everyone has one. Even me."

My eyes meet Maria. It's true—on a dark night, nobody could tell the difference between Maria's old, beat-up white car and April's shiny new SUV. If Maria had been the one following Brianna, she never would have known the difference. In the dark, it would've looked exactly the same.

But why would Maria kill Brianna? She had no motive. The only possible reason she could've done it is because of the way April threw herself at Sean. Revenge. And a way to get rid of April. But God, nobody is that diabolical.

Are they?

Maria winks at me. "Let's try the cookies."

She stands up and grabs a couple of plates from the counter over the sink. She's humming a little tune to herself. She drops a couple of cookies on a white ceramic plate and slides it across the kitchen table to me.

"Go ahead," she says. "I promise. They won't be disgusting."

I feel her eyes on me as I pick up one of the cookies and take a bite. It's delicious.

Just as good as April's.

EPILOGUE

JANET

The police came to talk to me about April.

The policeman was nice. He said his name was Hanrahan and he was young. So young. And also handsome. I liked his light blue eyes. It made me want to tell him everything. I've been wanting to tell everybody what I know for so long. I've tried, but nobody wants to listen. When you are in a place like this, when people think you've lost your mind, nobody listens.

Anyway, he was asking me about April. Some woman named Brianna Anderson, whoever she is. I told him I didn't know anything about it. His light blue eyes looked disappointed, but he just nodded.

Then he asked me about Courtney. That was the question I was waiting for. I told him everything I knew.

I've been waiting so long to tell that story. And I knew it was coming.

He told me he thought April was going to get in a lot of trouble for this. But I don't understand that part at all. My brain is still fuzzy. Even now. Even though they're weaning me off the medications, I still have trouble thinking. It could last a long time, they say. But I still don't quite understand.

But here's what I remember.

It was one of the nights when Peggy was giving me my evening meds. I know this, because she never gives me all my medications. Usually, when the nurses leave, I feel foggy. But after Peggy gives me my medications, I can still think. When she left for the night, she hugged me and said, "Hang in there. We're going to get this fixed."

The nurse on the unit that night was Deborah. Deborah spends the whole night on her phone. She doesn't notice when you hit your call button. She doesn't notice *anything*. Sometimes it's annoying, but that night it wasn't. That night, I didn't want her to notice.

I left my room and went to the nurses' station. Deborah was nowhere to be seen. She was probably out on the balcony, talking to one of her friends. She had left her big red purse on the counter. I fished around inside and found her keys.

The exit to Shady Oaks has a code on it. Over the years, I've heard the nurses talk about the code. *What's the code again?* Everyone is always asking. I've heard it enough times that I've committed it to memory.

9419

I used to be a math teacher a long time ago, in my other life, back when I was young, and that's how I know that all the numbers in the code are perfect squares. That makes it easy to remember. 9419. I punched it into the keypad and then I jammed my thumb into the red button below. I heard a click and the door unlocked.

It was that easy.

It was night time, so there were only a handful of cars in the lot outside the building. I looked down at the keys in my hand. One of them was a key fob. I pressed the unlock button and I saw a set of lights flash. It was a white SUV, just like the kind April used to drive.

My loafers sounded like gunshots on the pavement as I walked over to the SUV. Any second, I was sure Deborah would come running out of the home after me. It didn't seem possible I was getting away with this so easily.

I opened the door to the white SUV and slid into the driver seat. I stuck the key into the ignition and the car roared to life. I stared down at the dashboard in amazement. I hadn't been behind the wheel of a car in so many years. I hadn't even been in a car in years. But I was sure I could still drive. That sort of muscle memory never leaves you.

A little camera lit up on the dashboard. I had never seen anything like it before. The question stared at me on the screen. *Where would you like to go?*

Where did I want to go? I wanted to escape. I wanted to get away from that awful nursing home where they held me down if I didn't want the medications that made me feel like a zombie. But what could I do? I had no money. I was wearing pajamas.

And then an address popped into my head. My son-in-law's office.

If I went there, I could talk to Elliot. I always liked that boy. He would help me. I would tell him the whole story, away from April's prying eyes. I could ask him for money. I would promise him that I would never do anything to hurt his family, if only he would let me get away.

It was as good a plan as any.

I typed in the address, and the screen lit up with directions. I pulled out of the spot and got on the road. I was right—I hadn't forgotten how to drive. It came easy for me. And fortunately, there were very few cars on the road. I drove slowly and carefully though. I knew if I got pulled over, it would all be over.

It was a ten-minute drive to Elliot's office. I parked in the empty lot, but I couldn't make myself get out of the car. Maybe I couldn't trust Elliot. Maybe he would go right to April. And then I would be back where I started. Worse, because they might find out Peggy hadn't given me my medications. Without Peggy, it would be like entering an endless fog I could never get out of.

I thought about driving away. I could go as far as the car would take me, and then hitch a ride. But what could I do without any money or identification? In *pajamas*!

While I was trying to figure out my next move, the door to the building swung open. I couldn't believe my eyes. It was April.

I squinted through the dimly lit parking lot at my daughter. She was dressed in a red blouse and a skirt that was far too short for somebody her age. She had let her hair grow out a bit since the last time I saw her too. She had been keeping it shorter, but now it was long and flowing. She looked good. Better than good. She looked at least ten years younger.

She was happy. She had a great life. Thanks to me.

April looked in my direction. She squinted into the darkness, and for a moment, our eyes met. Then she quickly ducked her head down so that her blond hair hung in her face and hurried the rest of the way to her car. A blue Kia. It didn't seem like April's style, but I never really understood my daughter. She had never really been the same since her father died when she was five. He was watching her that day, and he had a heart attack while they were playing dollhouse. Dropped dead right in front of her.

April's car started up, and she sped out of the parking lot. My fingers tightened around the steering wheel, then I threw the car back into drive and followed her.

She knew I was following her. Her driving became more erratic. She was making turns that were taking us in a circle. I was worried I was going to get pulled over trying to follow her, but I couldn't stop. I kept following her.

It seemed to go on forever. Finally, I hung back a bit and shut off the lights. Maybe she thought I stopped following her. I watched as she pulled over in front of a somewhat broken-down house in a quiet residential neighborhood. I could tell it wasn't a good neighborhood. Did April live here now? It didn't make sense to me.

I pulled over a few car lengths away. I watched her get out of the car, her pretty blonde hair swishing around her. She was going home to her family. Something I couldn't do anymore, because of her. Again, my fingers tightened around the steering wheel as I filled with rage. And I looked in the backseat. There was a shovel on the seat, like the kind for shoveling snow.

I reached back and grabbed the shovel. And I got out of the car.

The street was completely dark. There was a street light, but the bulb had blown out, and April was nothing but a dark silhouette. She startled as she looked up at me. She opened her mouth as if to say something, but then her shoulders relaxed.

"Oh my God." She clutched her chest. "I thought you were someone else!"

I squeezed the handle of the shovel in my right hand as I stared at my daughter under the dim light of the crescent moon. She looked so pretty. She didn't look her age at all—she looked no older than twenty-five. She must have had plastic surgery to look good on her show. Anyway, she looked like somebody who had a wonderful life. Who didn't have a care in the world.

A flash of blinding rage came over me. All the indignities I suffered over the last several years came rushing back to me. How could she? How could you do that to your own mother?

And then I lifted the shovel and brought it down on her skull. Again. And again.

She went down easier than I thought she would. I've always thought of April as being tough—a fighter. But in the end, a shovel was all it took.

I lost count of how many times I hit her. But eventually, she wasn't moving anymore. There was blood everywhere. In a puddle on the sidewalk and leaking from her skull, obscuring her face. And I realized she was dead.

I killed her. I killed my daughter.

I stood there, trying to feel some emotion—love, regret, sorrow. But I felt nothing. Only a sense of relief. Maybe it was all the medications.

My first instinct was to run. I had finally gotten free of that wretched nursing home and I was free of April forever. I could disappear somewhere so they would never catch me. After the medications had completely worn off, I'd be able to think straight again and make a new life for myself.

But then it hit me. I had no money. No ID. In another few hours, Deborah would report her car stolen and me missing. How long would it take for the police to catch up with me? It would be so easy for them to find me. They'd know I killed April, and then I'd be in a place much worse than a nursing home. I'd be in jail. With no chance of escape.

But if I went back to the nursing home and returned the keys to Deborah's purse, she would never know I was gone. Even if she suspected it, she wouldn't be able to say anything to anyone, because it would mean her job. And then I would have the perfect alibi when they found April's body. How could I have killed her if I was in the nursing home all night long?

And now that April was dead, there would be no one there to keep me locked up anymore.

Ten minutes later, I was walking back into the nursing home. 9419. The thought of being back here made me sick, but I knew I would be free soon. April couldn't keep me locked up anymore. Deborah was nowhere in sight and I dropped her keys back in her purse. I had thrown the shovel into the wooded area by the nursing home. It probably wouldn't snow for weeks—by the time it did, she wouldn't make the connection.

The next morning, I expected somebody to tell me April had died. But they didn't. And then that policeman, Hanrahan, came to ask me questions about April. He wanted to know all about her and what she did. He told me she's probably going to go to jail for a long time thanks to me.

But I don't understand. How could April go to jail? Because April is dead.

And I'm the one who killed her.

THE END

ACKNOWLEDGMENTS

Whenever I finish a book, the first thing I think to myself is, "Oh God, now I have to show this to people." Thank goodness I've always got people who are willing to have a look! Thank you to my mother, for your boundless and unbridled enthusiasm. Thank you to Kate, for the positive supportive feedback. Thank you to Jen for your always insightful critiques. Thanks to Rebecca, for your great advice. Thanks to Nelle, for your thorough corrections. Thanks to Ken, for your no-nonsense advice. Thanks to Rhona, for always being ready to look at another cover. Thanks to my amazing writing group.

Thank you to the rest of my family, for letting me share my own baking secrets with you. The secret to a delicious meal is having someone to cook for.